RAVENS AND RUINS

WOLF SHIFTER ALPHA KINGS
BOOK ONE

BELLA MOONDRAGON

For Nancy

CONTENTS

1

LITTLE RAVEN

Blanca

I TRAIL MY FINGERTIPS ALONG THE ROUGH STONE WALL OF THE dungeon as I walk briskly along, keeping my shoulders hunched and my head down. In my other hand, I carry a bucket of water and a ladle. Down here, I should be safe from the ridicule I face on the upper levels of the castle, but occasionally, a guard or two will mess with me. It's easier to avoid them if I'm invisible.

When I was a little girl, I got it into my head that not looking at people somehow made them unable to see me. Now, I know better. Yet, I still find myself staring at my holey boots most of the time.

When I reach the first cell, I pause. "Water?" I offer the man caged inside of the small space the ladle. This cell has no windows, and it's hard to see because the light from the few lanterns on the walls only reaches so far. But I know his face. I know his name. I know his story.

I know all of their stories.

He comes over and takes the ladle, drinking thirstily before I refill it, and he empties it again. "You're an angel," he whispers.

"You're welcome, Clive." I smile at him, glad to be appreciated, even if it is by alleged murderers and thieves, and then move to the next cell.

I make my way as quickly as I can, hoping to make it to every cell before I'm discovered and hauled back up the stairs. My parents have forbidden me to come down here, but I do it anyway. I've seen the slop and dirty water these poor people are given, and I can't stand the thought of them suffering for a drink when I can help them. If there was ever such a thing as a trial in all of the kingdom of Dun's Crossing, perhaps I wouldn't feel so inclined to help, but in my mind, it should be innocent until proven guilty, not the other way around.

I move to one of the cells that has a window and pause to watch the man inside. Tall, with dark hair the same shade as my own, this prisoner has always been my favorite. When he makes a low humming sound in the back of his throat, several large black birds move to perch between the bars of the small opening high in the ceiling. I can never tell if they are ravens or crows, but their shimmering blue-black feathers are beautiful to me.

"Water?" I ask, like I always do.

He turns to look at me, an amused expression on his face as he saunters over. His long black tunic and pants are filthy and torn, but he looks majestic anyway, like he would be better suited for a wizard's study or a throne room than a dirty dungeon beneath Wilbury Castle.

"Still playing fast and loose with the rules, huh, Princess?" he asks as he takes the ladle from my hand.

I shrug. "If I get in trouble, it wouldn't be the first time, Mr. Blake."

"How many times have I told you not to call me mister? You're a princess and I'm–"

"What are you exactly?" I interrupt him. I've never been brave enough to ask the question of him. Unlike the others, his story is hazy in my mind because he doesn't want to tell it. I tend not to speak to anyone when it can be avoided. While Mr. Blake has always made me feel comfortable, I've never asked that burning question. I'm not sure what makes me ask it today. Yet, here it is, falling from my lips.

Rather than offering me a suitable answer, he chuckles and finishes the water from the ladle. "I am a prisoner."

"Yes, I know that." I practically roll my eyes, but I don't. Mother slaps me in the face when I do that. "I mean…." I gesture at the birds that are still sitting on the window ledge, patiently waiting for his attention. "What are you?"

"Some say I'm a madman," he begins, dipping the ladle back in and taking another drink before he continues. "Others say I'm a murderer. Or a magician. The king thinks that I'm his arch nemesis."

"But why?" I ask. "Why are you here?"

"Why are any of us here, my little raven?" He reaches up and tugs a strand of my hair the way a father might a beloved daughter. I smile up at him, wishing my own father would take such an interest in me. "Your king spoke the words, and now here I am. And here I shall be until he says otherwise."

I want to tell him that when I am queen, I will release him, but we both know I'll never have a chance to rule Dun's Crossing. That honor will fall to Prince Kieran.

Even thinking of him makes my stomach tighten up. The high and mighty Kieran–Crown Prince of Dun's Crossing. Tall, muscular, and handsome, with white-blond hair like the rest of the royal family. All the women want to be his mate, his bride. If they knew the truth–that he is mean, viscous, and cruel, they would gather their skirts and run.

He also happens to be my twin brother, but no one would ever guess that to look at us. And he treats me like he thinks I belong down here with the very prisoners I do my best to help.

"I wish I could let you out," I whisper.

Mr. Blake reaches through the bars and pats my cheek. "You're a good girl, little raven." He always calls me that, probably because of my black hair.

I open my mouth to thank him, but I don't get the words out before I hear footsteps pounding toward us and look over to see my brother coming toward us in a rage, his icy tresses flowing out around his shoulders as he rushes over. "There you are, you worthless filth. Father has us all searching the whole damn castle for you. Get your ass upstairs to the throne room now, you little bitch."

For just a moment, as I stare into his light blue eyes, I wish one of those birds on the windowsill would fly over and poke his eye out. It's a flash of a thought, one I'd feel embarrassed to admit I've ever had in my life. He is my brother, after all, and I shouldn't be so cruel to him just because he hates me.

But before I can even open my mouth to tell him I'll come along with him, I see a flash of black and blue careening toward him. Kieran raises his hands to protect himself as one of the birds comes flying at his face, squawking, raising its talons, and aiming directly for his eye!

"No!" I shout. Kieran swings at the bird, cursing and trying to knock it away. I cover my mouth in horror as blood drips from my brother's face.

Mr. Blake makes that sound in the back of his throat, and the bird immediately flies back through the bars. Kieran stands there for a second, one hand pressed to his face, blood dripping down his arm.

"Are you okay?" I move to help him, but he swats at me, pushing me away.

"Leave me the fuck alone!" he says. "You stupid bitch! And you!" He turns toward Mr. Blake, one hand still pressed to his injured eye. "You did that, didn't you, you psychotic asshole!"

"I'm sorry, Prince Kieran, but I can't take credit for that," Mr. Blake says calmly. "I wish I could."

"You fucking jackass. You're going to pay for this. Guards, give him fifty lashes!" Kieran shouts as he turns to walk back upstairs. I see some guards moving in Mr. Blake's direction.

Turning to him, tears prickle in my eyes. "No!"

"It's all right, little raven," he assures me. "I will live to see you another day."

My mouth drops open as the guards brush by me. I hear Kieran shouting for me near the stairwell and remember that my father has called for me. If I don't go now, I'll end up getting a beating myself. "I'm sorry," I tell him.

He says, "Don't be. It's not your fault."

The guards grab him and drag him to the back of his cell, and I have to go. I can't stand here and watch them beat him for something he didn't do.

One thought burns in my mind as I follow my brother up the stairs, his crimson droplets of blood on every other step: I hate Prince Kieran Solberg with all of my being.

2

IT'S COMING

Kieran

My cheek stings where that blasted bird pecked away my skin, but at least it didn't get my eyeball. Because of my wolf shifter abilities, I feel it healing already. When I draw my hand away again, there's no fresh blood.

I hear my twin sisters' footsteps lightly following me up the stairs and can feel her glaring at me. It's nothing new. We've been at each other's throats since we were old enough to walk.

Well, that's not exactly true.

I've been at her throat. She's mostly passive, just stares at me. Sometimes she cries. I used to laugh hysterically when she'd cry. It made me want to hurt her more. Now that I'm older and more mature, it just makes me want to tell her to grow a pair.

We are finally out of the dungeon stairwell. I hurry along to my father's office where the rest of the family is waiting. I know he will be displeased, especially when he sees my eye. Mother will likely start having a conniption. Perhaps I shall lie and say something else happened to me.

"There he is." Father sounds annoyed, as if it's my fault we are late, as I step into the room. I can't help that Blanca is taking forever. I find a spot on the couch between my younger brother, Anwen, and my younger sister, Candace, who reluctantly scoots over a tad. The two younger siblings, Finn and Ingrid, sit across from us, with our father, King Gavin Solberg behind his desk, and our mother, Queen Rowena, standing behind him. I keep my hand pressed against the side of my face for now.

"Where is she?" Mother demands. "Did you find her?"

Before I can answer, Blanca bumbles through the door. "Pardon me." She has lost the bucket and ladle at least, so they might not guess what she was up to. I'd say the filth on her long black dress should be enough of a tell, but then, she's always filthy. She sits down on the floor next to the couch where our younger siblings sit, knowing she's not allowed on the furniture in here. She is a stark contrast to the rest of us with her dark hair and eyes, her olive toned skin. The rest of us are blonde, blue eyed, fair to the point of almost being translucent.

A stranger wouldn't think we were related at all, let alone twins.

Maybe that's why no one has ever thought twice about treating her like she's not part of the family.

"It's about time." Father glares at her. "You haven't been down in the dungeon again, have you?"

She won't lie. Instead, she drops her head and stares at her arms, folded around her knees. Slowly, she nods.

"I've told you a thousand times not to go down there!" Mother sounds like she's about to cross the room to slap her. As she takes a step in that direction, Father raises a hand. It'll have to wait until later.

Normally, it doesn't bother me when someone slaps my sister in the face. She always deserves it, after all, but recently, I've felt a bit peculiar about it, like maybe I shouldn't let it happen. It's almost as if my wolf has decided to defend her. Perhaps that shouldn't surprise me. She will be one of my subjects one day, after all, and my wolf has been taught from a young age to defend the weakest of our pack. But I can't quite reason out what it is.

Father clears his throat and picks up several missives from his desk, stacking them loudly. "We've received word from the leaders in the conquered territories letting us know that a mist is forming around the borders. It's already taken over our neighbors to the north and west and will envelop those in the south and east in a day or two.

Ingrid sucks in a deep breath. "Already?"

"Yes. The full moon is still about five days off, but it will take a while for it to settle in completely. This one will be different from months prior. This is a silver Haze, named as such because it is the first Haze to encompass us once a royal has become of age." His heavy stare lands on my face, and I am compelled to lower my hand to look at him fully.

"Your eye!" Mother gasps, ruining the moment.

Again, Father puts a hand out to stop her. It's already beginning to heal. I can feel it.

He continues. "As you know, as the Haze settles on us, dignitaries from far and wide, as well as commoners and others who have recently reached their age of maturity will descend upon the land. Everyone will be pining for their chance to be mated to the Crown Prince of Dun's Crossing."

I can't help but lift my head a little. I've always been proud of my station. I would like to imagine one day soon I'll be married to a princess from a distant land, one that will be a good ally to my kingdom. There aren't many kingdoms left nearby since my father has a penchant for war. I think of all the areas he's conquered even in my lifetime and wonder if I will ever be as mighty a king as he. Hopefully, my mate can help me fulfill my destiny as a great and powerful ruler.

"You four are too young," Father says, gesturing at Anwen, Candace, Finn, and Ingrid. "You shall stay inside, out of the way."

"Oh, but Father! Can't we go outside and see all the magic taking place?" Candace whines. Normally, all she has to do is ask, and she gets her way.

It's not to be this time. Our father fixes his darkest stare on her. "Absolutely not. A Haze is no place for a young woman of your stature, not until you are old enough to find your mate. And even then—Goddess help me." He closes his eyes and shakes his head. I know he can't stand the thought of his little girls meeting their mates and being marked in a sexual romp out in the open—maybe in a tent if he gets lucky. I almost snicker and bite it back.

My eyes fall on my twin. Of course, she is old enough to take part because she is the exact same age as I am. But she doesn't ask to be included, and no one says a word. I can't imagine who she might be mated to anyway. Probably the son of some distant Beta. He will likely reject her. Marrying Blanca will not make a good match for anyone. Everyone knows she is the black sheep of our family.

"We need to get tents set up throughout the woods," the king continues. He looks at me and Anwen. "You are in charge of that. I want as many as possible. The last thing we need is people frolicking all over the place."

"Yes, Father," we both say in unison.

"Borrow from the army if you need to. Remember, this is an important Haze. Not an ordinary one. There will be tons of people here. We must make them feel welcome."

It seems unlike my father to want to welcome anyone, but perhaps he has ideas about what to do with these visitors that he has yet to share with me. I agree with him again.

"Remember, we only have five days." Mother wears a tight-lipped smile as she makes her unnecessary contribution to the conversation.

"You may go."

As soon as Father dismisses us, I am up off the couch and through the door before Mother can even ask about my eye again. The only person who leaves faster than me is Blanca, and that's because she knows if she sticks around, she'll be punished for going back to the dungeon.

All of us walk together toward our quarters. Blanca's room is in another wing of the castle, so she will break off eventually, but the others completely ignore her, as if she doesn't exist. That's better than hitting her or calling her names, which is what I usually do.

"You're so lucky," Anwen tells me. "You finally get to find your mate and fuck her real good."

My prim sisters squeal at his use of a swear word, but Finn laughs. I ignore him—as does Blanca. She seems to have something else on her mind.

"What the hell happened to your eye, anyway?" Finn asks me.

"Nothing." I don't want to explain it to him. Blanca breaks off and goes down a dark hallway by herself as the others head upstairs. I hesitate at the bottom of the stairs, realizing I need to know what my parents have planned for her. I'm not sure why, but if my sister is out there during the Haze, I need to know about it. I may treat her like garbage, but if anyone else were to misuse her, I'd be pissed. "I'll catch up with you later."

I turn and head back to my father's office. The door is ajar, and inside, I hear my parents talking. They aren't bothering to keep their voices down, but I pause anyway. "We can't let her anywhere near the Haze," my father is saying. "If she were to discover the truth—"

"She won't." Mother interrupts him. "I'll see to it."

"Good. That is your only job." My father's voice is stern.

I stop, deciding not to interrupt them. Even though I have no idea who they are talking about, I suddenly feel like I no longer need to ask the question. I turn to go back to my room when I hear a scream peel through the castle. Instinctively, I take off running. I'd know that scream anywhere.

3

SHE'S A WITCH

Blanca

I almost made it to my room.

When Nessa Winters steps out of the shadows near the last turn that takes me to my chambers, I leap backward, not out of fear but out of surprise. I hate it when she does that. Recently, she's been doing it more and more. I'm not sure why. Maybe the fact that we are all considered of age now and our wolves are more active has something to do with it. I don't know, but I don't like it.

"Well, well, well, if it isn't the nasty bitch who calls herself a princess," Nessa says, stepping closer to me. Out of other nearby shadows two of her friends appear. I'm outnumbered. That's not unusual. Not that I ever fight back anyway. If I did, I'd get it worse from my parents.

Nessa's father is an ambassador from an allied pack. They've been staying in the castle for years now, negotiating treaties or something like that. I don't know why she's here. I just know that she hates me.

"Leave me alone, please," I say. "I'm just trying to go to my room."

"Oh, is that what you're doing?" Nessa's dark eyes widen, and she shakes her head as she presses her lips together in a mocking fashion. In her best impersonation of my voice she says, "Just trying to go to your room?"

I take another step back and run into a wall. "That's right." I see one of the castle cats standing over in the distance, licking its paws beneath a table, and wish I could switch places with her. If I were a cat, all I'd have to do is sit around and eat scraps the cooks drop or maybe chase mice.

I wouldn't be the one who is constantly being chased.

"Well, I'm afraid if you want to get to your room, you'll have to get through us first, you fucking bitch!" Nessa swings her hand in a semi-closed fist so that her fingernails connect with my cheek.

My head snaps to the side, and my arms go up instinctively. I can't hurt her, but I really don't want to be hit anymore. "Stop!" I shout at her. "I mean it."

"Stop!" She uses that mocking voice as her friends laugh, and she hits me again. I wish I could do something to protect myself that didn't involve hurting her back, but the last time I hit her, my mother beat me so badly, I could hardly walk the next day.

I can't take another beating like that. Not this close to the Haze. If I can find my mate, maybe I can get out of here.

As she hits me another time, I press myself against the wall and wish, for an instant, that the cat across the hall was a wolf or a bear, that it would attack her, sort of like that bird trying to peck Kieran's eye out.

"Stop!" I say again, but before the word is even fully out of my mouth, I see a blur of gray fur and hear a hiss, and Nessa is no longer hitting me.

Instead, she's falling to the floor, screaming so loudly, my ears ache. I cover my ears and plaster myself to the wall as her two friends begin to scream as well. Neither of them are trying to help her, though. I wish with all my might that that cat would stop attacking her. I know that I will get in trouble for this, even though I had nothing to do with it.

Did I?

I remember what happened with the bird and how Mr. Blake said he didn't do that. Now, this cat has done something similar. Could I...?

No, there's no way.

But just in case, I make that sound I heard Mr. Blake make in the back of his throat, the best I can, and wish that the cat would stop.

It doesn't.

I reach down and grab the cat just as I hear my brother's voice shouting down the hallway. "What in the world is going on?"

I fully expect the cat to rip my hands to shreds. Instead, as I hold it, it begins to purr. I set it down on the floor, and it runs away, just as Kieran arrives.

"You–you psychotic bitch!" Nessa shouts at me, wiping blood on the back of her hand as she scoots across the floor away from me on her ass. "You witch!"

"What the fuck happened?" Kieran asks as he looks from Nessa to me and then back again.

"It was a cat." I wipe my own blood off my face on the back of my hand. Nessa hit me hard enough with her claws to draw blood from a few places. "It came at her, the same way the bird attacked you."

Kieran's eyes are practically glowing, he's so mad. I know Nessa has a thing for him, but I always thought she wasn't good enough for him. Now, I am beginning to wonder if maybe he likes her, too. "Go to your room right now, bitch. When father hears what you've done–"

Out of nowhere, the cat is back. I hadn't wished for it to happen this time, but it jumps on Kieran's back and sinks its claws in.

He shouts and reaches around to grab the cat. I scream, thinking he'll kill it, but the kitty sinks its claws into his hands, and he shouts and lets it go.

I watch in shock for a moment before I decide not to press my luck any more. If Kieran thinks I did that, too, he'll do more than slap me a few times. I rush between the girls and head toward my room, praying I can get there before he catches me.

I'm almost to my door when I feel his hand clamp down around my arm. He spins me to face him, pressing me up against the wall right next to my room. His eyes narrow as he lifts a hand and presses it against my neck.

It's been a long time since Kieran hit me. He usually just calls me names and leaves the dirty work to someone else. But I can feel his wrath coursing through his veins as he seethes, his lips twitching with words of damnation he has yet to spew in my direction.

He's so close to me, I can see the tiny flecks of blood on his nose that must've splattered there from the bird attack. He squeezes my throat, and I go completely still, staring into his icy eyes.

He leans in so that his nose is practically touching mine, and I know he's either going to choke me out or punch me so hard I'll crumple to the ground.

But he doesn't do either of those things. He just stares at me. as if he's in a trance of some sort.

Electricity prickles deep inside of me, my lower abdomen clutching in a way it never has before. My heart thrums in my chest. I can hear the blood whooshing through my ears.

Something strange is happening; I've never felt like this before–especially not when I was looking at my brother, but the wolf inside me stirs in a way she never does.

He must feel it too.

And as quickly as it comes, it goes–at least for me. I grab his arm trying to push him back, and even though he is much stronger than me, it works, in a way.

He releases me with a cry of anguish. "What the fuck? You little bitch! Have you been studying magic down there with that wretched Blake?"

Grasping my throat with both hands, I rasp out, "No! I didn't do any of it. I don't have any powers." My legs feel weak beneath me, but I fight to stay upright.

"Whatever the fuck it is you're doing to me, knock it off! I know how badly you want the throne. Father told me you've been scheming. Well, it won't happen!" He turns his back to me, leaving me leaning against the wall wondering what the hell he's talking about.

I want the throne? Why would I possibly think I could ever get the throne?

"Stay away from Nessa!" He turns around and glares at me. "Touch her again, and I'll break your hand."

I don't wait around to see if he means it. Instead, I dart for my room, lock the door, even though I know he has a key, and sink to the floor. With my arms around my knees, I begin to sob. I have no idea what's going on, but something strange is in the air.

I cry for several minutes before I remind myself that I have to be strong enough to survive this, to get out of here. Lifting my head, I look out the small window across my tiny room—and that's when I see it for the first time.

A fine, light, misty cloud—of Haze.

4

BEYOND THE BLACKNESS

I CAN STILL FEEL THE SHARP RIPS IN THE SKIN OF MY BACK WHERE THAT fucking cat sunk it's claws in, and my hands ache from the scratches that forced me to let it go before I ripped it in half. I don't know what the fuck is happening in this place, but something is wrong, and I don't like it.

I rush past Nessa and her cronies where they still stand in the hall. One of them calls out to me, but I wave a dismissive hand. I don't give a fuck if Nessa Winters is bleeding to death all over the Goddessdamn marble floor. What I do care about is my stupid sister getting herself into trouble again. How many times does she have to be told to stop fucking with Nessa? Last time, I thought Mother was going to break her legs. She came pretty damn close. Mother and her fucking fireplace poker. Thank the Goddess she never turned that on me or any of my other siblings.

Why is it okay that she beats the living shit out of Blanca then?

I don't have an answer for that. It's just always been that way. My parents have always treated her like garbage, except for the few times they've put a nice dress on her and made her stand with us on the platform to wave at the people below the balcony. The rest of the time, she's treated worse than trash by them. By everybody.

By me.

A spark of electricity washes over me again, but I refuse to acknowledge it. That woman has gone too far this time. She's been down there talking to Blake, finding out about his magic, and I don't like it. Father told me a long time ago to keep an eye on her. She's my twin, older than me by a few hours. She could try to claim the throne.

My throne.

"Where are you off to in such a hurry?" My best friend and will-be Beta, Taner, asks as he falls into step beside me. Thankfully, he's walking on what will now be considered my "good" side and can't see my fucking eye.

"Nowhere," I tell him. "My room."

"Did you hear about the Haze? It's moving in so fast, it'll be here before the full moon. It's wild. Of course, nothing will happen until the moon is full, but it's kind of crazy not to be able to see anything more than a few yards away."

He continues to babble on about the fucking weather as I storm down the hallway. I fully intend to go to my room, but with Taner refusing to shut the fuck up, I storm right past the hallway. I have another idea of where to go.

Taner moves in front of me before I reach the dungeon door. "Hey, your room's that way. Oh, fuck. What the hell happened to your eye?"

"Move, Taner. I have important matters to attend to." I try to side-step him, but he moves in front of me, fascinated with the condition of my face.

"Looks like a Goddessdamn bird tried to fucking peck your eyeball right out of your skull!" He chuckles, the mop of blond hair on his head dancing around as he does so.

"Get the fuck out of my way, asshole." I push him aside, throw open the door, and take the steps two at a time. It's dark down here and smells like body odor and shit. I have no idea why anyone would want to come down here, especially not a princess.

Not that we've ever treated Blanca like she's a princess.

Thoughts of what happened between us in the hallway come to mind again. What the fuck was that? Something about being so close to her stirred my wolf in a way that I've never experienced before. Rather than squeezing her throat so tight she couldn't breathe, I just stood there, staring into her black eyes.

They aren't black, though. I noticed then that they have little flecks of silver and blue in them. They're actually quite beautiful. My sister is beautiful.

"What the actual fuck?"

I say it aloud this time. My mind is all kinds of fucked up. I don't know if it's the Haze, the animal attacks, or the idea that there's a psychotic magician living in our basement, but I need to seriously get a hold on myself.

"Your Majesty?" one of the guards says as I briskly walk by him. I don't acknowledge his existence as I make my way down the dark corridor to Blake's cell. He's leaning against the far wall, his tattered clothes even more a mess since he was given a lashing earlier. I can hear the blood dripping on the stone floor. He doesn't turn to face me, but I know he senses my presence, and I can assume he knows it's me.

"Whatever the fuck you did… whoever the fuck you are… you need to leave Blanca alone. Life is already awful for her, if you haven't noticed. If you continue to play your mind games with her, you're going to end up getting her beaten—to death."

He's quiet for so long I think maybe his ears are ringing so loudly from the punishment that he can't hear me, but then he speaks, in a low growl of a voice. "I have done nothing. But I find it amusing that you, of all people, pretend to care what happens to her."

"What the fuck is that supposed to mean?" I grab hold of the bars between us and shake them. Certainly, I have never been kind to my sister, but I haven't beaten her like my mother has or locked her up without food or water for days like my father has.

He turns slowly, and I can see not only did they give him the lash, but his eyes are swollen to slits, dried blood caking his crooked nose and lips. "You have done nothing to help her, and that makes you just as guilty as the others."

A squawking sound at the windows has me turning my head up. Four large ravens sit there on the sill, staring down at me. I want to dare the bastards to come at me so I can shift into my wolf and rip them in half, but my conversation with Blake is more important.

"It's never been my place to question the king and queen–her own parents." I feel weak speaking the words, knowing they aren't the truth. As a child, I could've done nothing to help Blanca, but we are adults now. In the last several years, I could've done something.

I could've done anything.

Blake wheels around to face me, and even though he should be weak from the punishment, he stalks toward me on steady legs. "You may think you know who I am, boy. But you don't. Your father has filled your head so full of lies, you wouldn't know the truth if it tried to peck your eyes out. This Haze that's accumulating right now will change everything for you, and when it clears, I hope your eyes are no longer blinded to the truth."

"What the fuck are you–"

He interrupts me. "None are so blind as those who choose not to see!" Behind him, the birds begin to squawk. He takes another step toward me. "If something sounds false, looks false, and feels false, Prince Kieran, how can it be the truth?"

"Hey! Get away from the prince!" I hear a guard shout as Blake is practically nose to nose with me through the cell bars.

I want to reach between them, grab his throat, and squeeze as hard as I can. I want to feel the life evaporate from him, to leave my father's mortal enemy that he captured on the battlefield over twenty years ago nothing but a rotting carcass lying on the floor of this dungy, Goddess-forsaken dungeon.

But this close to him, even in the dim light casting shadows from the lantern on the wall, I can see his eyes. They're black like obsidian, deep, pools laced with insanity–and power.

But that's not what catches my attention.

Dancing around in that black pool of nothingness, I see something familiar, something that sends a bolt of shock down my spine.

Little flecks of silver and blue.

5

THE HAZE DESCENDS

IT'S BEEN FIVE DAYS SINCE THE INCIDENT IN THE DUNGEON, WHICH WAS followed by the incident with Nessa–and then the incident with my brother.

I've hardly left my room since then.

I have chores I must do every day, like muck the royal stables and scrub the toilets in my parents' bathrooms. I've done those things and then swung by the kitchen to take a little food. The chef there is nice to me. She never scolds me for plucking an apple or even a turkey leg.

That's it, though. The rest of the time I've spent sitting on the edge of my thin mattress staring out the window at the disappearing landscape. The misty fog has continued to roll in, its thick fingers moving mysteriously to intertwine around every building, every tree, every creature that dares to step out into it.

It's not a normal fog. The first time I went out to make my way to the barns and encountered it, I could feel it wrapping around me, the energy inside of it pulsating, moving. Breathing. I had to close my eyes for a moment to get my bearings. Not only could I see nothing through its milky whiteness, I lost my ability to think clearly.

It seeps into a person and changes who they are on the inside.

And it only has one purpose, one intention.

To find a mate.

Why the Moon Goddess saw fit to create such a wild, feral phenomenon to match people up, I can't say, but now, as a sliver of silver begins to appear in the sky, I know that the full moon is out there. I just can't see it through the misty magical mayhem that is the Haze. Once the moon hits her apex, chaos will ensue.

I close my eyes for a moment and draw my knees to my chest. In my mind's eye, I picture my wolf, black and sleek, gliding through the fog, guided by the same all-encompassing sensation I'd felt every time I'd walked through the Haze. Paired with the full moon, that feeling will be even more intense until I'm not even able to register a clear thought of my own. I will cut through the rolling dense barrier until I find him.

I have no idea who my mate may be, but in my mind, he is a large silver wolf with blue eyes. It's not a stretch to think he would be. Most of the people in my kingdom have blue eyes–like my family. Most of the wolves are white, gray, or silver. Though only those with great strength are the latter.

Like my father.

Like my brother.

I physically shake my head. No. I can't think about Kieran. He'll be out there, but he'll be paired off with his own mate, likely a beautiful white wolf with crystalline eyes.

Back to my mystery mate. I picture the two of us finding a tent on the outskirts of the forest. We go inside, shift, and fall into one another's arms. I'm not exactly sure what happens during a mating ceremony since my mother would rather lick the underside of a livery worker's boot than speak to me about anything important, but I know that it's magical.

It's wonderful.

And it will get me out of here.

Once I've found my mate, and he's marked me, that's it. I'll belong to him. Not as his property, but as his family. Nothing can undo that. We will be bound together. There's no rejection or divorce in our world. We simply trust that the Moon Goddess knows what She's doing.

And there's no magic strong enough to mess that up either. Sure, there are people who have some sort of magical powers. I think about Mr. Blake and his birds, and what I somehow did with the animals myself, but no one is stronger than the Moon Goddess. What She says goes.

So... I will be free of this place in a matter of hours, and the thought has a genuine smile grazing my face for the first time.

I'll know it's time to go when the longing inside of me begins to burn. I'll try to get outside before my wolf bursts free, but I can't promise anything. I haven't had much of an opportunity to shift since I found my wolf at eighteen, a few weeks before my brother found his, which is odd, but I know how to do it. I can't wait to run free and feel the wind whipping through my fur again.

I take a deep breath and try to remain calm. It's hard to believe it'll all be over soon, and the man who can save me will hold me in his arms.

As the hours go by, and the moon continues to climb, I feel that fire inside of me igniting, and I know it's almost time. The night sky fills with howls, some echoing out in the distance, others much closer to the castle. The urge to answer in kind bubbles up inside of me. I need to shift into my wolf. I need to feel the warmth of the silver light of the moon wash over my fur. I need to tear through the night and search for my mate.

And I need to do it now.

Even though I've yet to step foot into the Haze tonight, I can feel the carnal urges within me beginning to take over, clouding my mental acuity. I'm operating completely on instinct.

In a flurry, I rush to the door and yank on the handle, intending to fling it open, already planning to head out into the hallway to the closest exit to the castle.

But when I grip the doorknob and pull, nothing happens. I check to see if it's locked from the inside, but it's not. Confused, I pull it again. It doesn't budge. "Is it locked?" I don't know who I'm asking, and it doesn't matter because it's clear, even to my discombobulated mind, that the door is locked.

I'm trapped.

"No!" Inside me, that burning itch to escape grows stronger. I want to scratch my chest and stomach, as if I could somehow claw that uncomfortable feeling out of my body. I can't stop pulling on the unyielding door, though. With my other hand, I slap the wood. "Hey! Is anyone out there? Anyone?"

There's no answer.

Frustrated, I spin around and rush to the window. I'm on the fourth floor of the castle, and there are no roofs beneath me. Even if I shift, I won't be able to safely leap down to the ground below me. I have to get out through the door.

For a moment, I think I should use the mind-link to contact my parents and let them know I'm locked in my room. This has to be some sort of a mistake, after all. Everyone knows I'm old enough. I belong out there in the Haze with the others.

Where my mate is.

But the mind-link has never worked for me. I've never been able to get it to work to even contact my twin, and I've never heard another voice in my head. I have no idea why that is the case, but it sucks, because now would be the perfect time for me to be able to get someone on the other side of this door to let me out.

Not that they'd probably come to help me anyway.

Desperate to get out into the Haze, I return to the door and bang on it with my fists. "Hey! Is anyone out there? The door won't open! I need out!"

I'm met with only silence.

Actually, that's not true.

Leaning against the door, I can hear my heart thundering, my breath coming in loud, shallow bursts.

But that's not the only thing I hear. I also hear a sharp squeaking sound. Confused, I look around and see that my distress seems to have alerted a few of the mice that inhabit my room. They're sort of like pets to me. We all live here together, and I share my food with them. I've even given them names.

"Sorry, Harry. I didn't mean to alarm you," I tell the one looking at me with wide eyes from the corner. Behind him, Zelda peeps out of the hole in the wall, and I can see the shadow of Ralph behind her. "I can't get out."

The three of them come closer, their faces somehow seeming concerned–if mice are even capable of expressions.

I slide down the door in defeat, fighting tears. "I've got to get out of here, and the door is locked."

The trio scurry over to me. I lay my palm on the floor and they climb up so I can pet them with my other hand. "I wish that you could help me."

Before I even get the full sentence out, all three of them scamper out of my hand and disappear under the door. Confused, I lie down on the floor and peer under it. I see them running up the wall next to the door where they disappear from my sight. A second later, I hear a jingling sound, and then my mice friends reappear–carrying something.

They slide back under the door carrying that metal object.

My mouth drops open as I see what they've managed to retrieve from the hook in the hallway.

It's a key.

6

CUTTING THROUGH THE HAZE

I RUSH DOWN THE HALLWAY, MY BARE FEET SLAPPING ON THE STONE that makes up the floors in this dreary part of the castle. I don't dare look behind me as I hurry toward the closest exit before someone discovers I've left my room.

Someone locked me in there. Someone who wanted me to miss the Haze. Someone who wanted me to miss my only chance at escape.

I can't think about that right now, though. I have to find him.

I need to find my mate.

Pushing through the closest exterior door, I step outside and into another world. The Haze pulsates around me. No longer the milky white shade it has been the last few days, it is a shimmering silvery mass that engulfs me immediately. I can't see anything, and with every breath, it sinks into my soul.

My wolf cries for freedom, letting out an excited, primeval howl as I leap into the unknown. My clothes shred, my bones pop, my skin disappears into my body as black fur takes its place all over me. It

31

doesn't hurt; in fact, it feels incredible, like I am meant to be in this form all the time.

I land on four paws and peer through the cloudy substance around me. With my wolf eyes, I can see better, but it's still murky. It doesn't matter. I will not rely on the use of my eyes to find him.

Taking off at a fast gallop, I cut through the trees in the castle courtyard, skipping along the path that leads to the gate. It's been left open so that those of us who need out tonight don't have to wait for someone to open it for us. Thankfully, the guards standing there cannot see me well enough to question whether or not I'm allowed to go out. I move like a shadow through the iron gates and out into the open.

Once I'm far enough away from the castle, I let out another howl. This one is answered in kind by the others who are searching the forest nearby.

Guided by nothing but instinct, I move through the Haze, feeling my mind clouding over completely. I only have one thought on my mind. Find him.

Find my mate.

Around me, I sense other wolves. I fly past tents, some moving as the lovers inside mark one another. I hear human sounds as I hurry past them. Gasps. Moans. Whispered endearments.

I keep moving, picking up speed as my wolf hones in on some-thing. It's as if she's telling me he's not far away. *Move faster. Run this way. Cut left. Turn right. He's here. I can feel him.*

I've only been searching a few minutes when I see movement in front of me, and the Haze lifts just enough to reveal a sight that has me skidding to a stop.

He's huge, majestic, his silver fur glistening in the moonlight. His eyes are the purest blue I've ever seen, and only one word fills my mind.

Mate.

My Mate.

A howl burst from deep within me. He throws his head back and lets out a melodic sound that twists through the air, tangling with my own cry so that we are singing in perfect harmony.

My mate moves toward me like liquid flowing down the path of least resistance. He nuzzles against my neck, his fur soft on mine. I nip at him, wanting him from a part of me buried deep in my core.

When he turns and cuts between the trees, I follow. I know he is fast, probably far speedier than I am, but he waits for me. The two of us come across an empty tent and jut inside. My back is to him as we both shift, and he zips the tent. Naked and in total darkness, I close my eyes as his lips find mine.

The Haze is still in my blood. My mind is controlled by my wolf. This is primitive, animalistic, and everything I could ever crave with my body and soul.

HIs hands glide over my skin, setting me on fire. He tastes like mint, like the freshest water from a mountain stream. He lays me down, his mouth tracing down my neck. I reach up and tangle my fingers in his soft hair, pulling him to me as my tongue twists around his.

The ache between my thighs is all consuming. I feel a dampness there as my thighs slip against one another. I want to open my legs for him, but he's got me pinned, so I continue to kiss him, thankful that the first man to taste me in every way is this perfect creature.

My mate.

When he rests his hand on my breast, his fingers tugging on my hardened nipple, I arch my back, wanting more, longing for his mouth to close around my most sensitive area. He doesn't disappoint me as he lowers his head to do just that. I bite my lip to try to keep from crying out, but I can't contain myself. Like my wolf howling, I begin to moan.

I feel something hard and long against my leg, and though I'm not quite sure what it is, I know I want it inside of me. My body knows what we are meant to do, even if I do not. My wolf instinctively knows. I let her guide me.

His hand slides down my flat belly toward my apex. We move so that my legs are free, and I spread them wide for him. Without a word, he finds my opening, slipping his fingers along my wet slit before probing inside of me. He only sticks one finger inside at first, but I find myself taking hold of his wrist, demanding more. He gives me want I want, working his finger in and out of me, loosening me for what I now understand is supposed to go inside there—and it is massive. We continue to kiss until my body is on fire, his fingers spreading me, readying me, and then I feel the tip at my entrance.

I buck my hips, longing for him to take me, to make me his forever. He presses inside of me, and pain slices through my body, but it is quickly replaced by something else as he continues to move his hips, working in and out of me.

The same feeling of electricity I had out in the Haze pulses inside of me. My mouth opens in a silent scream of ecstasy. Everything about him is perfect—the way he moves, the way he touches me, the way he sets my body on fire. I wrap my arms around him, holding onto a sheer wall of muscle that is his back as he continues to thrust inside of me.

At the same time, our bodies tense. Leaning forward, I find the spot on his neck near his shoulder, and my fangs elongate. I feel his mouth on my skin just above my breast. We both lock down. His flesh rips between my teeth, the sweet taste of his blood filling me as I fall over a cliff, feeling no pain as he bites into me. The world explodes around us, my head spinning uncontrollably as an overwhelming sensation of pleasure wraps around me. I release my grip on his skin, letting out another moan as he goes rigid, grunting, and his warmth spreads through my belly.

Panting, sweating, tingling with electricity, I let go of everything, and still tangled and twisted in the loving arms of my mate, I surrender to the darkness that claims me as completely as he has.

Right before I lose consciousness, I feel him pull me tight against his chiseled chest, his hand on my stomach. He kisses my shoulder and whispers, "My mate. Mine."

A smile forms on my lips as I fall asleep to a chorus of howls in the distance.

I know this night, and every night for the rest of my life, I will dream of him, my mate. Everything is right and perfect in the world, and now that he is here, that will never change.

I've finally found my happily ever after.

7

THE MOON GODDESS WAS WRONG

I can smell her. I don't open my eyes yet as flashes of memories from the night before wash over me. I haven't seen her yet, but it doesn't matter. I feel her warm body pressed against me, her flat stomach beneath my palm, her small hips situated so that her perfect, round ass cradles my hardening cock.

She tasted like strawberries, like a warm summer's day. The way she'd moved beneath me was perfection, even though I quickly discovered I was her first. This makes me smile because I never want anyone else to claim her. She's mine.

My mate.

In a moment, I'll open my eyes and look upon her beautiful face, maybe for the first time. I wonder who she is. Maybe a princess from a distant land or the daughter of a noble. I'm the Crown Prince of Dun's Crossing, so she must be someone majestic. Someone important.

It doesn't matter, though. She could be the lowest scullery maid, and I would protect her to my last breath.

I feel her stirring beneath me, breaking me from my reverie. I imagine her long white hair fanning out all around her on the pillow we share and slowly open my eyes.

What I see has me shouting in shock as I scurry away from her, her black eyes staring at me in the same terror I feel now.

"What the actual fuck?" I grab hold of the blanket we'd been tangled in and try to cover myself, but she's doing the same, and it's a tug of war that rips the blanket in two. She takes her half and snaps it in place over her body, one arm wrapped around her breasts. I take my part and slap it over my lap. Over my dick.

"Oh my Goddess!" Blanca screams. "What the actual hell?"

"No!" My mind can't catch up with what's happening around me as I fight to put this all together. This is not possible. How the actual fuck did this happen? The Moon Goddess knows everything, right? Well, how did She not know that this woman staring at me like she wants to die, feeling the same horror I'm feeling now, cannot possibly be my mate?

Blanca shakes her head. "This… this is some kind of a sick nightmare. There's no fucking way."

I agree with her. This has to be a bad dream. The woman I was with last night… she was everything I ever wanted in a mate, and even though I never saw her, I knew we were meant to be together.

This? This is something out of a sick story someone from the back hills must've written just to get a rise out of people.

I'm not sure what to say or what to do, but I want to boil my entire body to get every trace of her off me.

Unless… "Did someone switch us in the middle of the night?" I ask. "Is it possible that we didn't…"

Blanca shakes her head. "I don't think so. Goddess. I think I'm going to vomit." I see her fighting the urge to spew the bile rising up in her throat, the same way I am.

My mind flies through the events of the night before, how I'd felt the urge to leave the castle as soon as the moon rose above the horizon. I'd shifted, taken off running through the dense fog, guided by my wolf. My thoughts are hazy after that. I'd been running totally on instincts, letting the Moon Goddess lead me to my mate.

We'd definitely had sex.

How the fuck is this possible?

Only one answer comes to mind.

"You're some sort of fucking witch!" I yell at her. She's reaching for the clothes that had been left in the tent for happy couples to wear on their way out to make the announcement to their friends and family that they'd found their fated mate.

She pauses with a dress in her hand. "What? You think I did this?"

"That's right! First, there was that fucking bird in the dungeon, then that demonic cat." I grab a shirt off the tent floor and shove my arms into it, pushing my head through the neck hole. "You're so fucking greedy for the throne, you'd do anything to get a hold of it, even something as sick and twisted as this."

She drops the dress on over her head without moving her scrap of blanket away and speaks to me in a tone I've never heard from her before. "Are you insane? I'm not a witch. How could I be? I'm your own—"

"Don't fucking say it!" I warn her, reaching for the pants next to me. "Not now."

"Well, you know I can't be a Goddess-damn witch. I'm just as disgusted as you are." She grabs a pair of shoes and thrusts her feet in them. Thankfully, she's turned away from me while she does this, so I manage to get the pants on without her seeing me naked. Goddess! The thought of where my skin has been. "I don't want the stupid throne either, Keiran!"

"Like hell you don't." I shove on another pair of shoes, which are too tight, but I don't care. "Father told me you were after it. I just never thought you were capable of doing something like this."

"I'm not! No one is. Only the Moon Goddess can control the Haze." She doesn't turn to look at me, and I don't know if it's because she's afraid I'm still getting dressed or because it's easier for her to lie when she's not looking right into my face.

"All I fucking know at this point is that we aren't breathing a word of this to anyone. Whatever the hell you did, we'll find a way to undo it. I'm going to walk out of this tent and head back to the castle. You'll wait at least a half an hour and then follow. You don't even so much as look at me for the rest of your days, or I'll kill you." I spew all of that at her through gritted teeth. "Goddess! To think you'd do all of this just to be queen."

"I don't want to be queen." She turns and looks at me now, her eyes overflowing with tears. "I just want to leave this Goddess forsaken place and never come back."

I see sincerity in her eyes when she speaks and know she means it—at least the part about leaving. I don't understand why anyone would want to leave Dun's Crossing. We are the most powerful kingdom in the world. Yet, when Blanca says she doesn't want to be here, I believe her.

"So you thought doing something this sadistic would get you banished?"

"I. Didn't. Do This." Her eyes are narrowed, her lips pressed in a thin line.

I want to believe that's the truth, too, but the only thing that makes sense in my mind at the moment is that she tricked me.

I shake my head. "Don't follow me."

She says nothing. I pull myself up off the ground and move to the tent, listening for a moment before I unzip it. I pray that no one else is up and about, that no one is close enough to hear us, and that no one sees me. If anyone else finds out about this, who knows what will happen? Who could possibly hear a story about siblings—twins, no less—doing what we did and not think they were absolutely fucked in the head?

No, I've got to do everything I can to make sure that no one in the world ever finds out about this.

I hear a few birds singing in the trees, but that's it. Not another sound. I hope that means we are alone. We were shouting at each other pretty loudly, so if there were other tents nearby, we would've had to wake the inhabitants up.

I yank the zipper down and stick my head out. I do see a few tents littered around us, but I don't hear anyone, and I don't see movement from anyone stirring about inside.

Still being cautious, I pull myself out of the tent and stand, breathing a sigh of relief.

Then, a rustling in the bushes in front of me catches my attention. A familiar giggle hits my ear, and I freeze.

This is my worst nightmare come true.

Scratch that—second worse.

"Well, well, well. What do we have here?"

I take a deep breath and shake my head. Goddess. I'm absolutely one hundred percent fucked.

"Looks like someone is in a bit of a pickle," she says. "Thankfully, I have an offer. One you can't refuse."

I brace myself and ask Nessa, "What the fuck do you want?"

8

THE DEAL

Blanca

Vomit rises up my throat as I wait as patiently as possible for Kieran to leave the tent. I can't allow myself to think about what happened last night–what we did. If I do, I'm likely to throw up everywhere.

Tears sting my eyes for so many reasons, I couldn't possibly name them all. Here I was thinking the Haze would be my ticket out of this hellhole, that I'd meet my mate, and he'd sweep me away.

Instead, the Moon Goddess made me the butt of Her own sick, twisted joke. What the hell will our parents do to us if they find out about this? They'll kill me. Like Kieran, they'll assume I've learned some sort of magic that would make this possible.

I truly don't think there's any magic in the world that would make this happen, but nothing makes sense at the moment. I need to do some research.

I turn around to look at the unzipped tent, wondering if Kieran is gone. I see his legs through the flap and then hear another voice.

"Oh, Goddess no!" I whisper. I never would've thought that this

43

day could get any worse. When I hear Nessa's voice, I know I am doomed. "Why does the Moon Goddess hate me?" Did I wrong Her in another life?

I move over to the tent opening so I can hear better, but I don't dare show my face. Kieran would kill me.

"You can come out, little whore," Nessa says to me. "I already know it's you, Blanca. Goddess, what a fucking sicko."

I don't move. I'm not getting out of here, not unless my bro– Kieran tells me to.

"Come on, Blanca." His voice is so full of defeat, I hardly recognize it. I've never heard him sound so depressed before, not that I blame him.

Slowly, I crawl out of the tent and stand a few feet away from them. A quick glimpse around makes me think there's no one else nearby. I hear birds singing cheerfully, which seems like a mockery to me at the moment. I sniff the air, but no other wolf or human scents hit me. Just me and Kieran and Nessa–and sex.

"Here's my proposition." She folds her arms under her boobs, pressing her chest up. "If you don't want anyone to know what the fuck you two weirdos just did, Kieran, you're going to tell everyone that I'm your mate. We'll get married. I'll be queen. And you, little bitch, will tell everyone you didn't find your mate, and when we are in charge, you'll just go away."

I stare at her for a long moment trying to figure out how this is a problem for me. Two things come to mind. "What about the pain? We marked one another." My hand goes up to the spot above my right breast that is already throbbing a bit from all of the rejection Kieran spewed at me earlier.

"You'll learn to live with it, bitch," Nessa tells me. It's like she thinks bitch is my name. "Kieran is strong enough to get through it."

I shift to look at him. His icy blue eyes are fixed on the forest floor, unblinking.

"And what about your mate?" I ask. Nessa is our age. She should have found her mate last night, too. But she's not from Dun's Cross– ing, and it's possible her mate isn't here.

I get my answer when she scowls. "I don't have one, I guess."

Rather than argue with her that she may meet him one day, I take a deep breath and swallow hard. "It's not really my decision," I remind them both. "I don't want to tell anyone what happened. My mark isn't where you can see it."

Kieran's is. I can see part of it peeking out of his collar. "Fine." Again, he doesn't even look up. He is choosing the lesser of two evils, and as much as I can imagine no one would ever want to marry Nessa, I sure as hell know no one would ever want to marry me.

Especially not Kieran.

My twin brother.

It's not even legal, for obvious reasons. In fact, I'm pretty sure there's a law that says we can both be put to death for what we did.

Not that we had a choice or any control over it.

"I won't tell anyone." I barely recognize my own voice. I start to walk between them toward the castle when Kieran's fingers grip my wrist, pulling me back toward him.

"See that you don't," he seethes, lifting his eyes to look into mine. "If you tell anyone what happened, for any reason, I swear to the Goddess I will cut your heart out. Do you hear me? I don't know how you did this or what your motivation was, but do not ever mention it to anyone."

His eyes cut right through me, squeezing my heart even harder than his fingers bite into my wrist.

I don't bother to try to wrench my arm away from him. "I told you I won't," I whisper. "I didn't do this."

He tosses my wrist out of his grasp and wipes his hand off on his shirt like it's covered in garbage. I try not to let the tears fall again, not because of his cruelty; I'm used to that. But in the back of my mind, I keep thinking that my mate will save me.

Jokes on me.

I turn and begin my trek toward the castle. I'm not even sure where I'm at, honestly. I never leave the castle grounds, so I could be anywhere in the dense woods that spread out across the rolling hills around the castle.

Birds chirp in the trees as if nothing horrific has happened recently. They are probably just happy that the Haze is over, and they can see during the day again.

"It's too bad you can't show me the way," I murmur to a particularly beautiful bluebird perched on a tree branch above my head.

Whistling a cheerful song, the bird flutters in front of me to a tree a few yards away and lands again, continuing with his tune.

My forehead furrows as I look at him. Is he… waiting for me? When I catch up with him, he does the same thing again, jumping to another tree. I follow. For the next half hour or so, we play this game where I walk and he flutters away and I catch up to him until I see the top of the castle in the distance.

Surprised, I lift a hand, and he flies over to me and lands on my finger. "Ca-can you understand me?"

In response, he sings his little song, and I gasp. It's like he really does know what I'm saying. I don't understand what's happening. From the bird in the dungeon, to the cat, to the mice that helped me escape my room, to this little friend, it seems like the animals can understand me.

None of it matters as I hear the guards at the gate shouting and know that they are alerting my parents that I've returned.

My feet drag beneath me as I close the distance, walking through the gate and up the stone path to the castle. The bird has long since left me, and I don't blame him. No one needs to witness what is going to happen. I have no idea what's going on with the animals or how I could possibly be mated to Kieran, but I have worked out in my mind that my mother and father have to be the ones who locked me in my room last night.

When I reach the front door, my father's main advisor, a white-haired older man named Leo, growls, "Blanca, you are wanted in your father's office."

"Yes, sir," I say, despite the fact that I am royalty and not him. I tip my head and make my way to the office, wondering what would happen if I turned around and ran back out of the castle. How long could I live in the forest on my own? Would they send troops to find me? Surely, they would.

Bears. I could ask the bears for help....

"Blanca!" My father's voice roars out of his office, causing a shiver to go down my spine. "Get in here."

With no other choice, I walk into his office. My mother stands behind him, her hands folded in front of her. "Where the hell have you been?" she demands.

"I went out for the Haze," I whisper.

"But how did you–"

My father lifts a hand and stops my mother from talking. I already know what she was going to ask–how did I get out of my room. Apparently, Father doesn't want her to confirm that the door was supposed to be locked.

Rather than try to explain how I got out of a room she probably locked herself, I am tasked with a different question from my father. "Blanca, did you find your mate?"

I open my mouth to answer.

Visions of the man I had so hoped to find flood my mind. Where is he? Why didn't he come for me? Why didn't he rescue me?

I think of Kieran and get hazy flashes of his body moving in the dark. The feel of him. His scent.

I lift my head and look my father in the eyes, knowing what my answer must be.

9

SHE'S MY MATE

Kieran

"Wh-what?" my father stammers as he stares at me standing in front of his desk, holding Nessa's hand in mine. "Nessa is your... mate?" His face is ashen, his jaw slack, and in his eyes I see the disdain I feel in my heart–along with a great deal of uncertainty.

I, too, know how that feels. Another shudder goes down my spine at the thought of what happened last night, but I can't let my father see that. He has to think I'm happy about this. I cannot, under any circumstances, let Nessa have a reason to tell anyone what she stumbled upon.

Or was she stalking me?

"Well..." Mother, who is standing behind Father's chair, one hand on his shoulder, clears her throat and makes a little face like she's swallowing down her own vomit. "Isn't that... lovely." She doesn't mean a word of it, I know. Nessa is the most annoying girl any of us has ever met. Even more annoying than my fucking sister.

Oh, Goddess. I'd better stop using those two words in the same sentence!

"Have you told your father yet?" The king leans back in his chair, as if he's doing his best to suck in a lungful of air and failing.

"Not yet." Nessa is practically vibrating with giddiness. She keeps squealing and grabbing my arm. Ordinarily, I wouldn't allow her to touch me.

I guess I'd better get used to it.

"We wanted to tell you straight away," I explain.

"Yes, yes, I understand." Father drags a hand down his face, tugging on his long white beard. "And you've… marked one another?"

"We have!" Nessa lifts up on her toes and drops back down before she leans in a bit too close to my father so that he backs away and whispers, "Mine is in a place where no one else can see. Just me and my matey-watey!" Another squeal. Another giggle. Another mouthful of vomit my mother is swallowing down.

"Good, good." Father presses his lips together so tightly they are a thin line. "Nessa, dear, why don't you go out in the hall for a bit so we can talk to our son?"

"All right." She turns to me, and I have no choice but to face her. "Goodbye, Kieran Wieran. I love you sooooo much." She rubs her nose against mine before pressing her lips onto my mouth and then shoving her tongue down my throat so far I really do think I might throw up. Then, she prances out of the room, practically dancing, her hands in fists out to her sides as she rocks back and forth.

As soon as the door is closed, my father says, "What in damnation? How is this possible?"

If only he knew the truth. Then… well, he'd be saying more than "damnation."

"Believe me," I begin, "I was shocked as well." I let that moment I'd registered who I'd slept with sink in for a moment and try to stay lucid. "Is it possible someone messed with the Haze?"

"Messed with the Haze?" Mother repeats. "That's impossible."

"Is it?" I'm staring earnestly at my father, thinking he must know something Mother doesn't–because obviously, someone messed with the Haze, and my reason for knowing this is true has nothing to do with Nessa.

My father slowly shakes his head. "No, son. It isn't possible to mess with the Haze. There's no magic more powerful in the world than the Moon Goddess's pull."

My forehead wrinkles as I consider what he's saying. "But... she can't be my mate, can she?"

"You felt the pull to her?" Mother asks.

I nod, thinking of Blanca, not Nessa. "It's all a blur, of course, but there was no question when we were... together... that we were mates." I take a deep breath. My own words don't make any sense to me. They go against everything I know about my very existence. "Aren't there more powerful wizards in other kingdoms who might be able to do this? Magicians?"

"No." Father cuts me off with eyes sharp enough to slice through me. "Even the most powerful wizard alive couldn't mess with the Haze, son. I'm telling you, it's not possible. If the Moon Goddess led you to Nessa, then she is your mate, and there's nothing we can do about it."

"Well...." Mother has one finger under her bottom lip, twisting it there. I know that look, but whatever evil thought has just slipped into her mind, there's no way my father will let her say it aloud.

He stops her with a deep growl in the back of his throat, and she drops it. For now.

"You must be tired, son. Go to your room, take a shower, and get some sleep." He tries to smile, but I see the worry behind my father's eyes.

"Take a long shower," Mother suggests. "And use a lot of soap."

They both chuckle, but if they knew the truth, they wouldn't think it was funny at all. Nessa Winters is annoying, and her status isn't nearly high enough to marry me and become the next Luna Queen. But at least she isn't–I cut the thought off. I have to find a way to forget.

"Very well." I bow in respect to my parents and then make my way out of my father's office. Thankfully, Nessa isn't waiting for me. She probably wandered off to tell all her friends.

As I head toward my room, I pray that no one sees me. I didn't get that lucky with my last request, and I don't expect to now, but somehow, I manage to make it to my room. I go inside, lock the door, and head straight to the bathroom.

All the while, I'm going over everything that has happened and what my father said. Steam wraps around me as I stand near the shower and strip out of these ill-fitting, cheaply made, borrowed clothes. I'm glad I can't see my reflection in the mirror. This fucking mark is going to be burned into my skin for the rest of my life, and that's going to make it hard to look at myself–ever. It burns now, even though I'm not that far away from Bla–the person who put it there. I wonder if that's because I'm essentially rejecting her, denying to everyone that she is my mate. Does the mark I left on her ache as well?

"I hope so," I whisper as I climb into the shower, grabbing the soap and beginning to scrub every surface of my body under the scalding water. "For what she's done, she deserves to be in as much pain as humanly possible."

Regardless of what my father said, he has to be wrong. He has to be unaware that there is a magic strong enough to mess with the Haze. It's the only explanation for what's happened.

The only alternative is that the Moon Goddess is fucked in the head and doing all kinds of shitty things to people.

"There can be no other explanation," I voice aloud, finally beginning to rinse the suds off my body. I've washed my dick so many times, it's raw. I have to get every trace of her off my skin.

After about an hour, I get out of the shower and wrap myself up in a towel, sinking down to sit on the edge of the massive jetted tub in the corner of the room. Absently, I consider which of these two worlds I want to live in–one where magic is strong enough to interfere with the Moon Goddess's will or one where the Moon Goddess lets us be mated to members of our own families.

Shaking my head, I get up and wander to the closet to get dressed in something that will be comfortable enough to sleep in but allow me to get up quickly if I need to. It is the middle of the day, after all.

Lying down, I begin to wonder if there's even a Moon Goddess at all. Sure, there had to be at one point or else we wouldn't be able to shift. The Haze wouldn't exist. But now, well, maybe She's dead.

Maybe the Moon Goddess decided She couldn't handle us anymore and left us to our own devices.

All I know for sure as I start to drift off is that I'm trapped in a hell where Nessa Winters isn't my worst choice, and that's enough to make me certain that even if I have the worst nightmare of my life it'll be better than my reality.

10

OH, THE IMPOSSIBILITIES

I AWAKE SOMETIME IN THE MIDDLE OF THE NIGHT. WHEN I FIRST GOT back to my room, I took a long shower and scrubbed my flesh raw. Then, I got dressed in as many layers as I could and fell into bed, exhausted. My mind had gone crazy, even in my dreams, trying to sort out everything that had happened.

I'd lied to my parents.

Father asked me if I'd found my mate, and I'd said no. Even as I'd spoken the words, the mark Kieran had left in my flesh began to throb. My wolf, my soul, seemed to want to claim him, even though it made absolutely no sense.

Curled up on my bed, I stare out the window, trying to ascertain what time it is. Judging by the placement of the stars, I guess it's around 2:00 in the morning, which means I essentially slept for sixteen hours. I don't want to get out of bed. I just want to go back to sleep and will this all away.

None of it makes sense to me, and lying here isn't going to fix that. I have to figure out how this happened.

When I consider who might be able to help me, only one person comes to mind.

I take a deep breath and pull myself up to a sitting position. I've been forbidden from going down to the dungeon for years, but that's never stopped me before. Still, after what happened last time, with the bird, I'm hesitant to do it again. I have a feeling I'll get more than a beating if my parents discover that I had something to do with that bird flying into Kieran's eye.

Nevertheless, thinking of the bird reminds me that there are other reasons for me to seek out Mr. Blake. With a deep breath, I stand and slip on my shoes before padding over to the door only to find it locked.

"Seriously?" I murmur. Why would my parents lock me in here again? It's not like the Haze is still going on. I don't know why they locked me in to begin with, but I did notice they were both relieved when I told them I hadn't found a mate.

Why didn't they want me to find him? Were they afraid I'd let someone know about how abusive they are? Or do they just not want me to leave the castle ever?

"Surely, they had no idea—"

I stop the thought before it can be articulated on my tongue. There's no way my parents ever would've considered that what did happen was a possibility.

With a sigh, I bang my head on the door, not hard enough to hurt. "Hey guys?" I say, but I'm not talking to any guards that might be standing outside. I'm sure there are none. I turn to find my mice friends observing me. "A little help?"

They squeak amongst themselves and then crawl under the door, but rather than climbing the wall as they have before, they just stand there in confusion. I can see their tiny feet from the crack beneath the door as I lie on my belly.

The key isn't there.

"Shit," I murmur. "Okay, I bet the queen has it. Do you think you can go to her room and fetch it?" I don't know for sure that my mother has the key, but it's my best guess. My father is usually too busy to put up with my "nonsense" which means I become the ward of the queen.

My mice friends squeak again and then disappear down the hallway. I lie there for a while before realizing they're not going to be back any time soon. My parents' rooms are far away. Finally, I sit up and wait until I hear the mice coming. It's taken them a while, but they're back, and I can hear the clank of metal on metal.

They've retrieved the keyring.

It's heavy, and they are tired, but they manage to get it to me. I unlock the door and thank them, placing the key in my pocket. I think I'll try to hold onto it this time, maybe hide it somewhere in my room. Mother will probably think she misplaced it.

I start to head down the hallway, but then I have an idea. "You guys wanna come?"

Zelda tilts her head to the side and peers up at me before squeaking again and nodding.

"Great. Bring your friends–all of them."

Ralph and Harry exchange a look before making some more noise that sounds like chatter, and the next thing I know mice are pouring out of the walls. I laugh as we head down the hallway together toward the dungeon.

Before we round the final corner that descends to the prison cells below, I tell them, "You guys wait here. Let me see if you're needed." With more confidence than I've felt in a while, thanks to my back-up, I approach the guards snoozing in two chairs on either side of the door.

As soon as I reach for the doorknob, the one on the right hops up. "Hey! You can't go down there."

"Sure I can," I tell him. "I'm the princess. I can do whatever I want."

"No, you can't." The one on the left is up now, too. "We have it on strict authority from the king himself not to let you down there no more, princess or no."

I stare at him for a moment before I decide I need to get through this door, no matter what happens when they tell my father. "Are you sure about that?"

As he opens his mouth to speak, I use my mind to call upon the mice, knowing somehow that they can hear my wishes. Immediately, they stream from around the corner. The guards don't notice them at first, not until dozens of my little buddies start to crawl up their pant legs.

Both guards shout, dancing around, kicking their feet, trying to get the mice out of their trousers. I stifle a laugh as I pull the door open, though I do hope that none of my friends get hurt while helping me. Some of them are so little.

I fly down the stairs into the darkness, not needing a light to know where I'm going. I'm not surprised at all when I reach the bottom of the stairs to see another guard there. This one is wide awake. He scowls at me and folds his arm across his muscular chest. "They let you down here? That's a no-no."

"They're busy," I tell him. It's not a lie. "And you will be, too, if you don't let me through."

He chuckles, a deep throaty sound. He's scruffy, with dirt on his face, and he smells like body odor. "How's that now?"

With a sigh, I summon the best help I can get down here. A half a dozen fat rats scurry from inside the closest cell, making their way over to the guard. When they ascend his pant legs, he screams in pain. Apparently, rats' claws are sharper than mices'. Either that, or they are biting him.

I rush past him and down the row of cells until I reach Mr. Blake. He's standing at the front of his cell, his hands wrapped around the bars. "You shouldn't have come, Little Raven." He shakes his head.

"I have to talk to you," I explain. "I know I don't have much time, but listen–the Haze. Is there someone powerful enough to mess with it? A wizard or a magician or… anyone?"

He swallows hard, his brow creasing. "What happened?" I hear the concern in his voice. "Did they actually let you go?"

I shake my head. "No. I snuck out." Why am I surprised that he knows my parents this well? He was, once upon a time, my father's greatest enemy, or so I've heard.

"How?" he wants to know.

I take a deep breath. Will it make sense to him if I tell him? "Uhm… I had some help. From… mice."

Mr. Blake's mouth drops open. "Raven…" he murmurs. "You know you have powers, then?"

Blowing out a breath, I say, "I know I have something. But I'm not strong enough to mess with the Haze, right?" Kieran accused me of such. What if I had somehow done it?

"Of course not," he says quickly. "No one is strong enough to do that. No, you didn't mess with the Haze. Did the Haze mess with you?"

All I can do is nod.

Slowly, he shakes his head. "I was afraid of this. It's almost time, Little Raven. You're going to discover everything, and when you do, there won't be anything anyone can do to stop you."

"What are you talking about?" I hear more guards coming and am too distracted to call upon the animals to help me.

"Which do you prefer, Raven? A world where the impossible is possible or one where the possible is impossible?"

"I don't understand." The guards are getting closer.

"If it's not possible for anyone to mess with the Haze, then that means that whatever happens during the Haze is true, and you must accept that as reality first. Then, everything else can fall into place."

"What?" I stare at him as the guards reach me.

"Hey! You can't be down here. What the fuck did you do to the guys?" the first one shouts as he reaches for my arm.

I dodge away from him just as a huge owl comes swooping between the bars of Mr. Blake's cage, aiming right for the man's head. I know I didn't do that, but I use it to my advantage, slipping between the guards who are now shouting and fighting the bird.

I head upstairs thinking I have more questions than answers.

11

MURDER OF CROWS

Kieran

THE LIBRARY SMELLS LIKE BINDING GLUE AND OLD PAPER. I HAVE NO idea why anyone would ever want to spend more than a few moments here. When I was younger, our governess used to herd all of us in here–Anwen, Candace, Finn, Ingrid, and me. We'd sit next to her and listen to her read from storybooks. Every once in a while, I'd see two big black eyes staring at us from the doorway. Why Blanca was so keen to join us, I never could figure out. It was just a damn book, nothing to get excited about.

As I approach the section of the library designated for books about magic and wizardry, it occurs to me for the first time that it probably wasn't the book Blanca was so interested in. I swear under my breath. How am I so stupid? Of course, she likes books. I know that. She has a dozen of them in her room, the ones Mother will allow. But she didn't want to listen to the story.

She wanted to be included.

She wanted to be part of the family.

I let out a breath and pull out the first book that looks like it might hold some clues as to what the hell happened during the Haze. In some regards, it seems a thousand years have passed since then, though it's just the day after I announced Nessa as my mate. Since then, she's barely left me alone. The only reason she's not hanging off me now is because I sent her to town to buy a new dress.

She's going to bleed me to death financially, I just know it. No matter that I'm the Crown Prince.

I flip through the book titled, "Powerful Magic," looking for any mention of the Haze. Nothing jumps out at me right away, so I flip to the glossary in the back and see there's a section about it. I find the right page, my eyes scanning quickly for anything that looks relevant.

Essentially, all this book says is that the Moon Goddess uses the Haze to help true mates find one another. Nothing is more powerful than the Haze, which should assure all participants that they've found their fated mate.

"Yeah, unless it ends up being your sister," I murmur, plunking the book back onto the shelf and pulling out another one. I look through several volumes, and none of them help me in the least. All of them talk about how nothing is stronger than the Haze.

Just as I'm beginning to think this search is futile, I hear footsteps and turn to find Taner gliding across the library like he's on cloud nine. I've only spoken to him briefly since yesterday, but I know he's thrilled to be mated to my father's Beta's daughter. I try not to scowl at him. I may have gotten a bitter deal, but he should be allowed his happiness.

"There you are." He grins at me. I don't think that stupid expression has slid off his face since he woke up to find Ayla on his shoulder. "Well, this is a first. Kieran Solberg reading a book."

I close the volume I'd pulled out a few moments earlier with a thunk that echoes around the large room. "What can I help you with, Taner?" I'm in no mood to joke around.

He chuckles. "I've been mind-linking you for a while. Lucias and Whyte got all the tents taken down. They found a few they can't use for next time. Should they toss them?"

I almost let out a sigh. How incompetent are my people that they have to ask me that? "Yeah, of course. We can always buy more tents. Anything else?"

"Man, you are in a foul mood since finding out you're mated to Nessa."

"Don't start," I warn him. I don't even want to think about Nessa.

He puts his hands up. "Sorry, sorry. No, nothing else. Why are you looking at books on magic?"

"None of your damn business." I slide the book back onto the shelf, knowing it's not going to help me. Nothing can. I even went to speak to my father's magician about the Haze earlier today, and he backed up what my father had to say. Of course, Wordsworth is probably the worst magician in the universe. My father just keeps him around to say he has one. My father always says brawn trumps power. That's why he was able to conquer so many kingdoms where the wolves have special powers.

"Did you even hear me?" Taner asks.

"No," I admit, shaking my head. "Sorry. What?"

"I said you're not going to find a spell in there that makes Nessa not your mate. You already marked her, right?"

I nod because I have to. If anyone finds out the truth, even Taner, I'm screwed–and I've already been screwed one too many times.

"Did you hear about the rats in the dungeon?" He snickers as he folds his arms and leans back on the bookshelf. "One of the guards got one of his balls chewed off."

Now, he has my attention. "Wh-what?"

"Yeah, you know that mean old fucker they call Albatross? The night guard who likes to piss on the prisoners' heads while they're sleeping?"

"Gross. No, I don't think so. What about him? He got one of his balls chewed off by a rat?" The instinct to grab the boys is real.

"Yeah, last night. Apparently, all the mice and rats went nuts and attacked the guards, crawling up their pant legs and shit. Then an owl saw all the mice through the window and swooped down to try to get them but scraped the shit out of a few guards' faces–kind of like you with that songbird."

"It wasn't a fucking songbird." I shove him hard in the shoulder, but he just laughs. "Fuck, that's a lot going on with the animals. Does it have something to do with the Haze?"

"I don't know. Probably not. There's no mention of animals going crazy during the Haze. It does remind me of that kingdom that used to exist north of here, though. Escuro. Some of those people could control animals. Mostly the royalty. But your father wiped them out ages ago. Anyway, thought it was a funny story. If it'd been someone a bit nicer, maybe I would feel sorry for the guy, but not Albatross."

Taner continues to talk for several minutes, but I'm stuck on a minor detail.

Escuro.

"Fuck," I mutter, dragging a hand through my hair.

"What? Are you ignoring me again?" Taner asks.

I shake my head. "No, I mean… sort of. That bastard Blake is from Escuro, isn't he?"

"Who?"

"That weird old guy in the dungeon? The one my father refers to as his mortal enemy? Didn't he capture him during the war with Escuro?"

"I don't know, man," Taner admits. "There's a fuck-ton of prisoners down there. I don't know who any of them are."

I'm already moving past my friend out of the library. He rushes to catch up to me. I need to talk to that asshole again. Is it a coincidence that I'd spoken to him just before all hell broke loose? I think not. He had to have something to do with all of this.

Including manipulating the Haze.

"I told him to leave her the fuck alone," I mutter as I approach the stairs to the dungeon.

"Who are you talking about?"

I ignore Taner's question and trudge down the stairs, past the guards, into the darkness. I don't stop until I'm standing outside of Blake's cage.

But he's not there.

Blood splatters mark the floor and up the wall. This is worse than when I ordered him to get the lash. This looks... fatal. "What the fuck?" I whisper.

Across the cell, a murder of crows begin to caw.

12

SUCH DEVOTED SISTERS

"AND IF YOU LEAVE THIS ROOM WITHOUT MY PERMISSION ONE MORE time," Mother says as she stands next to her henchman, Ardesia, "you can rest assured I will break your legs so that you cannot leave again."

The lash hits my upper thighs, my back, my bottom as I stare at the wall above my bed, trying not to cry. The last thing I need is to break down and let her know how badly she's hurting me.

It's not the lash so much, although it does sting. But this isn't the same kind of whip they use in the dungeon–the kind they use on Mr. Blake. This one is leather, but it doesn't have anything like bits of glass or metal on the end. Nevertheless, after twenty-five lashes, it breaks my skin. I know I'll have welts and scrapes for the next several weeks.

I keep my eyes focused on the wall as it continues, my arms folded over my breasts. She allows me to wear my bra and underwear while I'm being whipped, but if my arm wasn't over my breast right now, she'd see the place where Kieran marked me. My arm isn't thick enough to cover the whole thing, though I'm doing my best.

"Yes, Mother," I creak out every few seconds. I'm distracted from the pain by my laser focus on keeping the mark hidden.

"Good. I hope you've learned your lesson now. That man almost bled to death. I have no idea how you managed to train the mice to follow you about, but it's disgusting."

"Yes Moth–"

Before I can finish my statement, I hear another voice. I don't have to turn my head to know that my sister Candace has entered the room. I thought the whipping was over, but now that she's here, perhaps Mother will ask her if she'd like a try. None of my siblings have ever been the slightest bit kind to me. I've seen Candace giving food to beggars and caring for an injured dog, but she's actually hissed at me on more than one occasion.

"Mother? What's going on? Why is Ardesia whipping Sister?"

I can hardly believe my ears. Did Candace just acknowledge that I'm her sister?

"Never you mind, Candace. Get out of here. This is no place for a princess," our mother says.

"But... she is a princess." Candace isn't wrong, even if I haven't ever been treated like a princess for my entire life.

Mother lets out an exasperated growl. "Blanca is being punished for sneaking out of her room last night and going down to the dungeon. Now, unless you want to take her side and be punished yourself, I suggest you leave the room."

Candace gasps when she hears what I've done. By now, I'm sure word has spread about what happened down there, about how the guards were attacked by the mice. Only my parents and the guards know I was there at the time, and I'd like to keep it that way. If they begin to suspect I can control animals, things will get even worse for me. That's one of the reasons why I'm not defending myself now. Mother seems to think I trained them somehow, like they are circus animals.

"Let's go," Mother insists. "You'd better not leave this room again!" She walks out. I don't turn my head, but I hear the others leave as well. The door closes and locks into place.

I let out a sigh and drop my arms, finally. I quickly go into my small bathroom and clean my abrasions. Most of them aren't too bad, but a couple of the welts are already big and puffy. I twist to look at myself in the mirror and finally let the tears slide down my cheeks.

I'm not crying because it hurts, although it isn't the most comfortable. I've been beaten and whipped lots of times before. I've had bones broken. I've been pushed down stairs, starved, and once Ardesia held my head down in the toilet until I passed out.

I know what it's like to be punished, even if I'm not sure I've done anything wrong until now.

I shouldn't have gone down there last night. I not only got myself into trouble, but I probably got Mr. Blake into even more serious trouble. I don't even want to think about what they did to him if they thought he had anything to do with that owl swooping in and attacking the guards.

With my rag of a dress back on, I wipe my nose on some toilet tissue and walk back out into my room. The figure of a person sitting on the edge of my bed startles me at first, but then I realize it's Candace. Now, I'm just confused.

She holds up the key. "Mother isn't very good at keeping hold of this."

I almost laugh, but then, I have no idea why she's here. It can't be for anything good. I don't ask. Instead, I take a few hesitant steps toward her.

Candace is eighteen years old, three years younger than me. Unlike me, she looks so much like the rest of the family it would be possible for people to think she's Kieran's twin sister, not me. Of all of my siblings, she's probably the nicest one, but not to me.

No one is ever nice to me.

So why is she smiling at me and patting the bed now?

"Come join me." She scoots over a little. "Goodness, your blanket is scratchy."

I don't bother to tell her that everything I own is scratchy. Instead, I perch next to her, still wondering what the hell she wants, and ignoring the pain in my backside from the whip.

"How was the Haze?" Her blue eyes look into my dark ones, curiosity dancing there. "I'm sorry you didn't find your mate. I thought you would."

I shrug. "It was fine." It was horrid–the most awful night of my life.

Her head rocks back and forth. "Can you believe Kieran is mated to that awful Nessa?" She laughs. "Serves him right. Let him listen to her nag for the rest of his life."

My eyebrows furrow as I try to determine if she is just here to gossip or something else.

She continues to talk for a few moments about other people who found their fated mates during the Haze before she returns her attention to me again. "I really thought you'd find him. In fact, I had a dream about it. I dreamt you found your mate, and even though I couldn't see his face, you thought he was handsome. He was important, I think. And you were finally able to leave this place. You went away with him, and he made you happy. I thought... I thought that would happen."

I swallow hard, not sure what to say. I'd had similar dreams, though most of mine happened while I was awake. While I was slopping the animals or doing my other chores, I used to daydream about my mate.

Now, those dreams are over, and I have to accept that I'll be a prisoner here behind these walls forever.

"You see," my sister continues, "whenever I have a dream like that, they usually come true."

She has my attention now. "Like that? Like... what?"

"It's hard to explain," she admits. "It's just this feeling I get during certain dreams. That's how I know it's not just a dream but a premonition. I had the same dream about you and your mate for several nights in a row, so I was sure you'd find him during the Haze. When you didn't, well, I was confused."

Fighting tears, I manage to say, "Well, maybe I'll find him next time."

I see her eyes widen as she considers this, blinking a few times. "I guess that's possible."

"Just because it didn't happen this time doesn't mean that it won't." I hate the words that are coming out of my mouth because they are meant to give her hope, a hope I can never have. I can't find my mate next time because I already found him.

Even though I have no idea how it's possible.

Taking a leap of faith, I ask my sister something I know I will likely regret. But if she really can see the future sometimes, maybe she can help me decipher a riddle. "Candace, which do you prefer? A world where the impossible is possible or one where the possible is impossible?"

My sister's eyes bulge as her mouth drops open. "Wh-what?"

I know I've messed up. Whatever it is that has her making that face, I'm certain she's calling for the guards through the mind-link. They'll be here soon to take me to the dungeon where I'll be introduced to the real whip.

"N-nothing," I stammer, shaking my head. "Never mind."

"No, Sister." Her hand is warm on my arm. "Why did you ask that? Where did you hear it?"

"In… in a dream," I lie. "Wh-where did you hear it?"

She takes a deep breath. "Same place."

13

MIND GAMES

Kieran

The blood splattered all across the stone wall and floor is fresh. The birds continue to caw at me, and it feels as if they are scratching the inside of my brain. I want to yell at them to get the fuck out of here, but I also don't want to anger them.

Besides, I need to know what the hell happened to Blake.

I storm off toward the guards' station where the same fat fucker is sitting picking at his teeth that I passed when I came down. "Where the hell is Blake?" I demand. "Did you assholes kill him?"

He looks up at me, his face completely blank as if he doesn't speak the same language as me. "Wh-who?"

"Who—*Your Highness!*" I correct him. "Blake, you imbecile. The old guy with the dark hair. The one with the fucking birds!"

"Oh, him. Crowman. That's what we call him down here. Crowman. Because of all the birds."

I reach down and grab him by the neck, my hand wrapping all the way around the circumference so that my fingers nearly meet my thumb. "Where the fuck is he?"

"He's… in the… infirmary," he croaks out. I release him, my scowl telling him to keep talking. Not that he seems the type to need a nudge. He grabs at his neck. "After the incident last night with Albatross and the boys, some of the other fellas got a little rambunctious and beat the living shit out of him. The king wasn't too happy about that. For some reason, he wants the bastard alive. So he's in the prison infirmary… Your Highness."

"The prison has an infirmary?" Despite my status as Crown Prince there seems to be something new I'm learning about my own kingdom every single day.

He points a chubby finger to his right. "Over there. By the supply closet."

"Of course." I pivot and head in that direction, absently rubbing at my own neck. I'd like to think I'm having sympathy pains, but that's not the case. This fucking mark will not leave me alone.

I throw open the door to find a room smaller than my bathtub. There's one cot there with an older looking woman with frizzy, dirty hair pulled up in a messy bun on the top of her head sitting next to it. She's wearing a dark brown gown and looks nothing like the pristinely clean healers I'm used to seeing above ground. My best guess is she's either another prisoner or a whore who happens to know a thing or two about salves, and whoever is in charge of this miserable place now thought that was good enough.

Blake lies on the cot on his stomach. His exposed back is covered with strips of white fabric. His skull is wrapped in it, as are his limbs. He has a thin blanket tossed over his middle. Even that is dotted in crimson.

I gesture with my head toward the door, and the woman bows her head and gets out of the only chair in the room, careful not to touch me as she brushes past and closes the door behind her.

I take her place on the chair, leaning forward to look into Blake's swollen face. One eye is puffed up so much it likely won't open for several days. His lips are cut, and bruises and dried blood covers the rest of his skin. He looks like hell, and I am beginning to wonder how someone who is allegedly a wizard could let anyone turn his face into a pile of raw hamburger.

He says nothing when he opens the one eye that will budge and looks at me. I wonder if he can even speak. I'm probably wasting my time, but I need to ask him. Without spending any time on the obvious, like telling him he looks like hell, I ask, "You're from Escuro?"

His head moves slightly. I take that as a yes.

"Is it true your kind have magical powers?" I think of all the stories I heard as a child. While they were mostly about my father's triumphant conquest of our enemy's lands, no good story would be complete without a boast or two about the obstacles the hero had to overcome. My father and those who praised him shared accolades of how the people of Escuro were able to command animals and send them to attack our wolf-warriors. Bears and other large mammals tore them limb from limb while smaller animals served as constant pests to drive them mad.

Kind of like those fucking birds.

Blake's mouth twists slightly into a crooked grin. "Some."

"The royals?" That's how the stories always go. All of my father's enemies had such great magical powers. Yet, he was able to defeat them through his wit, power, and strength.

"Mostly." Blake's voice cracks such that it's difficult for me to understand. "Nobles."

I nod. "So which are you?"

A gruff chuckle escapes his throat. "I am no one now," he manages to say. It's as if speaking of his past is giving him strength. "What difference does it make, Your Highness?"

"I need to know something." My voice is demanding, despite the fact that I haven't even asked my most relevant question yet.

"You want to know about the Haze." It's not a question. When he says it, leaning up a bit so that half his face isn't plastered against the cot, I feel him regaining his strength—which begs another question. Why the fuck wasn't he chained up anyway if he's capable of something like this? I always thought my father had all of his worst enemies chained up with silver so that they couldn't hurt anyone. I guess I was wrong.

"I do want to know about the Haze," I tell him. My hand automatically goes to my neck. Fucking painful, itchy mark. I wish I could cut it out of my flesh. "How did you know that?"

He attempts to shrug but winces against the pain. "It's a popular question."

Confusion washes over me. What the fuck is he talking about now? Who else would've–

"Blanca," I mutter.

Everything falls into place. She was down here the night before. When all hell broke loose, the mice and rats going crazy, the owl attacking the guards.

It probably wasn't even Blake who did it.

"How the fuck does she have powers?" Again, I'm not talking to him. I'm speaking to myself aloud.

He doesn't answer, but he does chuckle, and it's a low, creepy rumble.

I lift my eyes to meet the slits that are his.

"You think that's fucking funny?" I glare at him, and for a moment, I don't care that he's essentially an invalid. I want to break his bones.

"I think it's sad," he replies, making me even more angry. "You'd rather believe something that makes no sense than accept the fact that you're on the wrong side of this."

"What the fu–?" I don't even finish the word because all I want to do is punch him in his raw-meat face. "Why does my father allow you to use your powers? Shouldn't he have silver chains on you so you can't hurt anyone?" Even though I'm almost positive he didn't do this, my mind can't wrap around the fact that he's taught my sister how to control animals and use them to do his bidding.

I knew she was a witch.

"I used to be chained to the wall with silver chains, but over the years, the guards got lazy. It's no matter. I've never tried to leave. For twenty-one years, not a single animal attacked a guard or anyone else down here, Prince."

I nod. "So it wasn't you."

"I didn't say that."

"But you didn't *not* say that," I remind him. I lean forward, and his swollen eye cracks open just enough for me to get a good look at both of them. They dance with flickers of silver and blue, and I lean back in my chair.

"I will tell you the same thing that I told her. No one is powerful enough to manipulate the Haze. What you think is true is a lie, and what you believe could never be is the truth is reality. Until you wrap your mind around that, nothing else in this life is going to matter."

With that comment, I am done. This man is my father's archnemesis. He's done something to manipulate my sister into not only fucking with the Haze to mess with my position in this kingdom, but he taught her how to turn common animals into weapons.

"Fuck you, Blake," I spit at him. "I hope you bleed to death, you asshole."

I get up and storm out of the room, but the sound of his cackle fills my ears, mingling with the call of the crows, and as I storm up the stairs I have to wonder if that bastard is starting to get to me, too.

My father should've killed him a long time ago.

14

SEPARATE AND UNEQUAL

Blanca

"I need to get out of here."

It's the only thought I can allow to enter my mind. It's the same thought that has kept me going ever since I was old enough to understand that I am not like the others. I need to get the hell out of here and never look back.

I'm sitting on my bed with my legs pulled up to my chest, thinking about where I would go. The door is locked from the outside again, but I have the key the mice stole for me hidden away in one of the mouse holes. I can get out.

But once I do... where do I go?

I hear my door knob rattle, and it startles me. "Blanca, open this fucking door!" My brother's voice booms, and my breath catches in my that.

"I... can't," I stammer, leaping off the bed and approaching the barrier. "It's locked from the outside."

"What?" Kieran swears under his breath and rattles the door knob again–harder this time. "Who the hell locked you in your room?"

79

"Mother," I tell him. I don't say more. He will either talk to me through the door or find someone to unlock it. In all of our twenty-one years, never once has my brother come to my room. I'm surprised he even knows where it is.

I hear a commotion outside as Kieran demands that someone unlock the door. The deep voice of a guard registers, "Sir, the queen said no one is allowed–"

I hear gurgling sounds and take a step back. I imagine my brother squeezing the poor guy's throat. "I said open the fucking door. I am the Crown Prince."

"Y-yes, sir." The guard can hardly get the words out.

The jingle of keys fills the air, and then my door swings open. Kieran has fire in his eyes as he walks in and slams the door behind him. It shakes the wall. If I had any pictures hanging up, I imagine they would fall.

Instinctively, I back away from him as he stalks near me. It doesn't take long for me to run into the window ledge, which bites into the back of my legs. I wince as my welts begin to sting.

Kieran's eyes lower slightly, his brow furrowed. He's actually noticed that I'm in pain. I doubt he'll say anything.

"What the fuck is wrong with you?" he asks, to my surprise.

"N-nothing," I mutter. I fold my arms. "I'm fine."

"You're not fine. Turn around."

My eyes bulge. Why does he care? I shake my head.

"Turn. The. Fuck. Around."

I can't disobey him, so I slowly pivot on my foot, wondering what he's going to do. He tugs up the bottom of my shirt and then gasps before he drops it. Thank the Goddess he doesn't look down my skirt. I look at him over my shoulder.

"Who the fuck did that?"

Like I'm moving in quicksand, I turn back to him. "Doesn't matter."

"It does matter," he disagrees. "Goddess, it looks gnarly. You're going to get an infection."

"I never have before."

His eyes widen slightly as he realizes I am used to this. Why he cares is beyond me, but this coupled with Candace actually being concerned for me makes me wonder what the hell is going on. Everything has been so strange since the Haze.

"You were down in the dungeon last night."

It's not a question. I nod.

"Did you fuck up all those guards?"

I swallow hard. "I don't know."

Kieran shakes his head and places his hands on his hips. "How can you not know? Either you did or you didn't."

"I don't know because… everything is weird." I lower myself down onto the windowsill. I want to tell him I think something changed during the night of the Haze, but I'm afraid to say that word to him.

"Was that your punishment? Did Father have you whipped?"

"Not Father," I tell him. "Mother. It was her punishment for me sneaking out. They don't think… they don't know it was me. With the mice."

"Holy Fuck." He sinks down on the edge of my bed. "You are something else, Blanca. I don't know what the fuck to do with you. You do realize that what you got is nothing compared to what happened to your friend, right?"

My back straightens as I consider what he is saying. I don't really have any friends, but if I could count one person as such, it's Mr. Blake. "What did they do to him?"

"They beat the living hell out of him," Kieran tells me. "He looks like a pile of rare steak."

Tears prickle in my eyes. I was afraid of that. After the owl swooped in, and I ran, I felt terrible because I knew he wouldn't be able to get away. They must've assumed he did all of it because of the birds.

"Crying isn't going to do you any good, witch." Kieran is angry, but his words are not as malicious as they were the last time he spoke to me. "When did he teach you how to do this?"

"Teach me?" I repeat. Then, I shake my head. "He didn't."

"He had to have," Kieran counters. "Otherwise, how would you know how to do it? It's not like you were born that way. Only people from Escuro can control animals, and you're obviously not from there."

I stare at him for a long moment, my mind racing. "People from... where?"

"Escuro! You know? The kingdom to the north Father conquered around the time we were born. He talks about it all the fucking time. At least, he used to when we were younger."

Shaking my head, I remind him, "I wasn't there for any of that, Kieran."

He stares at my face for a moment and then slowly nods. He gets it now. He remembers. I was never invited for story time. Or family time. Or dinner time. I was always separate from everyone else. Even when I was a baby, I had my own nursery on the other side of the castle and a couple of maids who took care of me. I was never with my brother. It was like we weren't related at all.

"Listen, I understand you're jealous, that you want the throne–"

The laugh that burst from between my lips is almost frightening. I sound deranged. His eyebrows furrow as he stares at me. I cover my mouth with one hand. "I'm sorry. It's just... I already told you. That's the last thing on earth I want."

"Then what else could it be? Why else would you let the crazy man in the dungeon, Father's arch nemesis, teach you how to control animals? Why else would you try to... do what you did... to take the throne?" His cheeks turn pink, and I know he's accidentally let some thoughts of what happened during the Haze sneak in.

I shake my head. "I didn't do any of those things. I told you, he didn't teach me, and during the Haze, my wolf was acting on instinct, the same as yours and everyone else's. I know you can't believe me because it's all so messed up, but it's the truth. As for the throne, the only thing I want for myself is freedom. To run as far away from here as possible and never look back. I don't care if I have to go slop hogs for a pig farmer twenty-three hours a day. I want out of here."

"Is it really that bad?" Again, his gaze locks with mine, his icy blue eyes sincere with his question.

I nod. "The worst part is knowing that even my own family doesn't want me." I wipe away a tear that's slipped from my eye. "And now, with no mate…." I yearn to scratch that spot above my left breast that itches and burns, but I don't. Not in front of him.

Kieran tosses himself backward onto my bed, makes a sound like someone who's just stepped barefoot in pig shit, and leaps up to standing. I might've laughed under other circumstances as he realized lying on my bed isn't a good idea.

He shakes his head as he starts to walk toward the door. "None of this makes any fucking sense to me, and I hate it. I hate all of it."

"Me, too," I agree.

He is starting to turn back into the asshole bully I have always hated. Pointing a finger at me, he says, "Whatever the fuck you're doing, stop!"

I nod. What else can I do?

Kieran leaves the room, and the keys jingle again. I'm a prisoner, as far as they know, but thoughts of escape fill my head again.

I dissolve onto my bed, the tears I tried my best to hold back earlier springing free. "I'm so sorry, Mr. Blake," I say from the bottom of my heart, wishing he could hear me. "I never meant for you to get hurt."

'It's okay, Little Raven. I'm okay.'

The voice in my head rings out so clearly, I gasp and sit up.

What the fuck was that?

15
SECRETS AND LIES

Kieran

I march down the hallway away from Blanca's room, wondering what possessed me to go in there in the first place. I should've known better. Even that close to her, my mark still ached. As long as two mates who had marked each other continued to fight against the Moon Goddess's plans, that would always be the case. But what the fuck else am I supposed to do? The alternative isn't even an option.

I'm almost to my room when I hear a voice behind me and freeze. "Hello Kieran Wieran!"

I grit my teeth, bite back a sigh, and slowly turn around to see Nessa standing in the hallway wearing a bright pink ball gown. It's the shade of bubble gum and looks hideous. What the fuck is she doing? Is that what she spent my money on?

"Hello... mate," I manage to spit out. "I see you've done some shopping."

"It's gorgeous, isn't it?" She does a full twirl, and the skirts swing out so far, I'm afraid she might knock over a statue sitting on a pillar not far away. Luckily, the bust is just grazed.

"It's… something else." That's not offensive–and it's true.

Her smile widens as she comes at me, a little too much like that cat that pounced on me the other night. I almost back away but remind myself she's in charge now. She pulls me to her and presses her mouth against mine. When she slides her tongue along my bottom lip, I start to gag but know I have to open up for her. She holds my entire life in her hands right now.

Eventually, I start to run out of breath and have to pull away. I plaster a ridiculous smile to my face because I don't want to offend her. "Let's leave something for our wedding night."

She giggles and covers her mouth with a gloved hand. "All right, matey-watey. I'll see you at dinner."

"I can hardly wait." She winks at me and does another spin before heading down the hallway, and I wait until she's gone to let my true emotions take over, my shoulders slumping as I shake my head. "It's too bad Blanca didn't have her attacked by mice."

"Hey, just the man I was looking for." Taner's voice cuts through the images in my mind of Nessa being eaten alive by a drove of vermin.

Slowly, I turn to face him, expecting him to say something out of left field that will make me question humanity, but instead, he points at my face and laughs hysterically. "Were you just attacked by a clown?"

Swearing under my breath, I pull a handkerchief from my pocket and wipe my mouth. When I pull it away, it's covered in bright pink lipstick. "Son of a bitch," I murmur. "Did I get it all?"

"Yeah, sure." Taner looks too amused for me to believe him, so I swipe at my face a few more times. "Man, I wish Ayla would kiss me like that, but she's giving me the cold shoulder until we're married."

"When's that happening?" I ask, wanting to tell him he has nothing to be jealous of. I'd rather lick the inside of a toilet than have Nessa's tongue in my mouth.

"Not sure yet. Have you two set a date?"

I shake my head. Somehow, I've managed to avoid that so far, but it won't be too much longer before my mother and hers will agree on a date.

"Well, I'm sure it won't be too much longer before you'll be linked to her for life. I bet you can't wait to hear her voice inside of your head." He laughs, and I grimace. No, I do not want to have the mind-link with Nessa.

But then, I won't, will I? She's not really my mate, so even when we're married and that should officially kick in, I won't have to worry about it.

"So I asked my dad a few questions about what we were talking about earlier." Taner lowers his voice to a whisper. "Can we go in your room?"

I'm still struggling to remember what we were talking about the last time I saw him as I nod and lead him the few steps to my room. I unlock the door, and he follows me inside.

My chambers are a stark contrast to Blanca's. While she has one tiny room with a bathroom the size of a small closet, I have an antechamber that leads to my bedchamber, a sitting area, and a kitchen. My bathroom is bigger than Blanca's bedroom. She wasn't kidding when she said things were different for her. I've never really thought about it before, but I probably should since it doesn't make any sense to me. I'll add it to the list.

"Do you want a beer?" I ask Taner as he makes himself comfortable on my couch.

"Sure, thanks."

I head to the refrigerator and pull out a couple of cold ones and walk over to him. By the time I'm sipping my beer and settled in the chair across from him, I remember what we were talking about before.

"Escuro?" I ask him.

He nods. "Yeah. My father wasn't a commander when the raids into the other kingdoms took place, but he was a warrior. I asked him what it was like, if the stories were true about the Escurotites sending bears and other animals to attack them."

"Yeah? What did he say?" I'm not sure why I'm nervous to hear his response.

"Well, he didn't want to talk about it at all," Taner admits. "It took some arm twisting on my part to get him to start talking. But he says a lot of the stories he's heard from various commanders and other nobility are not at all how he remembers the situation."

This is astonishing to me. "Really?" I ask. "How so?" It's hard for me to imagine Taner's father, an enormous man with facial hair and tattoos, afraid to talk about anything.

"He says that they headed to Escuro planning to fight, that they'd been warned that the royals and some higher ranking nobles could manipulate animals and send them to attack in large numbers. But by the time they got there... there wasn't really anyone left alive to fight."

My mouth drops open, and I have to set my beer aside because I don't understand what he's saying. "No one left alive?"

"That's right. The commanders were joking about it, laughing, even going into the people's houses to joke around about how they'd been outsmarted and all that, but my father didn't think it was funny. He had gone there expecting to prove himself as a warrior. Instead, they only fought a skirmish or two against a few smaller groups that hadn't been affected by... what had been done."

Swallowing hard, I stare at my best friend, trying to decipher what he's talking about. "What who had done?"

"Your father and his higher ranking commanders, I guess." He shrugs. "My father didn't say, but who else could give those kinds of orders?"

"But... what was it?" I demand. "Why would an entire kingdom of people be dead when my father and his warriors had just arrived? Were they attacked by another kingdom?"

Shaking his head, Taner says, "No. They were all foaming at the mouth. Some of them had been dead longer than others, like they hadn't figured out what had gone on in time to stop doing it but–Father says it looked like... wolfsbane."

"Wolfsbane?" I repeat the word–the one substance that can take us out faster than any other. "What do you mean?"

"Apparently, your father had poisoned their water supply. We have the same streams here, but they're downstream from us. The people who drank the water died–and that was almost everyone." Taner looks morose, but I'm already gritting my teeth together and shaking my head before he finishes.

"No fucking way," I tell him. "There's no way that's possible. My father is a great warrior. A proud warrior. He would never do something so underhanded."

"I was shocked to hear it, too, but once my father started talking, he told me more. He said when they attacked Starfall Mountain pack, they locked the entire royal family and all of their guests in a temple and set it on fire. The king's daughter was getting married. Your father was an invited guest."

"Fuck you!" I stand up, leaning over him, snarling. "How dare you! What you're saying is treason, Taner!"

"What I'm saying is the truth!" He doesn't move, only stares back at me, and I see in his eyes that he believes it.

I suppose I believe everything my father says, too. But this... he has to know it can't be true.

"I'm sorry, man. I'm not trying to be treasonous. I just want you to know that... maybe you should ask your father some more questions about what really happened. You wanted to know about Escuro, how we overpowered people with magical powers, now you know."

"We didn't poison them! We outsmarted them!" I insist. Taner shrugs and slides off the couch, steering clear of me. I've been mad at him lots of times in my life, but this is the first time I've wanted to rip him limb from limb.

"I'm gonna go." He walks to the door, setting his unfinished beer on a small table there. With his hand wrapped around the door knob, he turns to face me. I am still seething but I don't say anything. "By the way," he says, his voice quiet. "I asked him about that Blake guy. He is from Escuro, but he's not just one of their warriors or what have you."

"Who is he?" I demand to know.

Before he opens the door and disappears, Taner replies, "He was the king."

16

JUST THE VOICES IN MY HEAD

'It's okay, Little Raven. I'm okay.'

Mr. Blake's voice sounds in my head, and I freeze, afraid to breathe. This isn't just like when a person thinks they hear someone's voice because it's so familiar to them. No, this is completely different. It's as if I'm on the phone–something I'm never allowed to use–and I can actually hear Mr. Blake's voice, and he's talking directly to me.

"Wh-who? Who is talking to me please?" I say aloud as I also think the stuttering mess of a sentence.

'It's me, Blake. I can hear you, Little Raven. You're mind-linking.'

Shock ripples through me as I gasp and hold a hand over my trembling lips. "Moon Goddess," I murmur. The mind-link? But that's not possible. I've never had the mind-link before, not even with my own family members. It's not possible. There's just no way that Mr. Blake can hear what I'm thinking.

'Little Raven, have you given any more thought to what I said to you the other night? About all of the strange happenings that you and the Crown Prince cannot explain?'

I continue to sit with my mouth hanging open trying to determine whether or not I should continue to speak to this voice in my head or bury my skull in a pile of pillows to drown it out. Since I only have one thin pillow the width of a novella on my bed, I decide that's not going to work. "I have been thinking about it nonstop, but I don't understand," I tell him both aloud and in my mind.

'What is there to understand, dear one? Simply state the truth of the matter, and you can only arrive at one conclusion.'

A lump forms in my throat as I ponder what he's saying. For just a moment, I let my mind accept the only possibility that follows what I know to be true about the Moon Goddess. If only members of the same pack can speak through the mind-link, that means Mr. Blake and I are members of the same pack.

But he is from a distant land, the name of which I'm not completely sure of, so that's not possible. There's no way he's from Dun's Crossing, I'm almost certain. I remember what Kieran said about those special people who can control animals.

But I need to ask. "What pack are you a member of, Mr. Blake?"

'I'm from a kingdom known as Escuro,' he tells me. When he speaks of his lands, he is proud, I can tell. *'A special group of people who loved one another like family no matter their station. Kind, loving, thoughtful, selfless people. Those were the people of Escuro.'*

I can tell by the way he's speaking that there aren't many left of his kind. A tear forms in the corner of my eye as I think about it–of them. My father's warriors ripped his people apart. From King Gavin's perspective, we were the victorious winners who had extinguished some evil from the world. From the eyes of the vanquished, we were cruel invaders who changed everything for them, ending a great deal of lives, no doubt.

'Tell me about your people,' I say, still thinking about what it is Mr. Blake wants me to accept–that we are somehow from the same pack.

That either he is actually from Dun's Crossing...

Or I am from Escuro.

A laugh catches in my throat. It's not possible. I've been here my entire life. Most children don't have memories as old as mine, but I was born a woman, not a child, and the longing for any form of affection I'd had in my soul since I was an infant made images flicker and catch in my mind's eye that allowed me to hold onto time in a different capacity than most.

'I've told you, Little Raven, my people were kind and peaceful. That peace was sadly destroyed these many years ago. But I believe they can be resurrected, come back and be a beautiful, utopian kingdom once again.'

Listening to his words has me tearing up again. He speaks so fondly of them, I hate that my own father is responsible for what has happened. Others may see him as a great and mighty ruler, but to me, he is the cruel man who never even had a hug for his own daughter.

'How?' I gulp in some air, wiping my eyes on the back of my sleeves. *'How can they be brought back?'*

'All it takes is a little faith–and recognition, my Little Raven.'

I open my mouth to say more, but I hear a jingle in the door. "Someone's here," I whisper.

Mr. Blake laughs in my head. *'You can just think it. If you're thinking of me when you have a message to send, I'll hear you. I'll always hear you, my Little Raven.'*

I want to say more, but my sister's smiling face appears at the door. "Hi," Candace says, carrying in a tray of food. "Were you talking to someone?"

I sniffle and wipe my eyes. "Just myself," I tell her. "I'm sorry."

"Don't be." She sets the tray down near me on the bed and takes a seat near my feet. "I'm so sorry, Blanca."

"Sorry?" I ask. "For what?"

"For everything." Candace lets out a sigh, and I see her eyes beginning to glimmer as well. "We were never sisters, and I hate that."

I stare at her for a moment and know that she really means that. I couldn't tell if her concern the other day was genuine or just a matter of her getting all wrapped up in her feelings because of the situation with the Haze and all of that. But she'd been bringing me food a few times a day since the door was permanently locked, and if it wasn't for that, I'd be awfully hungry. And looking in her eyes, I believe her.

"When I think about all the fun memories I have with Ingrid–

picking out clothes together, choosing accessories, all of those fun moments. You missed out on that with us, and I missed out on it with you. I know how it feels to be the big sister in that situation, marveling at how beautiful and smart your younger sibling is, but I have no idea what it's like to be the younger sister, to be doted on."

I'm not sure what to say to that. Her reasoning sounds a bit selfish to me when she puts it like that, but since I don't say anything, Candace continues.

"Not only that. It's just not fair that you always miss out on everything." She sniffles and wipes her hand on the back of her nose. "And Mother having you whipped." Her head turns quickly so she's looking at me. "That wasn't the first time."

It's not a question, but I confirm for her. "No, it wasn't."

She nods and blows out some air. "Well, I don't like it. You're our sister, damn it. Why do we treat you like shit?"

"When—when did you realize that all of this was a problem?" I run a hand through my hair, trying to seem nonchalant even though my heart aches.

"It was about the time I had that dream that you met your mate," she says in a near whisper. "I started thinking about how sad I'd be if you left just like that, and I never even really knew you. I'd be happy for you, I realized. I've never said much, but I always hated the way we treated you. But yeah, it was just before the Haze."

I nod, not surprised. The timing coincides with when everything else in the world slipped on its ear.

"Well, I should let you eat. I'll come back and get the tray in a bit."

"Thank you, Candace." I smile at her, and she pats my arm. I almost flinch; I'm not used to gentle touches. But I don't, and we grin at one another for a moment before she goes to the door. I can't do anything about the past, but I can choose to have a sister now.

"Wish me luck at dinner," she says, her hand on the door. She makes a face that begs my question.

"What's happening at dinner?" I reach for the cloche on the tray she brought up to me for my dinner.

"Kieran is bringing his mate. Goddess, she's so annoying. That's something else I realized at the time of the Haze. Nessa Winters is just awful. Goddess, I can't believe our brother is going to have to marry her. Can you think of one other person on the planet that it would be worse for him to be mated to?"

I stare at her wide blue eyes, my hand frozen in mid-air, and murmur, "I can think of… one other."

17

VICTORY'S SPOILS

KIERAN

"OH, MY. THAT IS A BRIGHT SHADE OF PINK." MY MOTHER BLINKS HER eyes a few times before sipping her wine again. She's commented on Nessa's dress at least five times since dinner started only a few moments ago. Every time she does, Nessa giggles and squeezes my hand beneath the table, as if it's a compliment.

It's not one. My mother doesn't give a lot of compliments, but when she does, one can tell she is pleased. At the moment, she looks as if she'd rather down the rest of the bottle of wine sitting at the end of the table than look at Nessa again.

"Mother helped me choose it," Nessa gushes this time, smiling at her mother whose bright yellow gown is almost as capable of burning retinas as the one Nessa has on.

"We can't tell you how excited we are to further unite our two kingdoms," Nessa's father says. He's been practically giddy since we announced we were mates. He knows his own king will reward him greatly for creating such a tight alliance between Dun's Crossing and Snowcrest Canyon.

"Yes, Floyd. We were very pleased as well." The king speaks through gritted teeth. I know he's unhappy about all of this as well, but what my father doesn't know is how much worse it could be.

I continue to go over the conversations I've recently had with both Blanca and Taner in my mind, wishing I could ask my father if what Taner's father said is true. Is it possible they really did take out Escuro through the use of wolfsbane?

I look at my father, studying his face carefully as he lifts a forkful of beef and vegetables to his mouth and takes a bite. He seems so at ease, without a care in the world, though that changes when Mrs. Winters, Trudy, opens her mouth to begin a conversation about the wedding colors with my mother. Father looks as if he's trying not to listen at all.

As soon as there is a pause in the women's conversation, I find myself interjecting myself into the dialogue, wanting to hear anything but more blather about the wedding. "Father, I've heard from the dungeon guards that Blake, that old wizard, was responsible for the trouble down there last night."

The table goes quiet as everyone turns to look at me. My parents both blink a few times, but the others are motionless. Is this a topic we shouldn't be discussing at dinner? I can't say why not. We always talk about father's exploits into war. I just want to frame this conversation a bit more carefully.

"Yes, what he did to those men was just terrible. He's been severely punished for it." Father spears a carrot. "Has anyone noticed the new flowers in the west garden?"

"If he has magical powers, why is he allowed to just sit in his cell all day?" I press on. "Why didn't you kill him when you conquered the rest of the kingdom?"

Father lets out a loud sigh. "I'd rather not talk about it now."

"Oh, Father," my sister Candace leaps into the conversation from down the table where the rest of my siblings are gathered. They know better than to try to speak during dinner most of the time, but for some reason I can't understand, Candace is here to assist me. "I'd love to know as well. I've heard the tales about their magical abilities, how they can manipulate animals. Wouldn't it have been easy for you to end him when you wiped out the rest of the village?" Her blue eyes are wide and innocent as she looks down the table toward the man sitting over all of us.

"Of course, it would've been easier. It would've been a breeze," he says. "Everyone else had already been destroyed in battle. We'd ripped them apart."

My eyes travel across the table to check out the reaction from my mother and Nessa's father. Mother is as stoic as ever, obviously collaborating her husband's story, but I think I see a flicker of doubt on Floyd's face.

"How did you overcome them?" I ask. "Their powers are wicked if they can get rats to do that."

"Oh, it was just their royals who had those kinds of powers," Father shrugs absently.

"Could they teach others?" Candace asks, practically reading my mind.

"No, of course not. Just like the royals of Snowcrest Canyon can't teach others how to make ribbons of ice or the nobles of Starfall Mountain can't teach others how to create that ball of light they can toss."

"You managed to take out several other powerful packs all at once, Father. It's stunning. I should hope I can be as great a ruler." I give him a tightlipped smile, a forced one. Holes in his story begin to surface as I think back over the great tales he's spun over the years. Most of the time, they contradict one another. I'm not sure what is the truth, but I'm beginning to believe my father really did stoop to low levels to conquer all of those kingdoms.

I'd still like an answer to our question, though.

"Why didn't you kill Blake then?" I take a sip of my wine, trying to sound unbothered.

"Because... the old coward begged me not to kill him. I dragged him back here and locked him up in silver chains, hoping perhaps one day he'd use his powers to help me overcome other kingdoms."

This stirs Floyd. "What kingdoms? You've already conquered almost all of them." He clears his throat. "Naturally, not ours."

"No, of course not. Snowcrest Canyon is an ally to us. We're more aligned than ever before," King Gavin assures his table guest.

"He begged you not to kill him? You showed him great mercy, Father," Candace chimes in. She gives him a smile as well.

"Yes, well, I wish I would've killed him. He's never done a lick of good for me. He's refused to use his powers at all, saying he didn't have the ability any more. Obviously, he was lying. We should probably kill him now." Father takes a drink and sets his glass aside.

I don't want him to kill Blake, not now. I have some questions for the old man. I tell Candace, *'Let's let it go,'* through the mind-link.

She replies, *'He's not telling us something, brother. Something strange is going on. The dreams I've been having recently.'*

I turn and look at her. She looks so small and young sitting there next to our brother Finn who is a full year younger than her. Something is bothering my sister, and I don't like it. Candace and I have always been the closest of all, which is a bit ironic since I have a twin sister—and she's not her.

My eyes travel further down the table. There's not even an empty chair for Blanca.

Why not?

Why have they always hated her?

The women are talking about flowers again, which gives me an out. Dinner is almost over. I am finished. "I think… I'd like to go out to the garden and see some of these flowers you ladies keep speaking of for myself."

"I'll come with you," Nessa offers.

"Are you sure?" I had a feeling she'd tried to tag along. I really just want some air. "The staff has been seeing a lot of those black flying beetles recently."

"I'll be fine." She smiles at me in a way that says I'd better not try to ditch her.

"All right then, my dear." We excuse ourselves and head outside, and while I'm glad to be away from the table, I don't want to spend any time with Nessa.

"Why do I have a feeling you're up to something?" she asks as she strolls along beside me, her arm linked through mine.

"I don't know what you're talking about," I assure her.

"I think you're trying to figure out a way so that you don't have to marry me."

I stop walking and turn to look at her. "Nessa, of course I want to marry you." I manage to force myself to bend down and kiss her, even though I have to hold my breath and close my eyes tightly the whole time.

"Good," she says when I release her. "Because it would be horribly embarrassing for you and your family if I tell anyone the truth."

I take a deep breath and stare into her eyes. "No need for that. You and I will be married soon enough, and everyone will know that you're my mate."

She grins devilishly at me.

"I think I'm going to go for a run, just to get some energy out before I go to bed. I will see you tomorrow, my love." Over the years, I have learned to be charming. It works perfectly with all of the women that are smitten with me, and that include Nessa.

She blushes and reaches up to boop me on the nose. "Don't stay out too late."

I chuckle–as if there's any way I'm going to go calling on her.

Once she's inside, I meander around the garden a bit more, trying to decide what to do.

Father's story isn't adding up.

The Haze is never wrong and can't be magicked into doing something other than what the Moon Goddess wants.

Blanca has the same powers as Blake.

Only people from Escuro are capable of those powers.

Only royalty.

"Fuck," I mumble. "Blanca, who are you?"

18

STEPPING IN IT

AFTER CANDACE LEFT, I'D SAT THERE IMMOBILE FOR QUITE SOME TIME. Her statement about Nessa being the worst match for Kieran had made me nauseated. But I'd managed to eat the food she'd brought me, and now, I'm pacing in the small area of my room.

I can mind-link with Mr. Blake but no one in my family. Just to prove it, I try sending Candace a message that I'm done eating, but she says nothing back to me because she can't hear me.

My own family treats me worse than garbage. Why would they do that?

The Moon Goddess matched me with someone who can't possibly be my mate if everything I've been told my whole life is the truth.

But what if it's not?

What if I am from Escuro? I have no idea how that's possible since I have flickers of myself sleeping in a crib far away from everyone else in the castle except for the mean old maids who used to take care of me. I remember crying for my mother and being snatched out of that crib and shaken.

Maybe that never happened, and it's just a bad dream. Or maybe I have been here since I was a baby.

Is it possible that both could be true? Could I have been born in Escuro and brought here as a baby? But why?

I have no answers, and I'm sick of being locked in this room trying to figure it all out. For days, I haven't even been allowed to go outside to slop the pigs. I need air. I need–to go.

Without another thought, I rush to the closet and grab the old bag I have in the back. I shove a few changes of clothing into it, and that's pretty much all I have in the world. I have no idea how I'll get out past the guards and over the wall, but I have to try. What's the worst that can happen? They'll catch me, bring me back, and Mother will let her henchwoman whip me again. She did say it would be worse next time, but I am ready to take my chances.

I drop to my knees to reach into the mousehole to grab the key. When I do, I hear a bunch of squeaks from my little friends. "I'm sorry," I whisper to them. I pull out the key, and they poke their heads out. "I wish you could come with me, but it's too dangerous. Be safe."

They hang their heads in solemn expressions.

I want to say more, but I have no time. I look at their little faces once more, and then, I'm up and gliding to the door.

I press my ear against the barrier and listen for a moment. Hearing nothing, I slip the key into the lock and turn it. Then, I poke my head out into the hallway. I don't see or hear anyone, so I step out of my room and lock the door behind me, thinking that might give me a few extra minutes while people try to assess if I'm still inside.

With a deep breath, I turn to my right and head toward the door I use in the mornings to go out and slop the pigs. It's the quickest way out of the castle, and not many people should be coming in and out that way this time of night since all of the farm chores should be done.

I see no one else in the hallway as I make my way toward the door. Then, I slip out into the cool evening air and take a few deep breaths. The sense of freedom I'd carried with me during the first few moments of the Haze wants to settle around me, but I won't let it. I was wrong about that night, and I'm probably wrong about this one, too.

With no more time to stand around, I take off toward the barn, thinking about my best path out. I know where the gates are, and I know they are all guarded. I can't think of any secret tunnels or high ground that will give me a chance to scale the wall or jump over. No, I'm going to have to make it through a guarded gate at night.

I'm thin enough in my human form I can probably slide between the bars, but how I can get all the guards in front of the gate to look away for a moment is beyond me.

"Unless...." A thought occurs to me, and as I pick up speed running toward the nearest gate, I use my mind to call together any birds that might be nearby. I hate to use them because it'll either get Mr. Blake into more trouble or call attention to my abilities in a bad way, but I see no other way out.

I'm running so fast now I can feel my wolf chomping at the bit. She wants to be released. She wants to run free, to feel the wind in her fur, and I'd love to let her, but that would mean I'd have to stop, undress, pack my clothes, shift, and then run to the gate, shift, slip through naked, and shift again, and it really makes no sense for me to do that when I'm pretty sure no one even knows I'm gone yet.

No, I need to stay in my human form until I get through the gate. Then, I'll have every chance I need to shift and get out of here.

I run past the rose gardens where the rest of my family often gathers to admire the flowers and listen to the water tinkling in the fountains. I've seen them from the windows many times, but I've never once been invited to sit with them and take in the lovely scene.

Trying not to let it bother me, I push on. Maybe one of these days they'll all realize I'm gone, and they'll miss me. Maybe they'll wish they'd taken the chance to get to know me. I am their sister, their daughter, after all.

"Or am I?" I'm not sure where the thought has come from, but I can't help but echo it back to the one person who can hear me. To Mr. Blake, I ask, *"Am I even a princess at all?"*

His voice sounds very clearly inside of my head. *"Oh, yes, my little Raven. You are indeed a princess."*

"But... my family hates me," I tell him. *"They don't treat me like a princess at all."*

"Your family loves you," he counters. *"They will treat you like the queen you will be one day soon."*

"Queen?" I'm so confused. What in the world is he talking about? *"Mr. Blake, I'm leaving,"* I blurt out to him. *"I'm going to Escuro to figure out how the hell I can be a member of your pack."*

"Please be careful, my dear one," he says back. *"Use your powers to help yourself. Head due north, and you will find our homeland."*

"Our homeland?" I whisper. I'm running so fast, I almost trip over a tree root and have to slow down. I'm glad that happens, though, because I had almost reached the end of the garden, and I know the gate is up ahead.

Slowing my breathing, I dodge behind a large bush and look out. I can see the guards gathering around the exit. Above their heads, crows and other birds begin to circle. It's now or never.

I'm just about to step out of my hiding spot, my plan in place, when I feel a hand clamp down around my arm.

Sucking in a deep breath, I turn my head, wondering who the hell has caught me. When my eyes lock on Kieran's, I feel my stomach drop to the ground.

"Going somewhere are we, Blanca?" he whispers.

"Shit."

It's really all I can say because I just stepped in a big pile of it.

19

I DON'T THINK WE'RE RELATED

I'D SEEN HER RUSH PAST WHILE I WAS SITTING IN THE ROSE GARDEN, thinking about everything. My first instinct was to shout at her and tell her to get her ass back inside.

But I can't do that, and I know it.

She has to leave. Not just because she doesn't really belong here but because it's the only way either one of us are going to get any answers. It seems certain to me that no one in our family is ever going to tell us the truth, and everyone else is afraid to say anything. Even Taner's father, who's provided more info than he realizes, won't say anything more for fear that my father will kill him.

Still, with my hand wrapped around my sister's thin arm, I have to admit, I don't want her to go—not alone.

"Listen, Kieran," she begins, breathing heavily from the run, "I know you think I shouldn't be out of my room, but this is what you wanted, remember? You and Nessa?"

I wrinkle my nose and lean away from her at the mention of the woman who wants to be my queen. "Nessa is the one that said you need to leave," I remind her.

She shakes her head. "She might've said it, but you agreed. You said–"

"I know what I said, Blanca." I narrow my eyes at her. "I don't need any reminders of what happened that night."

She bites her bottom lip and nods at me, and I can't help but think there's something else she wants to say to me, but she won't. Not right now. She's trying to convince me to let her go.

Blanca lifts her eyes. That's when I first hear the calls of the birds circling overhead. "Fuck," I mutter, releasing her arm as I tip my head further back. "Are you sending them after the guards?"

"I don't want to." I believe her. She's practically whimpering as tears fill her eyes. "I don't want anyone else to get hurt, but it's the only way I can get out." The birds swoop lower, and even more of them come in in a large group from the south.

A murder. That's what they're called. A group of crows.

"Why are you crying about hurting the guards?" I ask her, practically snarling at her. "They'd beat the shit out of you without hesitation and drag you back to your room."

A large bird swoops down slightly, and I take a step backward. "I don't really want to hurt anyone," she says. "But it's not the guards I'm worrying about." She locks eyes with me for a moment, and that's when I realize what she's getting at.

My eye begins to twitch. I reach up and swipe at it. Even though the marks from where that bird attacked me in the dungeon healed up a few days ago, thanks to my good wolf shifter genes, it still hurts just thinking about it. "You wouldn't do that to me again, would you?" I smirk at her and shake my head. Who is this version of Blanca that has balls?

"I don't want to," she admits, taking a step away from me. "I just want you to let me go."

"Blanca, I understand why you want to leave. I don't blame you one bit," I tell her.

Her dark eyes widen. "You don't?"

"No, of course not. Clearly, something fucked up is happening here, and no one in this castle wants to help us figure it out." I drag a hand through my hair. "It's exasperating."

"Mr. Blake wants to help," she blurts out. "I can mind-link with him."

My mouth drops open as I stare at her. As she finally lost her ever-loving mind. "What's that?"

"I know it's crazy." She starts fidgeting nervously with the hem of her shirt. "But it's true. I called out to him, after you left, to see if he was okay, and he said he was. I could hear him. In my head."

I pull my mouth closed and stare at her because I don't know what to say, but I don't want to swallow a bug. "Listen, Blanca," I finally begin again. "That's not pos–"

"Possible?" She finishes for me. "I know. But he said the impossible is possible and the possible is impossible, and he's right. None of this makes any sense, but Kieran, if I'm from Escuro–"

"How can you be?" I blurt out. "You're my sister."

"Am I?" She tips her head to the side and looks at me like I'm an idiot. "Kieran, we look nothing alike."

"I know but–"

"We act nothing alike. I have these weird powers. I can hear a man we both know is from Escuro in my head." A nervous laugh erupts from her mouth. "I'm starting to think someone has been lying to us."

She makes a good point, and it would be easy to agree with her, but if I agree with her, I'm essentially committing treason. "If we're being lied to, it's from Mother and Father," I remind her.

She nods solemnly. "Your mother and father. I don't think they're mine. At least, I hope they're not because anyone who would treat their own daughter the way that they treat me is even more fucked in the head than I've ever even realized."

Again, she has a good point.

In the distance, I hear the guards start to yell as they notice the birds circling. We don't have a lot of time. Blanca knows that. She takes another step and peers around the bush I found her hiding behind.

"So you're just going to run to Escuro? And then what? Do you even know how to get there?" I ask, bombarding her with questions.

"Yeah, Mr. Blake said to head due North. I can do that. And I guess when I get there, I'll see if there's anyone alive who can help me. Mr. Blake told me they were wonderful, giving people."

"They might not take too kindly to someone coming through from Dun's Crossing." I'm making excuses now. I don't want her to go alone. I'm afraid she might get hurt–or she might never come back, and then I'll never know the truth.

"I'll be okay," she tells me. "But I have to go."

"What about the guards?" I ask her. "Not these guards. There are other ones out there, and these will use the mind-link to warn them that you're coming. They'll capture you, bring you back here, and I have no idea what Father will do with you, especially if you really aren't his daughter." A chill goes down my spine as I think of what the guards did to Blake. Would Blanca suffer the same fate?

"It's just something I'll have to worry about later, if I get caught. But I have to go." She takes a few more steps away from me.

Shaking my head, I tell her, "No. I can't let you do this."

"But Kieran–"

"Not alone," I tell her. I take a deep breath and pull my shirt off over my head, preparing to shift.

Her eyes bulge from her head. "You can't come with me."

"Why not?" I ask her, kicking off my shoes. "You got room in that bag for my clothes?"

Her head rocks back and forth, but she doesn't move. I pull the bag from her back and start shoving my clothes in it. When I unzip my pants, she turns away from me. Naked, I finish putting my clothes in and put the bag back on her before I shift.

We won't be able to communicate now, so I grunt at her, and she turns to look at me. Once again, she has tears in her eyes. "I don't think this is a good idea."

Wordlessly, I nudge her in the leg with my nose. Once again, she takes a stuttering breath. I give her another nudge, and Blanca swears under her breath before sucking in a lungful of air and moving forward, around the edge of the bush.

Then, Blanca takes off running toward the gate. The birds swoop down toward the guards. They are all in their human form as I tear after Blanca toward the exit. She takes her bag off, tosses it over and then slips between the bars, something I wouldn't be able to do even in my human form because I'm too muscular.

The guards are shouting, swatting at the birds. I see a glimmer of metal on the lead guard's waistband and run over toward him, snatching the keyring with my teeth and pulling it away. He doesn't even notice.

I rush back over to the gate where Blanca is putting her bag back on, looking at me with hesitation in my eyes. I can flip her the keys and hope she unlocks it from the other side–if I trust her.

Do I trust her?

20

RUN INTO THE NIGHT

"Hand me the key, Kieran," I tell him as I see guards coming closer to where he's standing on the other side of the gate I just squeezed through. Right now, the guards are preoccupied, fighting the birds I'm sending to distract them. But it won't take long before the birds get scared and fly off or the soldiers get the upper hand. If he is actually coming with me, which I still can't believe, then he'd better get his ass over here soon.

But he can hardly unlock the gate in his wolf form, so he needs to hand me the key.

"Give it to me," I whisper to him.

Kieran stares at me for a long moment before shaking his wolf head and dropping the key–on his side of the gate. I think this means he's not coming with me, and if I don't hurry up and run, maybe he'll change his mind altogether and work with the guards to get me back inside the castle. I take a few steps backward.

In a blink, Kieran shifts into his human form. He's standing there naked in front of me. Flashes of images from that night we shared together come back to me, and I have to pull my eyes away. Even though it's quickly becoming a reality to me that Kieran can't be my brother, old habits die hard, and I avert my eyes as he picks up the key, unlocks the gate, and steps through, locking it behind him. Then, he drops the key into my backpack. "Let's go."

He doesn't wait for me. Instead, he takes off running, leaps into the air, and shifts back into his wolf. I want to do the same, but I have the backpack. I take a few rushed steps away from the gate, hearing shouts from the guards as I do so. When I'm about ten yards away, I drop the backpack, undress, shove my clothes into the bag, shift, and slide it on. Then, I take off sprinting as my wolf, reeling in the feel of the air brushing through my fur. I see Kieran up ahead of me, even though it's dark, and the moon isn't much more than a sliver these days. Still, I can see his white fur in the darkness, and I push myself until I've caught up to him.

He turns his head slightly, probably surprised that I am this fast, but I think I see a smile as he bounds off even faster, and I have to kick it into another gear to be able to keep up.

I want to run as fast as I can to get away from the possibility of the soldiers following us. I'm certain they will once they realize the prince has also left the castle. They may assume I somehow kidnapped him. Best case scenario, Kieran can convince them that he's pursuing me. Then, maybe they'll back off, and if he does get caught, he can say that he was hunting me down.

Seeing how fast he is, how agilely he can slip between trees and over fallen branches, I'm glad he's not tailing me now. I'm not sure about any of the fumbling, bumbling guards we left back there, but I don't think any of them could be as fast as Kieran. He's graceful when he runs, too. He glides through the air, his light-colored fur falling softly around him with each descent.

We rush on through the night. After about an hour, I begin to think there's no way we'll be caught from behind. Those guards would've caught us by now if they would've been able to fight off the birds long enough to slip out. But I'm still concerned. There are other groups of guards stationed in various locations throughout the kingdom. They have a chain of mind-link relayers who can easily contact anybody at any time and then move it. So it's possible another group of soldiers will intercept us before we can get to Escuro.

My only hope is that Kieran is tapped into that channel and that they think they can trust him enough to prevent them from leaving him out of the messages. If he knows where they're coming from, maybe he can find us a path that goes around or behind them.

It's really our only chance of getting out of here.

I have to wonder if I ever would've been able to even get through the gate without him. I think I would have, but they probably would've caught me by now.

I want to trust him. I really do. Watching him fly through the air with every step of his majestic wolf makes me think we could be friends one day. Maybe once we figure out what's going on to make it seem like the impossible is possible, we can even discuss what happened between us again.

But in the back of my mind, I keep thinking about the brute who used to shout at me, call me names, and occasionally even hurt me.

What if he's doing this for some ulterior reason I am not privy to, and he doesn't actually want to help me at all?

I hate to even think that, but it's not like Kieran Solberg has ever done anything to help me for even one day in his life, and I doubt he's helped very many other people either. Charity is often left to the Luna and her wards, and since his mother isn't very giving, there's not a lot of it in Dun's Crossing.

The Crown Prince would be near the bottom of the list when it comes to generous individuals.

So it's nearly impossible for me to accept that he's here to help me. When he shifts directions and starts running away from the bright star we've been following and more to what I believe is the east, it makes me nervous.

Could he be taking me to someone who's going to punish me for what happened with him during the Haze?

If there's one thing about the Solbergs I do know it's that they often tend to mete out their punishments themselves.

I drag myself forward, despite questioning his motives, and press on. My lungs are beginning to burn. My back legs feel heavy, and my heart is thumping in my chest.

But I need to do this. Maybe the Crown Prince could make something up and go back to how things were before he followed me out into the night, but for me, there's no going back.

I can never go back.

Running to the east brings us into an obstacle of the sort I've not given too much thought to. Up ahead, even though it's dark, I can see the outline of several high mountains coming into view. Kieran slows his pace considerably as both of us stare ahead at them. He turns his head to look at me and makes a face I cannot read. Then, seeing that I don't understand, he lets out a little annoyed grunt and then gestures for me to follow him.

I continue to do what I've been doing for the past several hours and stick tight to his heels as he picks his way through the rocks. We are going up now, but we are also going back toward the north a bit, so the degree of ascent isn't that noticeable.

Kieran is keeping himself close to the base of the mountain. I'm beginning to wonder if he intends to just walk along their bases until we can head back due north, but then he makes another sound, like he's surprised, or maybe happy, and pushes his large form between two bushes.

I'm confused as it seems the bushes swallow him whole, but I follow, and when I squeeze through the bushes, I step inside a massive space and look up into the mouth of a cave.

Awestruck, I stare at the darkness around me. It's hard to see anything at all, even after my wolf-eyes adjust. But then, when I turn my head to where I'm expecting to see a large white wolf, I only see icy blue eyes.

Kieran is in his human form again. It's hard for me to see anything at all, but he tugs at the backpack, and I shimmy out of it. He pulls out his clothes and then tosses the bag back to me. I pick it up with my teeth and move away from him before shifting and getting dressed myself.

"Where are we?" I finally ask him, stepping back over.

Kieran lowers himself to the ground, shaking his head. He tugs up the sleeves of his shirt so that they're almost to his elbows and says, "Man, do I have a few things to tell you."

21

COVER YOUR TRACKS

Kieran

"Man, do I have a few things to tell you." I can barely see Blanca in the darkness of the cave. Her eyes are like polished onyx, and even the whites of them are difficult to make out. It's probably for the best. I don't really want to see her at the moment, not when I'm so fucking confused about everything.

"What's going on?" She sinks down across from me. I wish I would've had time to pack something–anything–before we left the castle because my stomach is killing me. Another hunger pang flashes through me as I pull a knee up to my chest. "Did you hear anything through the mind-link?"

"Oh yes," I tell her. "I heard plenty. That's what I wanted to tell you about." I take a deep breath and consider how best to spew this all out to her. On our way here, the chatter in my mind was almost over-whelming. I could tell when we crossed out of range of the castle because my father's booming voice stopped rattling my brain.

"I'm listening." Her tone is calm on the surface, but underneath that tranquility, I hear a tremor of apprehension.

I take a deep breath. "As soon as we got out of the line of sight of the castle, I used the mind-link to let the guard know I was chasing you." When I say the word "chasing" she giggles. It's a sound I don't think I've ever heard before. I've spent so little time with Blanca over the last twenty-one years, I can't even remember a time when we were together when she was smiling. Most of the time, she was upset when I was nearby.

For good reason.

"Yeah, so they took off after us," I continue, "and I kept them apprised of our location for a while. I told them the truth, so they will be able to follow our tracks until they get to that little brook we crossed a few hours ago. Then, I told them we went straight, and since there were some fresh tracks on the other side of it, they may mistake them for our sling enough not to pick them up again right away."

She pulls in a stuttering breath. "I didn't see any of that."

I'm not sure what to say to that. I'm not surprised. She has only been outside of the castle walls during the Haze, and no one has any idea about their surroundings when that's going on. I'm actually kind of surprised she found her way back to the castle from the woods.

I don't want to think about that right now, so I continue. "Once we changed directions and headed toward the mountains, I started to pick up messages from my father shouting at the guards in other areas of the kingdom, sending them out to try to head you off. He was unbelievably pissed."

"What?" She is obviously surprised to hear this. "Why? I mean, I know they don't want me to leave the castle, but why is it such a big deal?"

"I'm not certain," I admit, "but I have a feeling it has something to do with the pieces of the puzzle we have yet to put together. Whether or not he knows you have discovered your powers, I can't say, but my father is a pretty intelligent man. He has to know that you are capable of the same sorts of manipulation Blake can perform over the animals."

Now, I hate that I can't see her face. I'd like to know what her reaction to that is when she says, "Yeah, I guess so." I can't read her tone. "I guess Fath–" she cuts herself off. "Uhm, King Gavin must know more about this situation than either one of us can imagine."

"I think he does," I admit to her. "I think he knows a lot of shit he's not telling anyone, and the people who do know it probably know if they breathe a word of it to anyone they're dead." I consider how long ago my father's conquests went down and how often he's changed commanders in the army and in other key positions over the years and wonder if any of those people are even alive now. Sure, there are people like Taner's father who served as warriors in those escapades who are still amongst us, but something tells me my father probably gets rid of people who know information he doesn't want out if he has any inkling he might not be able to trust them fully.

"What's our plan now?" she asks. "Do we have one?"

I chuckle under my breath. She's such a different person than I thought she was. Whenever she questions me like that, like she doesn't care that I'm the Crown Prince, it impresses me for reasons I can't articulate. I'm so used to people treating me like I am perfect and the most intelligent person on the planet. Blanca isn't like that–apparently.

"I think we should sleep here tonight. I don't think they'll look over here. I've thrown them off our tracks completely, and it'll be hard to track us over the rocks. In the morning, we'll get up early, reassess the situation, and then head north, following the line of the mountains."

"Okay." She nods–I think. I still can't really see her. "And… you didn't just drag my ass out of the castle to lie to me, right? I mean, if you wanted to have me whipped and thrown into the dungeon, you could've done that without having to run for a bazillion miles."

At first, I'm a little offended at her question, but when I think about it from her perspective, something I've never really done before, I can't blame her. "Blanca, I'm sure I didn't sell you out. I've been keeping them off your trail the entire time we were running. I think, if I hadn't come with you, they probably would've jumped out of the woods in front of you."

"You're right." She yawns, and the whites of her eyes disappear for a moment. "I'm sorry. It's just... I'm not used to being able to trust you. Or anyone."

"No, it's fine. I don't blame you. I wouldn't trust me either if I were you. But you can." I look straight into her eyes, hoping she can see the sincerity in mine, even if she can't really see my face.

"Let's get some sleep then. Do you want to use the backpack as a pillow?" she asks me.

It's kind of her. This woman who has absolutely no reason whatsoever to treat me with any sort of charity has offered me the only slight bit of comfort either of us could have in this rocky, damp cave.

"No, you use it," I tell her. "I'm fine."

"Thank you." Her voice is meek as she finds a spot to lie down on the ground. Once she's settled, she says, "Maybe I'll send some skunks out to follow our tracks and spray them down... just in case."

I don't know if she's serious or not, but the idea of an army of skunks going out into the forest, following the path we followed to get here, spraying their noxious stench all over the place as they march along so that they cover up any possibility my father's warriors have of locating where we are.

A laugh escapes my lips, followed by another, until I'm laughing louder and harder than I have in a really long time.

"What's so funny?" Blanca sounds like she genuinely doesn't know what's tickled my funny bone.

"I was just imagining your skunks out there, spraying the rocks, farting along as they go," I tell her.

She laughs, too. "Well, I don't think they actually fart when they release their stench. At least, the ones I've seen out by the barn never do."

"You've seen a skunk by the barn?" I've seen a couple in the woods when I've been out on a run, but I always stay far away from them.

"Yeah. One time Horace, that big guy who handles your father's favorite horse, got sprayed. It was hilarious. He was so mad! He ran around screaming for people to bring him tomatoes."

We both laugh for several minutes. When it's over, my cheeks hurt, and my stomach aches worse. We quiet and try to go to sleep.

I've almost reached that tipping point where my conscious mind turns off and I sink into the black abyss of sleep when something Blanca said during her skunk story hits me like a ton of bricks, and my eyes go flying open.

I turn toward her, but I can't see her, and I'm not sure if she's still awake. From the even sounds of her breathing, I'm guessing she's not.

I'll have to wait until tomorrow to ask her why she said that–why she phrased it that way. Does she know something else, or was it just her instinct to call him that?

She'd said "your" father–not "our" father.

22

WHO'S YOUR DADDY?

Before I even open my eyes, I know that something is different. My back hurts, and the bed beneath me feels harder than usual.

The pillow beneath my head doesn't quite feel right either. It's familiar–but it's not the paper thin slip of fabric I'm used to resting my head on.

When the pillow moves, everything comes back to me. My eyes fly open, and I realize that Kieran and I have shifted our positions in the middle of the night. His eyes are closed, thank the Goddess, and he makes a small murmuring noise as he readjusts on the floor of the cave.

Somehow, he's got his head on the backpack I was using as a pillow–and my head was on his chest.

"Great googly moogly," I mumble, barely a whisper. The last thing I want is for him to wake up and look up at me, seeing me hovering this close to him. He'd probably think I was trying to make a move on him again.

I remind myself of everything I've discovered over the last few days and try to feel slightly more at ease about the horrific discovery we both woke up to after the Haze. I'm pretty sure that my entire life has been a lie, and that's easier for me to accept than the alternative—that Kieran is my brother.

My bladder shouts at me, and I quietly slide across the dirty, rocky floor of the cave and creep toward the opening, which is hard to get through in my human form. It's narrow, low to the ground, and covered by bushes. I manage to squeeze through and find another bush to squat behind.

I've barely finished when I hear panicked whispers coming from the cave. "Blanca? Where the fuck are you?" Kieran sounds alarmed.

"Just a second!" I whisper-shout back to him and then make my way back to the cave. When I squeeze my way back through, he's sitting on the floor with his arms folded, his eyes narrowed, and I know I'm in trouble.

"Where the fuck did you go? You scared the shit out of me."

"Sorry," I mumble, dropping back to the ground and sitting against the wall away from him. "I had to pee."

He drags his hand through his hair, and I'm not sure what to say. Why is he so alarmed? Sure, he wants to figure out what's going on as badly as I do, but would he really care if something happened to me? I doubt it. I think he's here more for the mystery aspect than trying to keep me safe.

"The patrols should be pretty far from here," he says, absently rubbing at his chest. He hasn't been doing that much. I noticed it when he stopped by my room a few days ago, but this is the first time I've seen him do it since we took off together. But then again, we were in the dark or our wolf form for most of the time, so maybe I'm just imagining it. But my mark doesn't hurt anymore.

"That's good that they're not nearby, isn't it?" I ask him.

He nods. "Yeah, but we still need to be careful. We've got a couple hundred more miles to go to reach the border of what used to be Escuro. I'm not sure what to expect when we get there either."

"Do you think it's occupied?" I ask. "I thought the story was that your father took over to free people who were being mistreated by their previous king. Wouldn't your father leave the area occupied to make sure that they are taken care of?"

He blinks at me a few times, shakes his head, and says, "I don't think so. I'll be back."

My eyes narrow as he disappears through the cave opening. It takes me a moment to figure out that he is probably also watering the bushes. In a few moments, he's back. "Why not?"

"Why not what?" he asks me. "Oh. Why do I think it's not occupied? Well, mostly because I think everything I've ever heard about Father is a lie. I don't think he was trying to free anyone in any of the territories he conquered. I think he used underhanded and illegal tactics to take over the lands of his enemies because he wanted to make sure they weren't a threat to him. Everything else he just made up. It's bullshit."

I listen, wondering how this can be the same Kieran talking to me now that I grew up with. I didn't spend a ton of time with him or any of my siblings, but when we were around one another, he was always completely loyal to the king. Even before he was old enough to walk, he was being groomed to take over the kingdom. Everyone was so proud of him. He was treated like the prince he is.

"So what happened to the people that lived there?" I pull on a thread on the hem of my skirt, not sure I want to hear the answer.

"Taner says Father poisoned them all."

I look up at him and see remorse on his face. He shakes his head slightly. "Really?"

"Yeah. His dad was there. Guess we'll find out. I'm sorry, Blanca." He moves his hand, like he's going to touch me, but then he doesn't.

"I'm sorry, too." I mean it, and I think he also means it. I can't imagine all of those people dying. Why would anyone do that?

I don't think Gavin Solberg is my father, but if he was, I wouldn't want to admit it.

Maybe that's why Kieran is here. He doesn't want to be related to him anymore either. I stare at a spot on the ground, wondering if there's anything that can be done about it.

"Can I ask you something?"

Kieran's quiet tone has me slowly lifting my head to look at him again. I nod.

"You keep saying 'your' father. Does that mean you don't think you're… a Solberg?" He bites his bottom lip and stares at me, his icy blue eyes as sincere as I've ever seen them.

"I don't think it's possible," I tell him. "I haven't quite figured out who I am or how I got there, but I'm pretty sure I'm from Escuro. And if that's the case, that means that the king and queen are not my parents. And you're–"

"Not your brother," he finishes for me.

Again, my head rocks back and forth.

He lets out a long sigh, and I know why. I didn't quite let the breath my soul's been holding since the Haze out like that, but I have felt the tension in my chest loosen the more it sinks into my mind.

We didn't do something horrific.

His father did.

"Do you…." He clears his throat, leaving me staring at him as I wait for him to finish his question. "Do you think that maybe Blake is your… father?"

"What?" My eyes narrow as I stare at him. It has never once in my life crossed my mind that Mr. Blake might be my father. "Why do you ask?"

"Well… you guys look a lot alike," he tells me. "Your eyes both have the same silver and blue flecks, and your coloring is the same. You have similar bone structure in your faces." He shrugs. "It would make sense, wouldn't it? That my father took you because he thought you might have powers he could use one day–against his enemies."

Not knowing what to say, I shake my head. "No. I don't think so. I mean, I guess he could be related to me, but I think he would've told me if he was my father."

"Why would he?" Kieran argues. "I mean, if he was afraid you might want to stay there and try to help him when you should be getting far, far away from there, then why would he tell you?"

"I hadn't thought of that," I admit. "I honestly don't know, Kieran. I guess he could be. But–" I can't finish the sentence. To think, all of those years while I was mourning not being included as part of the family, my real father might've been chained in the dungeon beneath my feet, suffering and miserable.

"I think we should head out," Kieran says, interrupting my thoughts. "There aren't any warriors around here right now from what I can pick up over the mind-link. I checked in with them and told them I was over by the Lavendale River."

I have no idea where that is. "Is that far?"

"It's about a hundred miles west of here," he assures me. "Most of them are headed that way. I told them I lost your tracks in the dark and took a nap, but now I've picked them up again, and I think you must've slept, too, because I can smell you. They're buying it." He gives me the confident, winning smile I'm used to from him.

"And your father?" I ask him. "Is he still pissed?"

"He's ballistic," Kieran tells me. "He's doing everything he can to try to get you back."

He seems to think that's funny, but it scares me. "Do you think he'll hurt Mr. Blake?"

"I don't know." Kieran's smile fades. "But try not to worry about it. Blake wanted you to, didn't he?"

I think about the conversation I had with Mr. Blake right before I left the castle and nod. "Yeah, he did."

"Then let's go." Kieran stands and pulls his shirt off over his head. I don't want to look at him, but it's hard for me not to. He notices and raises his eyebrows.

"Does it–still hurt?" I stammer, trying to think of a reason why I might be staring at his chest. *He's not your brother,* I remind myself.

His eyebrows furrow, but then he places a hand on the mark. "Actually, no. It hasn't been hurting since we left yesterday. You?"

"Same," I tell him. I think I know what that means. I think that our marks like that we are together. Maybe it's the Moon Goddess who is pleased that we have run away together.

I hope she enjoys it while it lasts because something tells me this isn't going to last forever.

Soon enough, I'll be in Escuro, and Kieran will be….

I don't know where he'll be, but something tells me he won't be with me.

23

SCENT OF DANGER

If I was smart, I'd rest during the day and run at night. But I guess I'm not that smart because the sun is hanging overhead, and Blanca and I have been running for hours. We hug the base of the mountains for shelter to exclude anyone coming up on that side. So far, despite the messages from the warriors in my range that my father is absolutely pissed, none of them have been able to find us. They still trust what I'm telling them and are fanning further away from us. No one is even questioning me.

It's a good thing, too, because there's no way in hell we'd be able to fight off a group of my father's warriors. They are the best trained fighters in the world, and there are just two of us. Not even an entire flock of birds would help us with that.

Blanca is keeping pace with me through the narrow, rocky path that has her a few steps behind me and not right next to me. Earlier, we killed a rabbit and ate it in our wolf forms. I could tell by her eyes that it made her sad to do so, but then, her relationship with animals is obviously different than mine. My stomach rumbles, and I consider asking her to summon another rabbit so I can eat it, but I don't think she'd like that idea.

For some reason, lately, I care a lot about what Blanca likes. It's different. My entire life, I've been taught to hate and ignore her, and now, she's the most important thing in the world to me. I tell myself that's because I need her to help me figure out this riddle and put the pieces of the puzzle together with me to find out what my father's trying to hide, but that's not all of it.

The Moon Goddess chose the two of us to be together. Why would She do that?

And can I wrap my mind around the fact that we are not related long enough to even think about what that means for the rest of my life?

We begin to cross a meandering brook, and I look down to see several large fish swimming around my feet. Immediately, I lean down and plunk one from the water with my teeth. With a wiggly fish in my mouth, I turn to look at Blanca. Her dark eyes widen, but then she looks down at the water, takes a deep breath, and sticks her snout in. A few seconds later, she pulls out a fish almost the same size as the one I'm grasping. She shakes her head wildly, like she could hardly stand having her face in the creek, and little drops of water fling all over. I want to laugh, but I'm afraid I'll drop my fish. I hook my head a few times and indicate she should follow me. Chomping on sushi, we continue to make our way toward Escuro.

We stop for a few minutes to rest now and then, but by nightfall, we're both beginning to grow weary, and I know it's time to find another place to sleep. I've purposely stuck close to the mountains not just for protection from enemies but also because there are networks of caves all through this range. I intend to find us a safe place to sleep when an odd smell hits my lungs.

Bracing myself, I stop and lift my nose. Blanca stops behind me, and I know she must smell it, too.

I can't quite place the scent–but it's feral. Wild, dirty, sweaty–it smells a bit like the dungeon. I turn to look at Blanca, and she shakes her head. She doesn't know what it is either, but I hear the fluttering of wings in the sky and know that she's being precautious and calling on her friends, just in case.

Turning toward the mountains at my right, I begin to look for any indication of a cave opening. Sometimes they are difficult to see, but I can usually smell the change in landscape when an opening is nearby because of the minerals that collect in moist caves that don't cling to the mountains otherwise.

Putting my nose down, I sniff along, but I can't make out anything because of that other smell. It's getting stronger.

Blanca growls, and I lift my head. In the distance, I see the glowing whites of four pairs of eyes. A moment later, two more sets join them. The sliver of moon we've been using to light the way is covered mostly by clouds now, making it hard to see them, but I know what they are.

Rogues.

"Fuck," I think to myself as I size them up. They are large, four males and two females, and by the looks of things, they are not from Dun's Crossing. Their fur is brown and silver. My best guess is that they are from the kingdom on the other side of this mountain range, and they've crossed over into my father's territory to do some hunting.

We'll, they won't be feasting on us.

Despite being outnumbered, I growl and howl, throwing myself in front of Blanca and hurtling toward the largest wolf. He seems to think it's funny, judging by his expression. He comes at me, teeth bared, and we meet in a collision of power and fangs.

These rogues don't intend to fight fair, obviously, as I feel a second set of teeth sink into my shoulder.

Blanca growls again, and then the force from the teeth ripping into the flesh of my left front haunch is relieved as the wolf goes flying backward. Damn, Blanca is a tough girl when she wants to be.

Still, we are outnumbered, and I see the other wolves headed toward Blanca as I continue to fight the largest one. I knock him onto his back with a little effort. Then, I use my front left paw, ignoring the pain in my shoulder, to wedge his head backward so I have access to the side of his neck.

A flurry of wings and feathers descends as I rip this fucker's jugular out and turn my attention to the next wolf in line. The birds are attacking, aiming for the eyes of our enemies. The wolves aren't sure how to react to that. A few of them pull away. Blanca has her claws dug into the face of one of the others. She seems to be holding her own despite her lack of training.

Somewhere deep in the woods to the west, I hear a low rumbling sound. All of us stop moving and lift our heads. It sounds again, and the ground beneath us begins to rumble.

That's a fucking bear.

A big one.

Immediately, the remaining rogues take off, most of them limping a bit. A few of them are obviously running blind thanks to the birds. They run into one another, the larger rocks, even a tree trunk, as they try to get away from here.

As soon as they are out of sight, save the corpse behind me, the rumbling from the forest stops.

I turn to look at Blanca. Her sharp teeth are pink in the moonlight. I smile at her. She jumped right in there and saved my ass from that second wolf. I motion with my head, and she follows me.

It doesn't take too long for me to find a cave. I walk inside first and have a look around. It's smaller than the last one, but it'll do.

My shoulder is killing me. I know it's still bleeding, and it probably needs bandaged up.

I hear Blanca's voice behind me. "Let me get dressed, and I'll bandage that up for you."

Knowing she's naked, I make myself keep my eyes on the wall in front of me. She's not my sister—we've all but proven that—and wolf shifters are used to being naked in front of other people, but the idea that I could catch sight of that amazing body I'd felt beneath me during the Haze has me afraid to look. I can't let the emotions that raged through me that night take over.

"Okay." I turn around at the sound of her voice, and she's dressed and ripping what looks like a skirt into ribbons. "Shift, put on your pants, and let me take a look?"

I nod, and she turns around to give me the same privacy I'd given her.

My shoulder burns as I shift, but it actually helps repair it some. Nevertheless, as I sink down onto the cave floor, the ache continues, and I know then that it's not in great shape. I put on my pants and tell her, "I'm ready."

Blanca turns, and her eyes widen. "Holy fuck, Kieran. That looks awful."

I glance down at the missing hunk from my shoulder, grin, and say, "I've had worse."

She shakes her head and starts to bandage me up. I close my eyes and try to pretend that the gentle feel of her fingers on my skin does nothing to my body at all.

But then, I am a liar.

24

THE HISTORY OF THE WORLD

I'm wrapping strips of my extra skirt around Kieran's shoulder wishing I had something to disinfect the wound with. Of course, I had nothing like that in my room back in the castle, so it wasn't like I just forgot it. I had very little. If Kieran would've known he was coming with me, he could've brought us a lot of supplies, but he didn't.

Sometimes I still can't believe he came with me. I'm not exactly sure I know why he's here.

"What's the matter?" His voice is just above a whisper, and I can feel the warmth from his breath on my cheek. I try not to let it affect me. He might not be my brother, but he's still not thrilled about being my mate.

My eyes go to the mark on his shoulder as I think about it, trying to figure out how to answer his question. "Nothing," I tell him, which isn't the truth. "I was just thinking it would be nice to disinfect this."

"Yeah, it would be. Oh, well."

He doesn't say more, and I find myself staring at his mark again.

It's different than mine. I try to ignore the scar on my chest left by Kieran's fangs, but it's definitely the shape of a sun. Every mark I've ever seen in Dun's Crossing is a sun.

Kieran's is a moon.

"What are you looking at?" he asks me.

Blinking a few times, I tie up the last strip I've wrapped around and tell him, "Put some pressure on that. It's still bleeding a little." Then, I find a spot across from him. It's a bit lighter in here than our last cave because there are no bushes in front of the opening. "Your mark." I hesitate, not sure whether or not we can discuss this.

He pushes on the wound as he raises his eyebrows. "What about it?"

I clear my throat, catching the edge of irritation in his voice. "Uhm… it's a moon."

He glances down at it, but he can't see most of it. I marked him near his neck. "So?"

"So… mine is a sun. Isn't everyone whose mate is from Dun's Crossing marked with a sun?"

His eyebrows furrow. "Yeah, I guess so. I never really paid much attention. Is the moon a sign you're from Escuro?"

I shrug. "I have no idea. I've never met anyone from Escuro. Except for Mr. Blake, I guess." My father? Maybe.

Kieran lets out a loud sigh and leans back against the wall across from me. "All of this seems so obvious now, but at the time, I was so fucking weirded out, I couldn't understand any of it."

"I know." I take a deep breath and think more about what I know about marks, packs, and all of that sort of thing. Not much comes to mind. Until I think about Mr. Blake again. He had told me something a long time ago, something I thought wasn't true, but now, I find myself wondering and hazard mentioning it to Kieran. "Do you know why Dun's Crossing is called that when all of the other packs around us have names that have to do with the sky or nature?"

"Doesn't Escuro mean dark?" His eyes are so narrow now, I can barely see them.

"I meant Snowcrest and Starfall. Aren't there more? Isn't there a kingdom across the sea called Sundrop Gem?"

He nods slowly. "Yes, but it's quite small compared to Dun's Crossing. I don't know why it's called that. Maybe the first king was named Dun."

"Didn't you learn about that in school?" I challenge him. "I thought the first king was your great-great-great grandfather or something." A few of the women who took care of me when I was little would tell me bits and pieces of history from time to time.

"True." He grumbles a little. "I'm not sure, Blanca. Why are you asking?"

"Well, when I was younger, Mr. Blake told me a story. I sort-of dismissed it because I thought he was just being bitter against Dun's Crossing, but now I'm starting to wonder."

"What was the story?" He yawns a little, and I know I should let him sleep. But he asked.

"He said that many years ago, the kingdom across the sea, Sundrop Gem, grew quickly and became a flourishing kingdom. They had a lot of horse drawn carriages and the like, and they needed all of the surrounding pasture land for animals, so with all of those horses, cows, sheep, etc., they soon had a shitty problem."

"A shitty problem?" he asks me.

"Yes. Literally."

That gets a chuckle out of him. "So what did they allegedly do?"

"According to Mr. Blake, they decided to load all of the poop up and take it across the sea and dump it. He said that the narrowest point of the sea from Sundrop takes you to Dun's Crossing. Originally, it was called Dung's Crossing."

Kieran chuckles. "I really don't believe that shit."

"I don't know if it's true or not, but he said that there was a group of people who rebelled against the king, and as their punishment, the king sent all of the rebels to Dung's Crossing to live or die. They were banished. That's where they started their new kingdom, and because that first king didn't want to have his lands named after poop, they called it Dun's Crossing, and he named his son Duncan."

Kieran doesn't say anything for several minutes, but when he speaks again, he asks, "Do you believe all of that?"

"I didn't. But now that I think about it, maybe the reason people from Dun's Crossing leave the mark of a sun is because you're really a pack member of Sundrop Gem."

"Or maybe it's because we are the light of the world. That's why we are named after brightness. Like our last name. Solberg means sun mountain."

"Yeah, that actually kind of convinces me more," I admit to him.

He yawns again, and I know we both need to get some sleep. "We might be able to make it to the border of Escuro if we hurry tomorrow."

"Really?" I thought we'd have to sleep at least one more time."

"It depends on how bad the terrain is, but maybe. If we hurry."

"And then what?" I'm afraid to hear his answer.

"I have no idea," he admits. "I hope there will be someone there who can help you, but I'm afraid everyone in the entire kingdom is dead. We might just find a land full of rogues and danger."

I bite back the idea that we've already run into that without even leaving his beloved Dun's Crossing, but I don't say it. Instead, I yawn. "Do you want the backpack pillow? It'll probably help your shoulder."

"No, thank you," he tells me. "I'm fine."

Has he even noticed he had it last night? I don't want to ask. "All right. Goodnight."

"Good night."

We both stretch out on the floor pretty far away from one another. My back aches from the rocky ground, but at least I have something to put my head on. I'm so tired, I think I'll fall asleep pretty quickly.

Part of me wonders if we are close enough to Escuro for me to use the mind-link to try to talk to someone there, but I'm afraid to do that. How would I know if I can trust them?

I start to doze off, still thinking about what lies ahead of us in Escuro. Soon enough, I'm dreaming of walking into a beautiful land full of smiling, happy people who are so glad to see me. Kieran is there, too, holding my hand, and we grin at one another. I finally feel like I'm home.

I awake to my pillow wiggling again. My eyes fly open, and I'm staring into Kieran's eyes, the light of day illuminating his handsome face.

He looks mad. "What the fuck is going on, Blanca?" he asks me.

Confused, I try to figure out what he's talking about and realize somehow we've rearranged ourselves again, and his head is on the backpack while mine must've been... on his chest.

"Fuck."

How does this keep happening?

25

SKIN TO SKIN

Kieran

It makes me uncomfortable to admit that she makes me feel comfortable.

It seems ironic, but it's true.

She's not supposed to make me feel this way because, in the crevices of my mind, the ones that haven't adjusted to the new reality yet, she's my sister.

Even though I know she's not, and even when I thought she was, I never once treated Blanca like she was a member of my family.

Most of the time, I didn't even treat her like she was a person.

Still, with her head on my shoulder like this, I start to think of her in a different light. She is my mate, after all. We are not related. We have never been related. Nothing about her being my mate or what we did during the Haze was wrong, and yet, whenever she touches me, it creates a war in my mind, a chaotic jumble of mixed emotions where I don't know what's up and what's down.

I don't know if I should smile and enjoy the tingling warmth spreading throughout my body and gathering in my groin or push her away and swallow down the first sour tastes of bile that threaten to fill my mouth.

When she lifts her head and those dark eyes stare into my face, the latter emotions win, and I find myself asking her, "What the fuck is going on Blanca?"

"Fuck," she mumbles, sitting up and staring at me, the tendrils of dark hair that frame her face lightened in the first rays of morning sun. "I don't know."

I scoot away from her, sitting up. "Did this happen yesterday, too?" I seem to recall waking up with my head on the backpack and not knowing how it got there.

"I don't know." She runs a hand through her hair, and I know she's lying. She does know. "I didn't mean to."

Swallowing hard, I check myself. She sounds scared, like she's afraid I'm going to hurt her or yell at her more. I can't blame her for that. It's not like I've always been nice to her. Sometimes, in fact, I've been down right mean.

I don't want to be that person anymore. Not just to Blanca but to anyone. If there's one thing she has taught me, now that I've matured enough to truly stop and think about it, it's that everyone deserves kindness. She went down into the dungeon and brought water to the prisoners there nearly every day not because she was ordered to or bored and had nothing else to do but because she was being kind. It makes me wonder what else she's done over the years just to be nice to the sort of people I've always overlooked. People like those prisoners. People like the servants I don't even know the names of.

People like her.

"I'm sorry, Blanca."

She stares at me, those wide eyes not seeming to comprehend what I've just said to her. That's probably because she's not used to hearing anyone say those words to her. Especially not me.

I take a deep breath and continue. "I shouldn't be blaming you, and I certainly shouldn't be yelling at you. This is all just really weird, you know?"

Slowly, her head rocks back and forth. "I know." That's all she says, and I feel compelled to continue speaking, but I bite my tongue because I'm afraid I'll reveal too much.

I'm pretty sure I had a dream about her last night, and it wasn't exactly family friendly. My dick twitches just thinking about it, and I realize it's time to get out of here. "Ready to go?"

She nods again and disappears out the cave opening, taking the backpack with her.

I give her a moment to undress, shift, and do whatever else she needs to do before I follow her out. Her large dark wolf stands off to the side. I take the backpack off the ground, step away from her, undress, put my clothes away, take a leak, and then shift. With the backpack on, I head off, and she follows close behind me.

In my head, I hear angry voices of commanders and Alphas who want to know where I'm at and how come I haven't checked in for so long. I tell them I lost her scent somewhere far away from where we actually are, naming a river on the western side of our territory while we are far to the east. I hear the forces formulating a plan that involves creating a line of defense along the northwestern edge of our kingdom's border with Escuro so that there's absolutely no way she can get through. I almost snicker but bite it back. That might work if we were anywhere close to that location.

I do wonder if maybe they'll continue to extend further east, and it's enough to make me increase my pace. We stop at a stream and grab some fish, but then we continue north, hugging the mountains as we go.

By dusk, we are higher up in the mountains than I intended. I think I may have swung us a little too far to the west. I start to think about going back down, but somehow I've lost my bearings. We are on a cliff, and it's getting darker by the moment when I start to think I might smell rogues in the distance again. I'm not sure, but that pungent odor from last time has me pausing to lift my nose in the air.

Blanca and I can't speak to one another in our wolf forms, which is unfortunate. I consider shifting to ask her if she smells it, too, but that will slow us down. It seems like the scent is stronger behind us.

There's no way to know for sure if there are rogues around if they are on our trail or if they just happen to be in the area.

When I catch Blanca's eyes, she lifts her eyebrows slightly, as if to ask if everything is okay. I have no response for that, so I turn around and continue on through the ever-increasing darkness, being careful of where I place my feet and hoping Blanca stays right behind me.

We pass what smells like the opening to a cave. For a moment, I consider stopping. It would probably be a good idea, but I was hoping we'd be in Escuro by now, and I know we have to be close to the border. Hesitating, I weigh our options and decide to press on just a bit further, telling myself we'll stop at the next cave. I've smelled several, so I'm confident there will be another one soon

The ridge we've been walking on grows a bit more narrow, and with the sun fading from view, we have to be even more careful about our footing. I take a few more steps and my front left paw slides out from under me. I pull it back and dodge to my right just in time to avoid falling down a steep incline.

Blanca, however, doesn't react the same way that I do. Either because she didn't see it quickly enough or because she hasn't had the training I've had, she loses her footing on the scree, and the next thing I know, she's tumbling down the mountain.

"Blanca!" I shift immediately so that we can communicate. "Shift!"

I see her dark eyes, the flecks of blue and silver catching the last rays of the fading sun. She looks up at me, and in that second, all I see is fear. Throwing myself on my belly, I reach for her, but she's too far away now. My hand grasps empty air.

She has to shift. It's the only way she can save herself. Most of the time, our wolf forms are better suited to perform whatever tasks we need, but right now, my mate needs hands.

I see Blanca's fur fade away as she slips out of sight. Pulling myself forward, I peer over the edge and see one olive-complected hand grasping a shrub about four feet below me.

"Kieran!" she shouts. "I'm slipping!"

With everything I have left in my weary body, I push myself forward so that I am hanging over the edge of the cliff and dangle off the side. I feel the rocks beginning to give way beneath me, but I can't think about that. I have to reach her. "Swing your other arm up and grab my hand!" I command.

I hear a whimper of fear and know she thinks she'll fall if she does what I've told her to do, but it's the only way. With a grunt of exertion, she swings her other arm around, and her fingers connect with mine. It's enough for me to pull her up until my grasp latches around her wrist. She lets go of the shrub, trusting me with her life.

I scoot back over the rocky terrain, tugging her along with me. Then, we are safe against the wall of mountain. She's in my arms, her body trembling against my chest. "Thank the Goddess," I murmur between pants.

Blanca's eyes meet mine, and I see the fear turn to gratitude and then something else. It's the same hunger I've felt burning in me for days. We are alive. We are intertwined. And we are completely naked.

I'm not sure which one of us moves first, but instantly, my mouth is on hers. She tastes like magic, like everything that's right in the world, and no matter how many alarms sound in my head, I know for certain she is my mate.

And I want her.

2 6

NO LONGER HAZY

BLANCA

MY HEART THRUMS IN MY CHEST, AND IT HAS NOTHING TO DO WITH THE fact that I almost died. With Kieran's arms around me, his muscular chest pressed against me, I don't even feel the scrapes and cuts I collected slipping down the mountainside. He pulled me back from the darkness, and now, here in his arms, I'm safe.

We are both naked, a thin sheen of sweat covering our bodies, and his lips are on mine. I remember his taste from the night of the Haze even if everything else is still hazy. When he runs his hand along my ribcage, I take a deep breath and brace myself for what's to come.

I want him. My body responds to his touch in a way that I can't comprehend. Even without the Haze, my thoughts are blurry. I'm reacting on pure instinct when I lean up to wrap my arms around his neck and open my mouth wider. I feel a soft tug on the back of my head as he intertwines his fingers through my hair and gives it a tug, eliciting a moan from my mouth.

There's no stopping this. Not only are we hyped up on adrenaline from my near-death experience, we have been denying the mate bond for weeks, pretending like the marks on our bodies aren't calling to one another. Without a word, Kieran stands, lifting me with him in a way only someone as strong and powerful can do. Carefully, he makes his way back the way we came only a few steps before he sets me down and ducks through a hole in the wall of mountain, grasping my hand and pulling me into the darkened cavern.

This space is about the same size as the one we were in last night, but I don't take any time to look around. His mouth is on mine again, and we are devouring one another. His hands roam freely over my body which hums only one tune: Kieran is my mate.

We drop to our knees, and I don't even feel the bite of the rock floor as the rocks dig in. Kieran's back is against the wall. His hands slide down my back, cupping my ass. I moan into his mouth, my tongue tangled with his, and move to straddle him.

One thing I've had flashbacks about from that night in the Haze is the enormous size of his cock. I feel it now, pressed against my belly, and wonder how in the world I will ever fit it all inside of me. His lips roam down my neck, his thumbs playing over my erect nipples. With each pass of his magical fingers, I moan louder, the tension inside of me beginning to build.

He lowers his head and takes one of them into his mouth, sucking and lapping at one of my most sensitive areas. I throw my head back, trying not to shout his name. Lifting up slightly, I rub against him, my slick juices sliding along his shaft. I want him inside of me so badly I can hardly stand it.

He must be feeling the same urgency because he lifts me up and positions himself at my entryway. I'm still concerned about his girth, but my body tells me that I can take him. I've done it before. Kieran's hands settle on my hips as his mouth finds mine again, and I lower myself down, consuming him. I go slowly at first, allowing my body some time to adjust, but when he begins to thrust, I can't handle it anymore, and I sink down, letting out a scream as pleasure and pain mix. I feel completely full, stretched to the max, and my body sizzles with satisfaction.

He isn't taking his time either. Continuing to hold me steady with his hips, he plunges deeper inside of me, letting out short grunts with every thrilling thrust. His mouth stays on mine for the most part, but every once in a while, he releases my lips to trace kisses across my cheek or down my neck. I keep my eyes closed and concentrate on the way that he feels. All I can think about is this moment–not the past when everything was topsy-turvy and all mixed up and not the future when I will arrive in Escuro and he will... I'm not even sure.

Despite our frantic pace, Kieran doesn't finish quickly. He keeps me at my peak for what seems like hours, though I'm sure it's not that long. My body buzzes with pleasure, and I whimper and moan, knowing I'm about to come unraveled all around him. When he slides his hand down my abdomen and between my folds to find my clit, I can't hold back any longer. I grind against him, crying out his name and losing myself, my mind as cloudy as it was that first night.

He continues to keep me there, his cock gliding in and out, deeper and faster, his thumb strumming me like I'm an instrument and he is a virtuoso. Just when I think I can't handle a second more, I feel him tighten beneath my grasp. He grunts even louder and then goes rigid. Warmth spreads between my legs, and then we both collapse against the cave wall, trembling, perspiring, and panting for air.

The moment we are finished, the haunting thoughts from last time fill my mind, and I'm certain he is thinking what I am. In fact, he's probably also just as disgusted as he was last time. I expect him to shove me off him and chastise me. If I was a smart girl, I'd move away from him now, but I can't move. Not only am I completely spent from the journey and our strenuous fucking, I want to be near him.

He is my mate. We can no longer deny that.

"Blanca?"

My name sounds like a prayer as it falls from his lips in a whisper. None of the harshness I expect can be heard in the utterance. I lift my face from his neck and look into his eyes.

It's hard to see in the dim light of the cave, but the only emotions I see in those light blue orbs are sadness and longing. The first I recognize as a constant companion. The second is completely foreign to me. That's not entirely true. I understand longing in the sense of wanting to escape, but I've never seen anyone with that look in their eyes with me as the object of their affection.

"Kieran?" I whisper back to him in the same tone.

He doesn't say anything for several seconds. My heart sounds like a bass drum in the small enclosed space as I patiently wait for him to say whatever it is that had him speaking my name to begin with.

"I think..." he begins, biting his bottom lip as he takes a deep breath in through his nose. "I think we have to start facing the fact that we are mates."

My mind goes blank. I'm not expecting those words to fall from his lips at all. In fact, I'd been expecting him to say the exact opposite, so all I can do is nod.

Kieran continues. "We've been lied to for so long, it's difficult to wrap my mind around what's right and what's wrong, what's up and what's down, but our bodies seem to know the truth. Our wolves and our marks call to one another, and fighting it because we've been deceived for all of these years doesn't seem to be working."

He isn't wrong. Once again, I nod along with him, but I'm not sure what to say. Eventually, I manage to phrase my most pressing thought into a question. "What does that mean exactly?"

"It means, we have to do something else I never thought I'd do."

I look up at him, my eyes wide, trying to figure out what he's talking about, but I can't ask, so I wait. After a long pause, he begins to talk again, and I can hear the betrayal he feels in every word.

"Not only did I never think you and I could be mates, a reality I've now grown to accept, but I most certainly thought never in my life would I have to do what we will need to find a way to accomplish next."

I take a deep breath and ask, "What's that?"

Kieran looks into my eyes and says calmly, "Kill my father."

27

KINGDOM OF ASHES

BLANCA STARES AT ME AS IF SHE CAN'T COMPREHEND WHAT I'VE JUST said. I don't blame her; I'm not sure I can comprehend it myself.

But then, I've said it, and I mean it.

"Kill your father?" she repeats.

I nod. "That's right. We need to kill him. Of course, it would be nice to hear him confess to all of his crimes first, but we can figure all of that out after."

Blanca, who is still sitting on my lap, both of us naked, blinks a few times. It's hard to see her in the darkness. The sun has completely gone down, and very little moonlight reaches us through the cave entryway, even though there are no bushes there this time. I'm not sure what I expect her to say, but since she's saying nothing, I continue.

"Everything he's ever taught me is a lie. He's mentioned time and again how he defeated all of these kingdoms around us where people were being mistreated by the royals, but none of that is true. It's just what he told himself and others in order to get his leaders on board with all of the horrible things he was doing. Poisoning people. Locking them in a temple and setting them on fire." She grimaces, and I realize she hasn't heard all of these stories yet. It doesn't matter–I have. I've heard my father's versions, and I've heard reality, and it's time someone made him pay for what he's done.

"What do you plan to do?" she asks me in a whisper.

"I'm honestly not sure yet," I admit. "We need to get you to Escuro, and then I'll return to the castle and assess the situation."

"You're not going with me." It's not a question when the words fall from her soft, full, pink lips. I'm fairly certain she's known all along that I didn't intend to stay in Escuro. At least, it hasn't been my plan to stay there long. I've thought I'd make sure I get her there safely and then go back home to figure out our next step. Now, I know what that is, though I'm not certain how I'll go about it.

"I'll make sure you're safe, and then I'll go back to the castle," I tell her. "Once I've done my work there, we can determine what's best."

"Will they let you be king if you kill your father?" I can hear the concern in every word she speaks.

"They'll have no choice. If I have to take out everyone who supports my father, then that's what I'll do."

"You'll need to be careful." She reaches up and touches my cheek. Her calloused fingers are nothing like other princess's. She has known long hours of tough work. But they feel like a balm to me.

"I'll be careful," I promise her. "Now, let's get some sleep. We are very close to the border, and I think we can easily make it to Escuro tomorrow before noon."

Again, Blanca nods. I realize I've dropped the backpack outside, so I go out to get it so we can get dressed. A few moments later, we are in our clothes. My head is on the backpack, and her head is on my chest, just where it should be.

Blanca's breathing evens out pretty quickly, but I lie awake, staring at the cave above me, wondering what I need to do in order to make sure my father can't harm anyone else. The betrayal I feel at knowing the man I've practically worshiped as a god has been lying to me for my entire life has my stomach twisting up in knots. How dare he pretend to be the exact opposite of what he truly is? He's led me to believe that he's some kind of hero when he's truly a monster.

Eventually, I fall asleep, dreaming of people foaming at the mouth and screaming from inside a burning building. When I open my eyes, I'm covered in sweat. Blanca sits near the cave opening, staring at me with concern.

"Sorry I woke you," she whispers in that tone that makes me think she's still somewhat afraid of me. "It seemed like you were having a nightmare."

I sit up and wipe the sweat from my brow. "What time is it?"

"I'm not sure, but the sun has been up for a few hours."

"Shit."

"I didn't want to disturb you."

"You should've woken me. We need to get moving."

She inhales in a way that makes me realize my tone is too forceful.

"Sorry." I look over at her, and she nods. "I didn't mean to yell at you. I was having a bad dream."

Her fear melts away, and concern takes its place. "Are you all right now?"

"I will be."

In near silence, we go about our morning routine and then get on our way. Seeing the spot where she fell the night before in the daylight is scary. If she hadn't grabbed hold of the bush a few feet below the ledge, she would've tumbled straight over a cliff and landed several hundred feet below in a ravine. She'd be dead. I'd be mateless, and I'd have no choice but to return to the castle and face my father as an ally. Without Blanca, I wouldn't have the strength or determination to take him on.

After we've observed the ledge, we go back the way we'd come a bit until we find a safer path down and then turn back north. In the daylight, it's easier to see danger, and we manage to pick up speed, no longer needing to hug the mountain wall. I know where all of my father's troops are, and none of them are within twenty miles of our current position. I don't smell any rogues either.

What I do notice is a vast change in landscape as we inch closer to

Escuro. Soon, the mountains are further to our west, and the arid desert terrain sprouts trees. They're few and far between initially, but the further north we go, the more the rare towering tree turns into a copse of several until we are in the forest.

Then, the ground beneath our paws begins to change as well. It turns from dry, dusty earth into something richer, something more capable of growing crops. I'm impressed with this area of land and wonder if we are already in Escuro. I've never heard my father speak about this part of our kingdom.

It's not until we start to see char marks on the northern sides of the trees that I realize we haven't yet crossed over. When we do, it's obvious. The good ground is covered in ash, and eventually, the trees giveaway to nothing but burnt wasteland. I can tell that what took place here happened many years ago as there are a few signs of life–some smaller bushes and plants–but for the most part, everything I see has been turned to ash.

I hear a sniffle and turn to look at Blanca. She's emotional at the sight of her homeland, and I can't blame her. We move forward, but everywhere we look, all we can see has been burned to the ground, save the occasional building that has a few timbers or a fireplace remaining.

Eventually, we make it to a cemetery where all of the headstones are covered in ash and residue from the fire. I look at the names etched in the stone, but I can't see many of them. We move along.

I want to ask her if she's trying to reach out to her people through the mind-link, but I can't do that because I can't speak to her in our wolf forms. We are definitely in Escuro now, so I could turn around and head back, but the thought of leaving her here where there can't be any food, and I have no idea if the water is safe to drink, simply won't do.

We trot on for another few hours, but nothing much changes. Then, I hear the cry of a bird overhead and look up to see what looks like a raven circling us. I turn to look at Blanca, and she nods. So she has managed to find a friend.

We follow the bird. It seems like the only choice we have. In my mind, I hear the angry shouts of commanders wanting to know where I am and where she is. Assuming the western portion of Escuro is the same as where we are now, I tell them it's a vast wasteland, and I'm getting turned around. They suggest I wait for them, but I tell them I must press on.

Which is what we are doing now. The last thing I want is to bring all of these troops into Escuro if there truly are people here, but I see no one.

Eventually, after what seems like hours of following the raven, it perches on the branch of a burned out tree. Shaking my head in confusion and irritation. I back up against the tree and lean on its trunk, wondering what we should do next.

The next thing I know, I hear a creaking noise, and then, I'm falling.

28

SOMEONE TRUE

Kieran is gone—swallowed up by a tree! I can hardly believe what I'm seeing. The tree simply opened, and now, he's disappeared. It takes me a moment to comprehend, and I have to wonder if perhaps all trees are capable of this, and my sheltered life has left me thinking otherwise, but then I realize that's not possible.

I gaze into the darkness where Kieran has gone and see a ladder. Instinct tells me to jump in after him, but it's so deep, I can't see anything down there. Instead, I take a moment to shift and get dressed. Then, I quickly climb down the ladder, hearing a creak as the tree closes itself above me.

Thankfully, it doesn't take too long to reach the bottom of the ladder, which means Kieran didn't fall that far, maybe ten feet. Still, I expect to see him lying on the ground unconscious. Instead, I wheel around to see him standing in his wolf form in front of several people who have sticks in their hands and are taunting him.

I want to look around at this place. It seems we've discovered some sort of underground city. I'd asked the raven to take me to where the people are, and he'd done just that, though I'd thought he was resting when he perched on the tree above us. Now, I realize, this was where he intended for us to go. But it's clear we are in danger. The young men with the sticks are taunting Kieran, stepping forward to poke him, and shouting at him.

"Why the fuck are you here, asshole?" one of them shouts. "You're not from Escuro."

"Let's pour wolfsbane down his mouth!" another says.

"And light him on fire!" calls a third.

"Stop!" I say, stepping up next to them. "He's not from Escuro, but I am, and he's here to help me find all of you."

The tallest man, who really isn't much more than a boy, turns his attention to me. I'm guessing he's a few years younger than me. "You're not from here," he insists. "Just because you have dark hair, that doesn't mean you're from Escuro."

"That's right. You're probably some sort of fucking spies." The first man who spoke is a bit shorter, with leaner muscles. All of them are thin and wiry, which makes me think they probably haven't had an abundance of food, something I can relate to.

Behind them, other people appear out of dark spaces and tunnels. The soft light of what must be hundreds of lanterns hanging from poles and sitting on the ground illuminates the space the best it can, but being underground makes it difficult, and I'm unable to see much beyond the crowd that's gathering. I'm guessing we are the first guests they've had, maybe ever.

"I am from Escuro," I tell them. "I was raised in Dun's Crossing, but this is my homeland."

The man who hasn't spoken yet, whose hair is darkest of all, shakes his head. "You're going to have to find a way to prove that or else we're going to kill both of you and send your heads back to that asshole King Gavin on a fuckin platter."

"How can I prove it?" I ask them, my mind going blank. "I was sent here by one of the prisoners in King Gavin's dungeon. He said I should find my people. He told me how kind and loving all of you are."

"He must not have visited since the war," the first one says, and they all laugh.

Beside me, Kieran growls. I wish I could mind-link with him to tell him to stop.

"That's it!" I say aloud, and they all turn and look at me, foreheads furrowed. Using the mind-link, I ask, *'Can you hear me?'*

Not only do the three men in front of me jump backward, gasps and shouts come from all over the space. I see some of the people behind them step back as well.

"We can hear you." The voice belongs to a woman who is probably old enough to be my mother. She steps forward, her dark eyes glistening in the light. "All right, boys. That's enough. Bruno, Donavan, Harry, go back to your assigned tasks."

"But Luna Delaney–"

"Go!" She uses the authority command, something only Alphas and Lunas have, and they immediately head off to do whatever it was they'd been doing before Kieran fell on them–or beside them.

Luna Delaney approaches us carefully, her face as ashen as possible considering she has a dark complexion like me. Her eyes are also dark, as is her hair, which is tied up on the top of her head. I see the crinkles around her eyes that say she's had a hard life, and I am again reminded of myself. A few other people stand in the shadows watching, but I no longer feel threatened as she stops before us. "You say you are from Dun's Crossing?" she asks, her tone soft, almost like she's holding something back.

"That's right," I tell her. "My name is Blanca, and this is...." I hesitate. Perhaps it isn't wise to disclose that I have the Crown Prince with me. What if everyone in Escuro isn't as polite as Mr. Blake thought they were? After all, we've already been accosted once, and we just arrived. "This is my mate."

"Well, Blanca, it's nice to meet you," the Luna says with an air of hospitality that makes me think perhaps she was also Luna before the war. Maybe she is accustomed to welcoming people into her home, into her kingdom, in a former life.

"Thank you," I tell her. Kieran nips at the backpack, and I take it off. He grabs it with his snout and steps into the shadows. I assume he's shifting and getting dressed. "It's been a long journey, and we had no idea what to expect."

"If you've come all the way from Dun's Crossing, that is a long journey. How did you manage to find our hiding place?"

"A bird showed me the way," I explain. "I was able to use my powers to find him and ask him to help us."

Again, I see a reaction in her obsidian eyes. "You can talk to the animals?"

I notice Kieran walking up beside me, but he has a slight limp. I am concerned and turn toward him, but he shakes his head and waves his hand slightly as if to say it's nothing, that I shouldn't draw attention to it. I'm having difficulty remembering that we are in enemy territory here. Well, at least he is, since this woman is so kind.

"I can speak to them," I tell her. "It's something I've only discovered recently. Right after the Haze."

She nods. "Ah, I see. So another Haze has come and gone, and that's when you discovered your mate...?"

She is waiting for him to say his name. "Kier-" he begins.

"Keery," I supply. "This is Keery... Light...man...guy."

Her eyebrows nearly touch her dark hair, and Kieran turns toward me with an equally questioning expression, but he doesn't correct me.

"All right then," she says. The Luna clears her voice and extends her hand. "Lovely to meet you... Keery Lightmanguy."

"You as well, Luna." I see him shaking his head slightly out of the corner of my eye.

"And what is your surname, Blanca?"

"I don't know," I tell her. "I'm hoping to find out that information while I'm here."

She nods in understanding. "Yes, I hope you can as well. When you lived in Dun's Crossing, were you told you had a certain surname that you now realize can't be correct?"

"That's right," I tell her, a bit startled at how quickly she is figuring everything out.

"And what name was that?" She gives me a kind, encouraging smile.

"Solberg," I tell her without thinking.

Everyone behind her suddenly becomes quiet. The chatter that had continued in the background as we spoke ends, and I realize everyone is staring at me.

"Solberg?" she echoes, only a tinge of kindness remaining in her tone.

Everyone, including the Luna, spits on the ground.

I swallow hard, glad I didn't tell them the truth about who Kieran is. Obviously, they are not happy with the Solberg family, and who could blame them?

"Yes, but I know that I was taken from here when I was a baby," I say quickly before everyone turns on us again. "Mr. Blake wouldn't tell me everything, but he did say–"

Suddenly, the Luna's face turns pale white, and her eyes nearly double in size. "Who?" she asks me, a hand pressed to her chest.

"Mr... Blake," I whisper, hoping his name doesn't make them even more upset.

The Luna stumbles backward a few steps, and another woman rushes forward to catch her before she falls. "Oh, Goddess," she says. "He's alive."

2 9

WHAT'S IN A NAME?

THE MOMENT BLANCA STARTS NAMING NAMES, I KNOW WE'RE IN FOR IT. I want to tell her to be more vague, but I also don't think it's a wise decision to be secretive right now, and we still don't have the mind-link. I was an idiot for not believing she was my mate and going ahead with the ceremonial shit before. Now, it might cost our lives.

She says my last name, and everyone in the whole damn—whatever the hell this is—freezes. She says Blake's name, and the Luna almost passes out.

Still, I stay back, right next to Blanca, and wait.

After Luna Delaney recovers from her near swoon, she continues to question Blanca. "You've seen him? With your own eyes?"

Blanca's head rocks back and forth. "Yes. King Gavin keeps him in a cell in the dungeon, but I used to go there often to bring the prisoners water."

"Why would you do that?" The woman who caught the Luna looks to be about the same age as Delaney, and their facial features make me wonder if maybe they are related. Sisters, perhaps?

"Because it's the kind thing to do." Blanca doesn't miss a beat. "I was mistreated in my time at Dun's Crossing, and whenever I could, I tried to take pity on others who were equally abused. Besides, Mr. Blake was always kind to me. He used to tell me stories. He's the one who encouraged me to come here. I discovered right before I left Dun's Crossing that I had the ability to mind-link with him. I also found out about my powers to control the animals." Her countenance changes as a solemn expression sinks into her face. "I'm afraid he was badly injured because I used my powers, and the guards assumed it was him."

"Badly injured?" Delaney presses a hand to her cheek. "Is he going to be all right?"

Blanca doesn't speak for a moment, and I see a tear forming in her eyes. I decide it's time to chime in. "I think he will be. Blake is a tough guy, that's for sure." I can't allow myself to think about how horrible I have always been to the man, to all of the prisoners really.

When I speak, the Luna looks at me for a moment and manages a nod, but it's Blanca she is most concerned with. "All these years, I've wondered why he didn't use his powers to set himself free. I assumed the fact that he never returned must have meant that King Gavin went back on his promise not to kill him."

"Why did my fa–the king–promise not to kill him?" The words almost slip from my mouth. I'm sure the Luna must've noticed, but she doesn't ask what I was going to say, only stares at me. Blanca sucks in a deep breath and holds my gaze for a second, but she also doesn't call me out.

"Why don't we take this conversation to my home?" Delaney offers. "It'll be more comfortable there."

"Of course." Blanca starts to trot off behind her, but I tug on her arm. She bounces back to me and turns with wide eyes. "What?"

"Are you sure this is a good idea? What if they're just luring us in so they can kill us?" I ask her.

She scoffs. "They won't. They're nice. Besides, why did you come all the way here if you thought my people were going to kill you?"

I am temporarily distracted by the feel of her slender fingers wrapped around mine but manage to pay attention enough to answer her question. "I couldn't let you come by yourself."

"You couldn't let me die by myself?" She snickers and shakes her head. "The Luna knows Mr. Blake. He's my friend. We're fine. Just… be careful what you say."

I mumble under my breath that I know she's right, and then we follow the Luna, who has paused for us to catch up a few feet away.

This place is all hollowed out tunnels with the occasional wooden beam to keep the ceiling from falling in. It's dark, save for the lamps, but it also seems like a massive space with lots of twists and turns.

A lot of people congregate along the path as we walk along as well. Most of them have curious expressions on their faces, which are clean despite the fact that we are walking on dirt and walled in by dirt. I have a thousand questions about this place, but now is not the time to ask them.

We pass mud houses carved from the earth. Some of them have straw mixed in for support. There are markets with fruits and vegetables, and I wonder where those are grown. Everything above the surface that we encountered was ash. I do remember the fertile soil we passed over, though.

I also see a well. That explains how everyone is clean. They have fresh water. I'm assuming they tapped into something my father and his men didn't poison.

The Luna's house isn't too far away. By the time we arrive, I'm glad I'll be sitting down soon. My back hurts from the fall, and I have a slight limp. I'd tried to reach out to grab the ladder with my paw but all that did was twist it. I should have taken the advice I'd given Blanca to shift, but I heard noises below me and wanted to be prepared to fight.

The Luna leads us into a modest house that appears to be one large room with a kitchen area, a bed, a couch, and a couple of chairs. The kitchen has a sink with a pump and a fireplace, which makes me wonder where the smoke goes, but again, I can't ask. The chimney is made of mismatched stone I assume they gathered from the remnants of their previous dwellings above. It's all very sad to me that they've been living this way for over two decades now because of what my father did to them.

The Luna offers us each a chair, and I gladly accept, thanking her. She doesn't ask if we want water, just brings it to us, as well as a few scraps of dried meat. I bite into the salty substance and think it tastes a lot like rabbit. Despite how difficult it must be to live this way, they are making it work.

"Now, Blanca," Delaney begins, sitting on the couch. "Tell me everything you can about your life, dear. It will help me to understand why Cole didn't use his magic to get out of prison and why you are clearly very important to him."

"Cole?" Blanca echoes.

"That's right. My husband–Cole Blake, the Alpha King of Escuro."

Blanca nods in understanding. She obviously never knew his first name, and neither did I. She starts off by telling the Luna about her childhood, how she was told she was a daughter of the Solbergs but was never treated like one. She talks about things I've never been aware of, like how her nursemaids mistreated her, etc., and it makes me angry at those people, but then, I am one of the worst offenders, though she doesn't mention that to the Luna.

She tells her how she snuck out during the Haze and found out that I was her mate. She is kind in not disclosing my reaction. She doesn't even mention the fact that we were told we were siblings since I am still Keery Lightmanguy. Then, she talks about discovering her powers, the friendships she's had with the mice, and how Blake took the blame for her when she used her powers to assault the guards.

"When I realized I could speak to him through the mind-link, I knew we had to be from the same pack. He told me to find you, his people–our people–that they would be kind to me. So I ran away, and Keir–Keery came with me."

The Luna takes a deep breath and says, "All this time, he stayed there on the promise that Gavin would fulfill his end of the bargain, and it sounds like he never did."

"What do you mean?" Blanca asks, leaning forward.

The Luna silently stands, crosses the room, and takes an object from beneath her pillow. When she brings it back, I can tell it's a framed photograph, but all I can see is the back.

"When we heard we were about to be invaded, we rounded up as many of the children as we could and hid them. Most of them we deposited in caves or other places where it would be difficult to find them. Our own child, we sent away with her loving nursemaid. She was on her way to our allies across the mountains. Gavin claimed he had found her and had her in his possession. I didn't believe him, but Cole said if there was even a chance that was true, he would go with Gavin. The king of Dun's Crossing promised to return our daughter to us if we surrendered. Cole did just that. They burned everything to the ground, took my husband, and I never got my daughter back."

Blanca has tears in her eyes as I wonder if it was a bluff, and their daughter is in that other kingdom. But then, wouldn't their allies have sent word by now? Unless they think everyone died.

"Can I see?" Blanca asks.

The Luna nods and turns the picture around. It's her, twenty years younger, Blake, and a small baby.

"This is our sweet girl," Delaney says. "My precious daughter. Raven."

30

WRAPPED UP IN LOVE

I BLINK A FEW TIMES AND AM GLAD THE LUNA HASN'T HANDED ME THE picture to hold because I would probably drop it and shatter the glass all over the packed-earth floor.

"What did you say your daughter's name is?" My voice is a whisper, and I hope that it doesn't betray the emotions that are welling up inside of me.

"Her name is Raven." Luna Delaney speaks as if she believes her daughter is still alive somewhere.

I believe she is, too.

"King Gavin said he found her?" Kieran asks, his voice stronger than mine.

"That's right, and from the description he gave of the location and who she was with, he was convincing. To my husband, at least. I suppose it was my prayers that she made it to our allies that has prevented me from accepting that fact." She lets out a sigh. "For years, I've been searching for her in our own territory. But the border between our lands and our allies, Dark Valley, is filled with rogues.

171

Most of the people who survived the attack from Dun's Crossing were children and their caregivers, not our warriors. Most of them were poisoned when Gavin dropped an overwhelming amount of wolfsbane in our main water supply to the primary villages. Thankfully, the castle and some of the outlying areas were not affected, or else we would all be dead."

I shake my head, unable to comprehend the cruelty the man I thought was my father for all of those years inflicted on these poor, innocent people.

My people.

"After the Alpha King was taken, Gavin burned everything. You likely saw the desolation on your way here?" Luna Delaney asks.

I manage to nod, but I don't try to speak for fear I'll begin to cry.

"With no other options, we relied on our animal friends to help us. No one else in the pack has control over the large animals like Cole did, and many of the animals didn't survive the fire, but those that were left, the smaller ones that we could influence, those of us with noble blood like myself and my sister, Nola, whom you met, we were able to get them to help us. The rabbits, moles, voles, and some of the other tunneling animals helped us start this system of underground dwellings. After that, we secretly cleared out some of the lands furthest from our shared border with Dun's Crossing. We started growing crops and herded up some of the farm animals that had survived so that we could feed everyone. We did all of it while fearing for our lives. It's been a long process. In the beginning, many people became malnourished because of the lack of food. We have managed to survive, though."

"And your water? It comes from another source?" I ask.

"That's right. We've tapped into a natural spring we wouldn't have been able to easily reach above ground. It feeds the river that was poisoned, but the water originates below any levels that could be tampered with."

She continues to talk about how difficult it was to start over, how they don't have many warriors, and how so many of the citizens are young and don't remember their old way of life. When she speaks of

Escuro before the war, her dark eyes twinkle in the lamplight. "We were a thriving kingdom, but even better than our riches and vast amounts of natural resources was the way our people flourished. We were peaceful, with our focus on gaining knowledge and creating beautiful works of art. It was only because Gavin thought we may someday become a threat that he tried to destroy us. He was afraid we'd rise up and use our powers to conquer his lands. That was his reason for destroying all of the kingdoms around him using under-handed means and going to any lengths necessary to kill even the most innocent."

I've listened to her speak about her kingdom for almost an hour before we get back to her family. "They kept Mr. Blake in silver chains at first." I tell her what I've heard from Kieran. "So he wouldn't be able to use his powers."

A giggle escapes her lips, and it's the first note of amusement I've heard from her in a while. "He's far too powerful for a bit of silver to stop him. No, Cole stayed there because he must've thought our daughter was being held there, but I don't think that's possible. If she never made it to Dark Valley, I'm afraid… well, I'm afraid it was the worst for her. I hate to think of it. She was only a few months old when we had to send her off in the dead of night."

I swallow hard, thinking of Kieran's theory. He nudges me with his knee, and I give him a slight nod. "Luna Delaney," I begin, wondering why the same thought that is in my head hasn't occurred to her yet. Perhaps she's too forlorn. "I was a few months old at the time of the attack," I begin.

She tilts her head slightly to the side and doesn't blink as she stares at me. Nor does she say anything.

"I'm obviously from Escuro, since I have the mind-link powers and look like the vast majority of citizens here."

This time, her head rocks back and forth, and I hear Kieran inhale sharply next to me as if he is bracing himself for what I am about to say.

"Do you think it's possible that Mr. Blake was staying there, doing what was asked of him by King Gavin because… of me?" I can't bring myself to say the words I actually want to. I hope that she will do that for me.

Her eyes widen. "For you?"

Taking a deep breath, I blow it out slowly, and nod. "That's right. Even though I told Mr. Blake my name many years ago when I first started visiting him as a small child, he never called me Blanca. Never. He invented what I thought was a nickname for me. He always had these birds perched on the window ledge at the top of his cell. I thought maybe it was because he was so fond of them, or maybe it was because of my dark hair. But he always called me... Little Raven. He called me Raven, Luna. Do you think.... Do you think I might be...."

I don't get the rest of the sentence out before Luna Delaney sets the picture aside and flings herself at me, wrapping me up in a tight hug. "Oh, my baby girl," she says. "I didn't dare dream that it could be you, even though I recognized Cole's eyes the moment I looked into yours. After all this time, you've come back to me. My sweet, sweet, Little Raven."

She's holding me so tightly that I can barely breathe, but I don't even care. I have a mother–one that loves me. One that has been dreaming about me returning to her since I was a baby. Images flash through my mind of the reality of my life–my alleged mother having me beaten, calling me names, even pushing me down the stairs–but they mingle with what might have been, and I see myself as a little girl running through the castle to hug my beautiful mother who embraces me the way she is now. I see myself sitting at a royal dining table with both of my parents, Mr. Blake clean, well, and smiling. I see a lifetime of missed memories unfolding before my eyes and find myself sobbing in my mother's arms.

I feel the warmth of Kieran's hand as he rests it gently on my back, reminding me that he is here, that as horrible as my past has been, that is all over now. I have a mother. I have a father. I have a mate. I have a *future*.

Finally, the Luna–my mother–lets me go and cups my cheek with her hand. "Raven, I can't believe I have you back. We have so much to catch up on. I love you so much, my beautiful daughter."

"I love you, too… Mama." The word falls from my lips like a promise. I turn to look at Kieran and see tears in his eyes.

And that's when I know there are two people in this room that love me.

31

ADMISSION

AFTER A TEARFUL REUNION WITH HER MOTHER, BLANCA–I MEAN Raven–is taken outside to meet the rest of the pack. I tag along in awe of everything I'm seeing. Unlike my mate, I've known my parents my whole life, and I've always felt like they loved me. But after seeing this, I'm beginning to realize I'm not sure I know what parental love looks like. At least, not until now.

Delaney doesn't stop crying the entire time she is speaking to her people. She calls them all to gather in a central area that is a little larger than the other tunnels, and when a great mass of them has congregated, she tells them all what she has discovered. The girl who climbed down the ladder a bit ago is her daughter–Princess Raven– the girl that disappeared twenty-one years ago.

At first, a hush falls over everyone. They're obviously surprised, and I have to think they also wonder if Delaney has lost her mind. How does she know this? What if this girl is lying? But then, the woman from earlier, whom I've now learned is Raven's aunt, Nola, steps forward and says, "You look so much like your mother–with

177

your father's eyes." Then, the crowd erupts with discussion of just how true that statement is.

Next, everyone wants to come and give her a hug and welcome her to the pack. This takes some time, and while I gain several curious glances, no one really speaks to me. I'm just fine with that. As much as I am proud of Raven and happy for her, I am not really a part of this. If I open my mouth too much, I'm bound to slip up again, so it's best if I just stay in the background.

Every once in a while, Raven turns to look at me, and we share a smile. This warms my heart in a way I've never experienced until now.

"What of King Cole?" someone finally asks. "If we have the princess back, does that mean he is still a prisoner?"

"He is," the Luna Queen says with a quiver of sadness in her voice. "I believe he was staying there because he wanted to protect Raven."

"We should storm the castle!" someone in the back shouts. "It's time those bastards felt the wrath for what they've done to us!"

Others in the crowd shout in agreement, but the Luna quickly calms them. "No, no, we can't do that," she tells them. "While I know how badly all of you want vengeance for our losses, we are not strong enough to stand up to King Gavin right now. His army is full of fierce warriors. Besides, he always uses underhanded tactics that would never cross our minds to guard against."

A pinprick of offense springs to life in my gut because it's natural for me to want to defend my father, but then I remember that she's absolutely right, and I nod along with the others who realize their Luna knows what she's talking about.

"How do we free our king?" someone else shouts. "We need him back!"

"Yes, King Blake would know what to do!" another person agrees.

"Now that Raven has escaped the clutches of King Gavin, I have no doubt that our Alpha King will return to us soon," Luna Delaney says, her voice loud enough to be heard over everyone else. "Let's give him some time."

"I'm going back to help him." The words slip from my lips before I am even prepared to hear them. Everyone is suddenly looking at me, including Raven and her mother. I clear my throat and wonder if I should say more. Since there's not another sound in the wide open space, I feel compelled to continue. "I'll make sure he is able to return here."

Raven gives me a grateful smile while her mother looks surprised. Then, someone shouts a question I don't think I can answer. "How?" he says. "How can you do that?"

Raven shakes her head slightly, a warning not to tell them the truth. I think for a moment before I say, "King Gavin trusts me. He's known me… my whole life. I can do what it takes to help your Alpha King escape."

"He's known you your whole life?" Nola repeats with a chuckle. "All of twenty-one years then? Little pup."

"Nola," Delaney chastises. "Keery has said he will be helping Cole return to us. Let's support that. We know, as much as anyone, what it's like to have your mate stolen away from you. In order for Keery to help us, he will have to leave Raven behind. That's difficult for anyone, especially newly found mates." Then, she turns to her daughter, a fearful expression in her eyes. "You are staying with us, aren't you?"

Raven nods, and her mother looks relieved while I feel my heart break in pieces–even though I knew that. Still, the thought of being away from her is physically painful.

"Let us celebrate!" Delaney shouts. "We shall have a traditional pack feast!"

Cheers go up and then everyone heads out to prepare said-feast. I have no idea what this will entail, but I'm starving having only eaten a few fish over the past few days. Nola whisks her niece away, telling Raven she's going to teach her how to cook a fatted pig in the way traditional to their people. Raven's dark eyes meet mine, and then she's gone. I try to follow after her, but before I can take more than a step, my way is blocked.

I look up into Delaney's dark eyes. "I think we need to have a chat–Keery."

Swallowing hard, I nod. This woman commands this entire pack.

If she wants to speak to me, I have little choice. I just hope I don't say anything to anger her or give away my true identity.

She makes a sweeping gesture with her arm which implies I should start walking back to her house, so I do. She falls into stride next to me, and soon we are back in her meager dwelling.

I sit in the same chair I occupied before, and she takes the one Raven had been sitting in before. "Now, Keery Lightmanguy, tell me who you really are."

I stare at her for a moment, wondering what my chances are of pulling one over on her. This is Raven's mother, and if there's one thing I do know about my mate, it's that she's smart as a whip. The look she's giving me tells me that I may as well not try to lie.

Yet, I can't tell her the truth without talking to Raven first, so I find myself stammering. "Wh-what do you mean?"

"I mean... my daughter is a princess. You are her fated mate. There's no way in hell the Moon Goddess would match her with just anyone. You must be someone important in your kingdom, especially if you have the ear of the king. Who are you–Keery Lightmanguy?"

"I'm... a noble," I tell her, hoping that's sufficient. She doesn't blink. "I've lived in the castle my whole life. My parents are very important in the kingdom."

"Yes," she replies. "Go on."

I shrug as if there's nothing else to say. "That's it, really."

"No, it's not. Who are your parents?"

"Uhm, royals," I finally say. "They're of royal blood."

She nods, and I wonder if maybe I've already said too much. There are royals who are not the king and queen–like my aunts and uncles and their families. Remarkably, she doesn't press me further. "Do you love my daughter?"

"I do." The words surprise me, but I try not to react in a way that will not let her know that. Even though it's the first time I've admitted it, even to myself, I know it's true.

Raven is my mate. She's a beautiful soul, inside and out, and I am the biggest dick alive for not noticing any of this before, but I intend to make it up to her, even if it takes me the rest of my life.

Even if it costs me my life, for that matter.

"Very well then," Delaney says dismissively. "If that's the case, then come with me." She stands and starts walking out the door.

I blink a few times, not sure what's going on, but what choice do I have? I follow her out the door wondering if I'll be called on to give up my life more quickly than planned.

32
MOTHER KNOWS

I have an Aunt.

Nola takes me to her home, and together we begin to bake a traditional dessert that is eaten during celebrations. She tells me all about how the dish is prepared and why it means so much to our people.

I am listening the best I can, but I am distracted. I keep thinking about my mother–I actually have one that loves me–and how she asked to speak to Kieran. I'm nervous that he will say something he shouldn't say, but I have to trust him. He is my mate, after all.

As we bake, Nola asks me all sorts of questions about my life. I am slicing apples, something I've never done before, and am slightly afraid I'll cut off my finger if I don't pay attention. I tell her the truth. "I was raised in the castle, mostly cared for by nursemaids. It's not been too interesting, honestly. Your life here seems far more intriguing. I'd love to know how you have apples underground."

Nola, who looks a lot like my mother, laughs and wipes the back of her hand across her face. "We grow them in the lands far from the border with Dun's Crossing. We've got tunnels that lead there. We can pop up and hide if we need to. We use the birds to warn us, but no one from Dun's Crossing has been in those parts for over a decade. Only rogues. Still, we want to remain unseen so that word doesn't get back to King Gavin." She spits on the dirt floor of her home. "We've left the land close to the border in the state he left it in so that he will, perhaps, think we are all dead or gone, but the land further north we've cultivated. We have rich soil here, so we are able to grow quite a bit. Some of our livestock survived, and it does well on the rich grasses that grow there. We get by."

I blink back tears at hearing more about their plight. All of it has been for naught, too, because these people never would've come looking to take from King Gavin. He simply wanted to eliminate a threat–or maybe gain a weapon.

Is that what I am supposed to be? I'm not even that powerful.

We finish making the dessert and put it in to bake over the fire when Nola invites me to sit, drink some tea she's just brewed, and discuss Keery. I accept the drink and take a seat on her meager couch. I take a sip and can tell she's used some sort of apple extract to flavor the beverage. It's sweet with a touch of sour aftertaste, and I love it.

"Tell me about before the Haze," she says. "Did you know him then?"

I don't want to lie, but I also can't say anything to put Kieran in danger. "I did know him, sort of. He's not really who I thought he was." That much is true, though I'm not sure what facilitated the change. Did he stop being such a jerk in the last few years, or has he always been kind and thoughtful to other people and just treated me like garbage because he was taught to do so? I don't know, and I don't think it matters now. He is my mate. I love him. And he's redeemed himself by coming on this journey with me.

"Were you friends?" Nola asks.

I shake my head. "I wasn't really allowed to have any friends, except for Mr. Blake."

She giggles. "I think you can call him Father now."

"Right. Gosh, it's so weird to think about that. I mean, he's always been the kindest soul to me, and now I understand why."

"And Keery? Was he nice to you?"

I shrug. "I wasn't around him too much, not recently, anyway. The king and queen wanted to keep me away from everyone else. I had chores to do each day until recently. They locked me in my room to prevent me from taking part in the Haze. I guess they didn't want me to find my mate."

"How did you get out?" She finishes her tea and sets the glass aside.

"My mice friends helped me," I tell her.

She nods. "And how was the journey here? Did the two of you get... acquainted?" She smirks and then winks at me, and I feel my cheeks warm.

"A little," I admit, which makes her laugh again, but in a good-natured way. I think about that night in the cave and feel my face flush even brighter.

"Well, he seems like a good man to bring you all the way here on a whim when you weren't even sure who you were or where you were going. Handsome, too."

"Thank you." Again, I blush and look away. Handsome isn't the half of it. He's gorgeous, just like all the princes in the storybooks I managed to swipe from the library over the years.

Aunt Nola starts to speak again but then goes quiet. I wonder if she's realized who Kieran really is and is mad until a wide smile brightens her face. "Your mother would like for us to meet her in the plaza." She gets up and takes the dessert carefully from the fire, putting it in a container to carry along with us.

I don't know what a plaza is, but I finish my tea and go with her. I know that Mother is with Kieran, and I hope that he's okay. I wonder if she's cracked him yet.

We walk outside to the same area where we were before, past that to a larger space that is decorated with even more lanterns. All of the people seem to be here now, decorating and setting up big tables full of food. Everything smells so good, my stomach begins to growl.

Then, I see Kieran and my mother standing under a large twisted vine structure at the far end of the space–the plaza. They turn and look at me, and smile, and I have no idea what is happening, but Nola leads me over. My mother is holding a large book with words written on the cover in a language I've never seen before.

"What's going on?" I whisper, not sure which of them I'm asking.

"This is your handfasting ceremony," Mother replies. "Since the two of you love one another and know that you are mates, there's no reason to wait any longer."

I look at Kieran who only shrugs. He doesn't seem alarmed or like he wants to fight my mother over this decision. Still, it seems rushed. "What about Father?" I ask. I know Kieran hates his own father now, but it would be nice for mine to be present if possible. I'm not sure how he feels about his mother.

"He will understand. The handfasting ceremony will strengthen your powers, Raven. It will also strengthen your bond to your mate and give you the ability to mind-link. Keery will be able to mind-link with our pack as well."

I nod, but something else has occurred to me. "Mother, may I speak to you alone for a moment?"

"You could use the mind-link," Aunt Nola reminds me.

"Right." I'm not used to having that power. In my mind, I ask, 'Can you hear me, Mother?'

'I can hear you.' Her voice is strong and true though her lips don't move.

'We may have not quite told you Keery's true name. Will that be a problem?' I admit.

She snickers. 'I know, darling.'

'How do you know?' Did Kieran tell her the truth?

She laughs again, and I bet the crowd that has gathered to watch the ceremony wonders what's so funny. 'Lightmanguy isn't a very convincing fake last name. At least you haven't learned to be too good at deceiving others in our time apart. What is his real name, my darling?'

I hesitate. She's my mother, and I know she loves me. I think she will protect Kieran, but I don't want to anger the entire pack. I bite my bottom lip and consider what to say. Finally, I settle on, 'Well, it is Kieran, but....'

'Solberg?' she asks me, and her expression doesn't waver.

'Yes,' I admit. 'I don't want to make everyone upset.'

'I will stick with first names, my darling.'

She doesn't bat an eye at the fact that I didn't tell her the truth. 'Thank you.'

"Now," she says aloud, "Raven, join hands with Kieran, and let's perform the ceremony."

As a woman I don't know comes and wraps a ceremonial silk cloth around our arms, Kieran whispers, "Did you tell her?"

I shake my head. "She already knew. She won't tell them."

He lets out a deep breath and nods. He's not mad, which still surprises me, even though it shouldn't.

In her Luna voice, my mother commands, "Gather around, my people. It is time to unite this man and this woman in matrimony through our traditional handfasting ceremony. Please, everyone, join me for the wedding of my daughter, Princess Ravin to her true mate–Kieran."

The people gather around with smiles on their faces, no one suspecting that their precious princess is about to marry the son of their worst enemy.

33

THE CEREMONY

Kieran

When Delaney first asked me to come with her, I was nervous, but as we walked along, she told me about what it was like giving birth to Raven, how she'd been asking the Moon Goddess to bless her with a child for many years and hadn't been lucky enough to have one until finally she found out she was pregnant. When it had turned out she was having a daughter, she'd been overjoyed.

Raven had only been a few months old when everything had happened with my kingdom. As she spoke, I got the impression she knew who I was, that I am the Crown Prince of Dun's Crossing, but I never told her the truth, and she didn't ask.

Now, here we are about to go through with the handfasting ceremony, something Delaney also explained to me. I figured it was like a wedding but not as complicated. As we walked, my mind went over all the planning my mother and Nessa had been discussing since the Haze and think about what a waste of time that's going to turn out to be. There's no way in hell I'm going forward with marrying Nessa yet, not that I've figured out how to keep her from telling everyone what she saw. I'll figure it out.

"Kieran," Delaney says, letting me know that Raven must've told her something through the mind-link since she's no longer calling me Keery. I hope she doesn't know my last name, but since no one is trying to kill me, or spitting on the ground, I assume she only knows my name and not who I am.. "Take Raven's hand."

I do as she says, and then Nola takes the fabric we'd been presented about and wraps it around our arms so that we are united–sort of. It's not as if we couldn't let go if we wanted to. But I don't want to.

"Kieran, today we celebrate the beauty of the Moon Goddess and the blessed experience from the Haze. Though you may not know everything there is to know about Raven yet, as the two of you grow together, you will quickly learn to love and treasure one another." Delaney's smile is sideways as she continues. "The two of you will have many years together to know your strengths and weaknesses and how to love and support one another. May you spend many years happily together, no matter what trials and tribulations you may face."

Not sure what to say or do, I only smile at her, and then she turns to Raven.

"My darling daughter, Raven, I am so happy to have found you. We are delighted that you are now part of our family again. You are a beautiful, kind hearted, intelligent woman, and one day you will lead our people and make our kingdom great again. We are all thankful to be here with you today to witness the uniting of two wonderful young people who have fallen in love."

Raven turns to look at me and smiles, and my heart begins to beat out of my chest. I do love her, I know that now.

"Kieran, will you please repeat after me?" I nod, and Delaney continues. "I, Kieran, pledge my love and life to you, Raven."

"I, Kieran, pledge my love and live to you, Raven."

"And I promise to always be here for you, no matter what."

I repeat after Delaney.

"I thank the Moon Goddess for joining our two hearts."

I feel my emotions begin to well up inside of me and blink a few times before I continue. "I thank the Moon Goddess for joining our two hearts."

"And I bind my heart to yours for all time."

"I bind my heart to yours for all time."

When I'm finished, I see tears filling Raven's eyes and can't help but smile reassuringly at her.

It takes Raven a few moments to get the words out, not because she doesn't remember what she's supposed to say but because she is overwhelmed. I wish I could kiss her to make her feel better, but I am afraid to mess the ceremony up. She finishes with the same remarks, "I bind my heart to yours for all time."

"Now," Delaney says again, "it's time for the two of you to seal your promise with a kiss. Let the Moon Goddess keep you bound together for all time, never to be separated by anyone. Kieran, you may kiss your wife."

With a wide grin, I lean forward and press my lips to hers. It's a sweet, gentle kiss, since everyone is watching us. A cheer goes up from the crowd. Delaney takes our bound hands and raises them, and more cheers go up.

"Let us celebrate!" the Luna says, and then we are rushed away to the area of the plaza where the food is ready for everyone. Musicians begin to play the guitar, violin, drums, and flute. With our hands still bound together, we are led out to the floor and begin to dance. At first, I'm a bit shy, but Raven is overjoyed and begins to sway in time to the music. She's actually quite the dancer, and soon we are dancing with one another. Others join in, and we laugh, and I spin around until the fabric is twisted up so I have to spin her around a few more times.

The song ends, and then Nola comes and removes the fabric. We are officially bound together, which causes the crowd to erupt in cheers again.

"Are you happy?" Raven asks, her eyes wide as she smiles at me.

"I've never been happier," I admit.

"Good. Me, too." Another song begins, and we continue to dance, not paying any attention to anyone until someone makes an announcement that it's time to eat.

We are led to a table and served all kinds of food I've never had before, including smoked meats, fresh vegetables, and a dessert Raven tells me she's never tried before that she helped her aunt make. It's delicious. We laugh and chat, and for once in my life, I feel like nothing in the world is wrong. In the back of my mind, I know that isn't true. In a day or two, I'll have to go back to the castle and face my father, but for now, I feel like all is right in the world.

An older man asks Raven to dance with him. She agrees, and I watch. The two of them have an amazing time dancing. For being older, he seems like he's in good shape, and I wonder if maybe he is related to her in some way.

"Are you having fun?" Delaney asks me, sitting down in Raven's empty seat.

"I am." I take a drink of a glass of mead that is constantly refilled every few minutes by friendly pack members.

"Good." In a quiet voice, she continues. "Raven told me the truth, that you're Gavin's son."

I swallow hard, not sure what to say.

"It's all right," she says. "I understand that you love my daughter, and you are her fated mate. But I must tell you, if your father finds out where we are hiding, I will never forgive you. Neither will Raven, I'm sure. She's been through a lot, and it's time she had the opportunity to be happy."

"I know," I say with a nod. "I promise, that's my goal. To make sure she's happy. She deserves that."

Delaney nods in understanding. "Are you going back soon?"

"I have no choice." I watch my mate dancing and smile, but my heart feels heavy. "I plan to go help King Cole kill my father."

"That will be difficult," she tells me. "He's powerful and has no scruples. Besides, he is your father."

"I know, but everything he's ever told me has been a lie." Bitterness radiates through me when I think about all of the lies he's told me over the years.

"Be careful." She squeezes my arm. "Make sure you get back here all right."

"I will, I promise her."

We lock eyes, and she nods. But then Raven comes over and takes my hand, and I laugh as we get up to dance again. For at least a few hours, everything is wonderful. I refuse to think about the future and how important it is that I find a way to kill my father. For now, all I want is to be with Raven–to laugh, to smile, to hold her. To show her how blessed I feel that the Moon Goddess has blessed me to make her my wife.

For the rest of the night, I intend to make the most of being with the woman I love. In the morning, I'll worry about everything else.

"I love you, Kieran," Raven says with a wide smile.

"I love you, too, Raven. More than anything." I lean over and kiss her, wishing I could carry her off to some place where we can be alone so that I can show her just how much I mean every word of it.

34

HONEYMOON

My legs ache from dancing. At one point, I took my shoes off and let Kieran spin me in circles across the rough cobblestone in the square. Now, I'm barefoot and hobbling beside my mate—my husband—along a trail through the tunnels lit by the same lanterns the villagers had hung in the square before our surprise handfasting ceremony.

My brain is still unable to process how fast this happened, but it's done. Kieran and I are husband and wife.

I curse under my breath when I step on a root jutting from the trail and stub my toe.

Kieran sighs heavily before swooping me into his arms. "My first order of business as your husband is buying you a new pair of shoes, *my dear.*"

My dear. I giggle, wiggling in his arms as we continue our walk through the lantern lit darkness. "Is that your new name for me now that you can never get rid of me?"

He rolls his eyes. It's nice seeing him relaxed and enjoying himself. I'm not sure I ever have, to be honest.

"Would you prefer sweetheart? Darling? My dearest, most beautiful, most powerful wife?"

"Okay," I laugh. "You're just trying to butter me up."

"Maybe a little," he growls low in his throat as he lowers his face to my neck and roughly nuzzles me, which causes another cascade of giggles to echo through the unending darkness around us.

"Where are you taking me?" I laugh.

He shrugs. "Hopefully not far. You're rather wiggly."

I swat his chest, but then his footsteps slow, and I follow his gaze.

There's a small cottage just ahead of us. The windows glow from within, and the chimney puffs whispers of smoke.

"What is this place?" I ask him.

"A gift from your mother," he says, but the care-free tone of his voice slips back into his familiar, somewhat icy drawl. "This is our house."

"Our house?" I look from his face to the cottage and feel my chest squeeze.

"Apparently." Kieran starts walking again, faster than before, and carries me up the stairs to the porch, which is decorated with potted plants and a patio table and chairs. It's much nicer than the houses we saw in the village proper.

I'm sure in the daylight this place would be beautiful. It's too bad it's never daylight here. I can hear dripping water nearby, and the insects around us chatter back and forth, whispering congratulations and warm welcomes as my mate opens the door and carries me through the threshold.

I don't say anything. I can't say what I'm feeling because it will ruin this new warmth between us. We can't live here. Not now. Not for very long, at least. Kieran has unfinished business to attend to, and me?

He sets me on my feet in the main room of the cottage and closes the door behind us, locking it.

I look around, taking it all in. Dirt walls, pounded dirt floors.

Comfortable furnishings. A small kitchen area. Two bedrooms–only one of them furnished–and a bathroom.

Fresh flowers in vases decorate every surface. Bottles of mead sit on the dining table beside a tray of fruit, chocolate, and pastries.

"This was nice of them to do for us," Kieran says softly as he turns to inspect the cottage just like I am.

I want to ask what needs to happen now. I want to know when, or if, he's leaving.

And I need to know if I'm coming with him.

I don't realize I'm staring absently into the fireplace until Kieran says from the bathroom, "Raven, come here."

I walk into the bathroom, which is roomy and clean, and look down at the copper, claw foot tub. It's steaming, the water spiced with lavender scented soap and rose petals. I wonder how they managed this underground.

Slowly, I look up at Kieran. "Do you think they're trying to tell us we stink?"

The corner of his mouth kicks up and he shrugs, then starts taking off his shirt.

I bite my lip as I watch him undress.

"Are you not getting in?" he asks, stepping into the water and sinking down to his chest with a groan. "Ah, this is so nice."

"You look very comfortable," I tease.

"Take off your clothes, wife," he growls, "and come here."

The dominance in his voice sends prickles of heat racing down my spine. I obey, shoving that nagging feeling that something is coming and this might be the last time we're together like this away.

I let my clothes drop to the ground, puddling around my feet. Naked and bared to him, I ease into the tub, very aware of how he's watching every move I make.

When I'm within his reach, he pulls me toward him, water sloshing over the sides of the tub, and sits me in his lap, my back pressed to his chest.

He takes a long breath and exhales deeply into my hair.

"You drank a lot of mead, didn't you?" I whisper as his hands come up to palm my breasts.

"Mhm," he groans, brushing his lips over my shoulder.

I close my eyes and lose myself to his touch.

I'm reminded of the Haze, and our first night together before we knew the truth.

Right now, Kieran's touch is gentle and exploratory.

But I don't want gentle.

I turn and straddle him, wrapping my arms around his neck, then kiss him soundly. My tongue slides along his lower lip before darting into his mouth, and I rise up on my knees.

"Raven," he rasps, clutching my ass.

His cock is hard between us, and I cant my hips over the head, which causes Kieran to tremble and blow out his breath through gritted teeth.

"I've been thinking about you all night," he groans. "I've wanted nothing more than to bury my cock inside you and hear that little sound you make when you come."

Oh, Goddess. Heat pools between my thighs, a dull ache throbbing to life as I continue to tease us both.

"But I'm not fucking you in a bathtub," he says, and stands up with me in his arms.

I yelp in surprise as he carries me out of the tub, ignoring that we're soaking wet and dripping water all over the place.

In a second, we're in the bedroom, and he deposits me on the bed and spreads my legs apart.

I almost move to cover myself, but the heat in his eyes has me in a trance.

It feels like a lifetime ago that I was sneaking out of my room in the castle to be a part of the Haze. I remember being so desperate to find my mate, to find a way out of the life I'd been living.

Now, I have that life. I have my mate. I have a family.

"Kieran," I whisper, my voice catching in my throat as he leans down, covering my body with his. He presses a kiss to my throat before rising up to look at me.

"I love you," I say.

His smile makes that heat curl through my veins.

"I love you," he agrees, and kisses me hard.

He lowers himself between my legs and thrusts his cock into me in one fluid motion. I moan as my muscles tighten around his length, squeezing in relief. He groans, whispering my name as he begins to ravage my body, kissing me everywhere he can reach.

Every thrust of his cock has me slipping closer and closer to a climax I know is about to rock my world and leave me senseless.

"Mate," he growls across the top of my ear. "I want to feel you come. I want you screaming my name."

I close my eyes, my breath coming in rasps. Kieran is close, and rasping praise against my skin as I grip his sides so tight I'm sure my nails are leaving marks.

"Kieran!" I shout, my back arching off the bed. Pleasure rips through my body like a tidal wave, leaving my skin tingly and muscles spasming.

Kieran clutches the sheets above my head and slams into me, spilling his seed deep inside of me. Warmth pools in my belly as I open my eyes and find him looking down at me with mingled shock and the deepest kind of love.

He lowers himself to rest on his elbows, hovering above me. His cock is still buried deep inside of me, and he makes no moves to pull out. His nose brushes mine.

"Raven," he whispers. "Tonight was the best night of my life. I will keep my vows to you. That is my promise."

My stomach twists. I already know what he's going to say.

"One day, we'll lay here in bed together and have nothing but our future to look forward to." He reaches between, resting a hand on my belly. "I want children with you. As many as we can. I want a family that rivals mine in size so we can do it the right way, and raise them with love. We will have a future, you and I. I'll make all of this, every-thing that ever happened to you, worth it."

Tears sting my eyes.

"Because I love you," he says. "I will return to you. I promise."

35
WHAT I MUST DO

Kieran

I wake to lamplight streaming through the curtains. It's early morning. Though I can't see it down here in the tunnels, I imagine the sun is still hiding beneath the horizon. I should still be asleep, but my mind and body are at odds with my heart, and rest hasn't come easy.

Raven and I made the most of the soft bed and total privacy we were awarded last night after our wedding and didn't fall asleep until well past the middle of the night. But I reach over to her side of the bed and find it empty, and cool to the touch.

I sit up and fumble for my clothes.

She has to know that this moment was coming. That I have to leave, and it may be a while before I can return. The idea of storming into my own kingdom, deposing my father, and putting his crown on top of my own head is appealing, but it can't happen that way.

I have to play the long game. I have to take out the enemies in his inner circle. I have to work my way to the top.

King Cole must help me, but I can't bring his daughter into this.

Raven has done enough. She has suffered enough.

She won't be going with me.

I pull my shirt over my head and work my belt through my pants as I walk through the cottage. She's not inside, that's obvious. Her scent is heavy near the front door as I push it open, finding her sitting on the steps in a nightgown, her black hair spilling out behind her and reflecting the lamp light.

"Raven," I say, mostly to myself. She doesn't turn to me as I walk up to her and take a seat beside her.

Silence hangs between us for a long time. We sit quietly together, and in the distance, I hear the sounds of the village awaking. She has tears glistening in her eyes; I'm not sure I've seen anything more beautiful.

"I couldn't sleep," she says eventually.

"Me neither." It's not like we really tried to get any rest. I'd love to pick her up and take her back inside to finish what we started last night, but this conversation needs to happen, unfortunately. "Raven, I—we need to talk about this."

She licks her lips and looks up at me. "How long are you going to be gone?"

"You know I can't answer that," I tell her. "Long enough to do what needs to be done."

She looks back toward the village, where we can hear people calling to one another, all in good cheer after last night's celebrations. Children are chattering back and forth. I look at my mate and wonder if she knows how happy she's made all of them.

"Look, Raven. I'm coming back for you. That's a promise. I don't want you to worry about me. You're home—with your family. I held up my end. I got you here. We always knew I'd have to return and finish my business with my parents."

"And Nessa?"

Shit. I sigh heavily and run my fingers through my hair before resting my arm over her slim shoulders. She leans into my side. "Yeah, Nessa." I promised myself I wouldn't think about that. We are betrothed, after all. But Nessa knows the truth, which means while I'm home, I need to keep up the charade as long as I have to in order to keep Raven, our mate bond, and the fact she's here and safe a secret until I can strike.

"I won't be going through the wedding with Nessa, obviously."

"But you might have to if this takes longer than–"

"It won't," I tell her. "I promise you. Plus, a marriage between Nessa and I wouldn't mean anything, Raven. I am married to you."

She swallows hard and looks up at me, and thankfully a smile touches her lips and brightens her eyes. "I know."

Her stomach growls, and now I'm smiling too. "Hungry?"

"Yeah, I am."

"I'll make breakfast and then we can go into the village." The words hang between us for a moment. We both know the second we walk into the village, I have to leave. I can't linger. Every second I spend with Raven makes me question going on this quest in the first place. I could just stay here. I could be Keery. I could have word sent to my parent's somehow, by someone, saying that Kieran is dead.

But then Raven would never be safe, and our kingdoms would always be at odds.

Inside the cottage, Raven makes herself busy going through the books stacked neatly on a shelf beside the fireplace while I rummage through the cabinets. I find coffee, some eggs, and proceed to cook a very simple breakfast that will hopefully tide us over for a few hours.

Look at me now, cooking breakfast for my mate. A few days with Raven have turned me into a totally different person.

I know the second I leave her side I'll fall back into my old ways. The worst part is, I have to. I have to be cruel and cold. Otherwise, this isn't going to work.

I watch my mate eat her eggs and sip her coffee. I wonder what she's thinking right now, but I don't have the balls to ask.

I just watch her, barely touching my food, until she lifts her head and stares at the window, where a small blue bird is tapping on the glass and chirping incessantly. I wonder how it got down here, but then, these people love animals. They must allow some of them in the tunnels.

"What is it saying?" I ask.

Raven smiles, then sighs. "My mother is on her way here to fetch us."

I rise from my chair and gather our empty plates, rinsing them in the sink. "We'd better go, then."

"Sure." There's hurt in her voice. It cuts me to the core as I follow Raven out of the cottage and along the path toward the village.

Sure enough, Raven's mother is in the square, having been caught up by some villagers and stuck in conversation while we made our way back.

She gives Raven a cursory glance between turning her attention to me. "Kieran."

"Luna Delaney," I say, and give her a little bob of my head in greeting.

"Raven, darling, Nola is waiting for you in the apothecary."

Raven nods, smiling at her mother before looking over her shoulder at me. "I'll come find you shortly," I tell her.

Raven takes a deep breath, grief flashing behind her eyes before she turns and walks into one of the buildings facing the square.

"I'm not going to ask why she's going to the apothecary," I say to Delaney.

"It's just for tea," Delaney says with a little smile. "Nola is going to make something to keep Raven's nerves calm while you're gone."

"What else will she be doing while I'm away?"

"Training her powers." Delaney looks sad for a moment. "I fear so much time has been wasted. She has so much to learn."

"She's in the right hands," I reply.

"Is my mate in the right hands?" Delaney asks without warning, her voice dropping.

I meet my wife's mother's eyes. "I will free your mate. King Cole will get the freedom he deserves, and he will return to you. I swear on my life."

"And will you return?"

"For Raven, yes." I know what she's asking. She wants to know if I plan to return for her daughter and take her away again.

The truth is, I have no idea what's going to happen. I have to kill my own father, a man I've grown to hate more than ever over the past several days, and I have no idea if I'll be sitting on his throne or thrown from my pack while one of my brothers rises to take the title.

All I know, and all I care about, is seeing Raven's family reunited.

"I promised her I'd return, and I mean to keep that promise, I just don't know how long that's going to take. There will be a mess to clean up if I'm successful."

Delaney lays a hand over my arm, and I resist the urge to jump at the contact. I'm still not used to how friendly everyone is here. "I trust you."

"Okay," I say quietly. What a fucking burden to carry.

"The pack has put together a bag for you with enough supplies for your journey. Clothes, food, weapons."

"Thank you. I can hunt on my way. The food isn't necessary."

"You are the mate and husband of our princess, Kieran. You are one of us now. Take the food and supplies, please. It would be rude not to." She gives me a loving smile I don't think I've seen on the face of my own mother, and my heart squeezes.

I hadn't realized how much I longed for this kind of belonging until the moment I watched Raven reunited with her pack and her family.

"I need to say goodbye," I tell her, practically whispering the words.

She nods and steps aside so I can walk past her to the shop Raven disappeared into.

The shop is quiet, clean, and smells sharply of herbs and spices. Raven's soft laugh flitters through the air down a narrow hallway. I follow the sound, and find her in a backroom seated at a table with her aunt and two other pack members I don't know.

Raven looks at me and knows what's about to happen. Her aunt and the two other women leave, and then it's just me and my mate.

Raven launches herself at me with tears in her eyes as I wrap my arms around her waist and pull her to my chest, breathing in her scent. "This isn't goodbye forever. Just for a while. I will come back."

"Promise me."

"I promise."

I take her face in my hands and kiss her deeply.

"I love you, Kieran. Remember that. Remember that I'm waiting for you."

"I love you, too," I whisper against her lips.

Somewhere outside the shop, I hear people gathering to send me off. I clutch my mate harder.

"Be good," I whisper into her hair. "Don't get into trouble while I'm away."

"Me?" she giggles through tears. "I've never caused trouble a day in my life."

36

CLOSE ENCOUNTERS

RAVEN

AN ODD SENSE OF CALM WASHES OVER ME, EVEN WHEN KIERAN HAS ascended back above ground, back into the sun. I pick up the teacup my aunt Nola gave me and sniff it suspiciously. She knew this would be hard for me, so she must have slipped me something to calm me down. The thoughtfulness touches me as I leave the apothecary to find her and my mother waiting for me.

"You look tired, my darling," Mother tells me with a knowing look. My cheeks redden under her gaze. "You should rest. There's much to do."

I shake my head forcefully, when I hear Kieran's voice in my head.

'Miss me already?'

What a strange thing to be linked to him after all this time when our minds have remained cut off from one another.

'Not as much as you miss me,' I tell him cheekily.

"Ah," Nola says with a gleam in her eye. "The joys of newly wedded bliss. You and Cole were like that once you were linked," she says, turning to my mother.

207

A brief sadness colors my mother's face, but it's gone quickly.

"And soon we may be again," she says with a cautiously hopeful expression. "We'll leave you to it," she tells me, squeezing my shoulder affectionately and grabbing Aunt Nola by the arm, dragging her away.

I meander through the corridors until I find my way back to my new home. Our home. One day it will be again, I have to believe that. He *will* come back to me safely.

'Our bed is cold without you,' I think sadly as I sink down onto our unmade bed. I know it's impossible, but I swear I hear a howl somewhere far away. My chest burns with the ache of being away from him.

'It's no picnic up here without you,' he tells me gruffly. *'How could my father do this? It's even worse now, somehow, after I've seen how they all survive down there. They did nothing to deserve what he did to them.'*

My blood boils hot in my veins as I look around this small cottage, cut off from the light and warmth of the sun. King Gavin took that away from them. From us. And I know that if he had any idea that they survived down here for all these years, he wouldn't hesitate to smoke them out and finish the job.

'Raven,' Kieran's voice comes in clearly now, and I hear the pain in it. *'You didn't deserve what he did either. What you- what my mother did to you. I will make them pay, I swear it.'*

I lie down against the comfortable mattress, pull the quilt over myself, and close my eyes, imagining that Kieran is lying next to me, that we're just having a normal conversation.

'Tell me something happy,' I say, wanting very much to never think of those people ever again.

I have a real mother, one who loves me and is happy to have me around. Back in Dun's Crossing, I have a real father. He watched over me my whole life, and I wasn't even aware. Those are my parents, my family. Not the cruel King Gavin and Queen Rowena. Not the monsters who beat me until I bled, who starved me, who neglected me

'I love you,' Kieran's voice rings in my ear. *'How's that for happy?'*

I smile and squeeze the quilt against my chest, hugging it to my mark, as if I had Kieran's hand hovering there to hold.

'I love you too,' I tell him earnestly, still amazed at how easily the words form and how right they feel when I say them. *'But tell me something else happy. Give me something I can hold onto when I can't hear you anymore and I'm waiting for you to come back. It could be weeks, Kieran.'*

There's nothing for a while, and I know he must be thinking. My heart aches already, even with the tea, and I can't imagine how I'm supposed to survive this. He really will be out of range soon, and I have no idea when he'll return. The truth of it comes crashing down on me, threatening to drown me.

'When I come back,' he finally answers, *'and my father is dead, I'm going to build you a house in the forest. In a meadow, where the sun can always reach it, but somewhere we can have privacy and only have to see other people when we want to.'*

'My parents can visit, of course,' I say with a laugh.

'Not too often,' he nearly growls. *'And not for several weeks after I return. Maybe months.'*

I turn my head and giggle into a nearby pillow that's still covered in his scent. I breathe him in deeply, and the ache is dulled.

'Trouble,' he says sharply, and my eyes open wide. In the small, dark cottage, I try to imagine what he's seeing, to hear what he's hearing.

'What is it?' I ask, my heart thumping in my chest.

'I can hear my father's men. They're close. They're searching Escuro trying to find you. You have to warn your mother.'

I'm already on my feet, running back toward the village to find my mom. She's not at the apothecary, but why would she be? I've been gone over an hour. Someone helpfully reminds me how to find her cottage, and I knock briskly, hoping to get her attention.

"What is it darling?" her dark eyes search mine, and her hand cups my cheek.

"There are soldiers searching Escuro for me. Kieran says they're close."

She nods curtly and grabs me by the arm, pulling me to the town square where she gathers some of her people. I follow the crowd through a maze of tunnels, sure that I'll never learn this place. We're heading north, toward the crops. If King Gavin's troops see them, they'll know that someone is living here. Even if they can't guess to what extent, they'll keep looking. They will literally leave no stone unturned.

"Fret not, my love," Mother assures me. "We've prepared for this. We're lucky to have someone like Kieran here to give us an advanced warning."

Rather than pierce me, as I expect it to, the comment enlivens me. My mate helped us. He's given us a chance to prepare, to survive. But what happens when I can't hear him anymore?

There's no time to worry about it now. We work for hours to secure the livestock in some kind of makeshift underground barn, which the animals don't seem to like at all. Thankfully, my mother, Aunt Nola, and I are able to encourage them in a way the others cannot. The animals are not happy, but at least they seem to understand this is for their own good.

While we work, another group harvests what they can of the crops and use an intricately woven grass blanket to hide the rest. From a distance, it truly just looks like an empty field, and as long as the troops don't get too close, they hopefully won't smell the fresh fruits and vegetables.

"Skunks," my mother says, as if reading my thoughts. "They'll spray far enough away from the crops to not damage them, but close enough that no one would be able to smell anything else for miles."

I smile, thinking of my plan days ago to do the same with mine and Kieran's scents.

When the work is done, we head back underground, and Mother calls a meeting of all the residents. It's a small community, of course, so word has already spread that the soldiers are nearby.

"We don't have to hide from them," a young man calls from the crowd. Even in the dim lights, I see his dark eyes burning with passion. "We could fight them. Surely, we could take on a few soldiers."

A cheer goes up from several of the young men, but Mother fixes them with a stern glance and they go silent. For a moment, I envision how differently my life would have been if my wrongdoings had simply been punished by that glance, and not from Queen Rowena's more severe torture methods. Of course, had I grown up here, many of my "wrongdoings" likely would not have been viewed so harshly.

"There will be time to fight," Mother promises, though her voice sounds more like a warning. "For now, you will do as I say and stay hidden. We've gathered enough of our crops to last a few weeks at least. We'll remain concealed until the danger passes."

The young men nod their consent, though disappointment is etched in their faces.

'Thank you,' I murmur to Kieran, not even sure if he's still within range. There's a stabbing pain as I think of the hours I've had to spend without talking to him.

'You're welcome, my love,' comes his tender reply. *'I'll always protect you.'*

37
ONE PROBLEM DOWN

KIERAN

Kieran

I travel southwest for an entire day through the remains of Escuro, my unease growing with each new step. A monster did this to their kingdom when they were already weak and defenseless. And he lied to us about it for our whole lives. If not for Raven, I might have become exactly like him. That's what he was training me to be. He wants me to be a king exactly like him, but I'll see him dead before I allow that to happen.

The trip back will be easier now, at least, since I don't have to dodge my father's men. I head to the southwest, where I told them I'd last seen Raven- *Blanca*, I remind myself. I miss her so much already, I have no idea how I'm supposed to pretend that I hate her. As far as Father knows, I chased after her to stop her. He'd want me to torture her, to kill her, even.

The thought alone turns my stomach now. There was a time when I might have considered it. He poisoned me so thoroughly against her, telling me that all she wanted was to be the ruler of Dun's Crossing. He pitted me against her, but she was never even fighting. She simply wanted to survive. Just like her people.

I growl and try to clear my head. It's been torture not hearing from her since I warned her about the soldiers.

'We're on lockdown now,' her voice comes, faint and distant. We'll be out of range within a few miles. I'll be cut off from her.

'Be safe,' I shoot back wearily. 'But if there's trouble, give 'em hell.'

I say a silent prayer to the Goddess that there won't be any trouble. I can't bear the thought of her being there defenseless. Without me to defend her, anyway. I know she can take care of herself, but she isn't trained to fight like I am.

Just another injustice inflicted by my father. I can't help but wonder if he left her weak on purpose. To what end? Why did he raise her as a daughter if he only intended to make her feel isolated and alone? Why let her live just to give her a half-life?

'Where the hell have you been?' an angry voice shouts inside my brain. One of my father's men, I know. He's close enough to have sensed me.

'Have you seen this Goddess-forsaken place?' I growl back, channeling the man I was before Raven. A man, I realize now, I completely despise. *'I've been wandering around aimlessly for days. I lost the bitch and then got lost myself.'*

I cringe internally talking about Raven like that, but better to get used to it now around men who don't really know her. All they know is the king's deranged daughter ran away, and the king's son went after her. It's probably good to practice with them now before I have to really put on the act for my father.

'Head south. You'll find us close to the border,' he tells me. *'We'll regroup and form a plan. We're not supposed to return to Dun's Crossing without her chained and muzzled.'*

Damnit. Somehow I'll have to find a way to convince these men that continuing the hunt will be fruitless.

'Can you still hear me?' my chest clenches as I wait for her response.

I'm worn out from the trip, and I'll need to stop for the night soon. It would be nice to still hear her for just one more night. Despite being away from her all day, it was nice to know I could still speak with her. There are no caves in this flat terrain, but now that we're linked, I don't need to shift. I find a large clump of trees situated close together. It'll have to do for tonight.

'*I can hear you,*' Raven finally says, and I feel my tense muscles relax. '*It's harder to hear now, though. How far are you?*'

'*I've been walking all day. I must be nearing the southern edge of the kingdom.*'

The soft ground is much more comfortable than the hard stone of the caves, but not nearly as nice as the warm bed I left this morning. The moment I curl into a ball and lay my head down, I'm nearly dizzy with exhaustion.

'*I won't last long,*' I tell her. '*I'm so tired.*'

'*Me too,*' her voice comes so faintly. It's almost as if I'm dreaming it. '*I love you so much. Please stay safe. You carry my heart with you.*'

'*I left mine with you,*' I say with the last ounce of strength I have left.

The dawn hits my eyes far sooner than I'm prepared for, and I stretch my tired limbs, an aching soreness spreading through my body. The last few days have been hell on my body, but the journey isn't nearly over yet. Better get this over with.

'*I love you,*' I think one last time, knowing Raven is probably sleeping. Maybe she'll hear it in her dreams. The thought cheers me as I shift quickly, just to check the pack Luna Delaney gave me. There's a small hunk of bread and fresh jam inside. I scarf it down, hungrier than I realized, and shift back, eager to get this journey over with once and for all.

The mark on my neck throbs more the further I get from Raven, so much so that it nearly distracts me from the familiar stench of rogues. The fur on my back stands up as I realize it's a large group—at least seven or eight. They're in such a tight formation it's hard to tell.

The leader is a dark brown wolf who immediately bares his teeth. *Shit.* I back away, trying to show them I don't want trouble. I can't take this whole group alone, and they don't look like they're planning to show any mercy. They're all snapping at me, feral.

A silver wolf who flanks the leader runs at me, and I quickly dodge him, forcing him to run into a nearby tree. I take advantage of his distraction, charging at him and aiming for his jugular, taking him out swiftly and easily. The victory is short-lived, though, as two more immediately flank me, attacking from both sides.

I spin quickly, backing myself against the tree so I'm at least covered on one side. The three of us brawl in a haze of teeth and fur, and I'm terrified this will be my last moment on earth. After everything, I'll be taken down by a group of rogues before I can reach my father. Before I can return to Raven.

Her face snaps into my brain, and it's as if I hear her voice, telling me to fight. I know she probably can't hear me from this distance, and I'm glad for it, but the thought of her spurs me on, and I gather my strength, overpowering the two wolves and ending them. When I look back at the group, I realize only the leader is left, the others having run away sometime during the fight. I growl lowly at him, and he takes off as well, clearly not willing to face me himself.

I relax for a moment, assessing my fallen foes. It's only then that I realize one of my attackers is a black wolf. A black female wolf. A plan quickly formulates in my mind, and I grab her scruff in my teeth, dragging her up the mountain, until I find a steep cliff. I throw her body over, watching as it falls, landing with a satisfying thud at the bottom.

For a moment, I get a vision of Raven's body at the bottom of the cliff, and my heart lurches, but I remind myself that she is safe with her mother. I will not let anyone hurt her. Especially not my father. I take off at top speed, more determined than ever to reach the border by the end of the day. I need to get back to Dun's Crossing.

I send a message to my father's men that I've discovered Blanca's body. I flash the image of the dead wolf in my mind, and I hear grumbling from dissatisfied men who were looking forward to bringing her home in chains. It's hard to control my anger at their thoughts, but I must get used to it.

These men simply want to receive my father's good favor; they don't care one way or another about Raven. I tell them I'll be caught up with them soon, and we'll deliver the news to him in person. They seem satisfied that they won't be the ones who have to deliver the bad news. My father probably will be furious, but this ensures her safety, and that's all I can possibly hope for. It's one problem, at least, that has solved itself.

3 8

NEW FRIENDS

The bed that was once so comfortable now feels as hard as a rock without Kieran there. I spend the entire night tossing and turning and unable to think of anything else but Kieran's safety. It's so quiet without his thoughts in my head. How strange when I've spent my entire life without them. Now the silence is deafening.

How far has he made it now? The trip here took days, but we took the long way, trying to avoid his father's men. Maybe he's closer to home already. Maybe he's safe. Anyway, it's not like his father would punish him for running after me. For all King Gavin knows, Kieran was trying to stop me, to bring me home. Even though he's failed, he won't suffer any significant punishment, and for that, at least, I can be grateful.

When I can't take it anymore, I finally get up and get ready for the day. I have no idea what time it is; my internal clock is so out of whack underground. A clock on the fireplace tells me it's nearly 6:00 AM. I get up and stretch my sore limbs, tired as I am from all of our work yesterday.

I make myself breakfast, though I'm feeling too nauseous to enjoy it. There are so many things that could go wrong while Kieran is away. While I've never seen King Gavin be cruel to him, the golden boy, things might change if he somehow figures out the truth. Will he be able to sense it somehow?

The thought alone puts me off my breakfast entirely. I quickly bathe and dress, hoping that today will offer me more work and distraction from my worries and fears. After all, there's truly nothing I can do here. I'm safe, my people are safe, and I have to believe that soon Kieran will return with my father, and we can all be together again.

I walk to my mother's home, knocking quietly in case she's still sleeping. The last thing I would want to do is disturb her sleep. She is the pack Luna, after all. To my surprise, though, she answers the door almost immediately and is fully dressed herself.

"Good morning, my love," she says warmly, reaching out to cup my face.

I lean into her touch, still so unused to this kind of affection. Until meeting her, I didn't know that mothers could be like this. Sure, I'd seen Queen Rowena show some level of affection to her other daughters. Her real daughters. Yet even they didn't receive the unconditional love that my true mother has shown to me.

"Have you eaten?" she asks, pulling me out of my revelry.

"I tried," I answer honestly, wondering if she would be able to tell if I was lying. "I don't have much appetite right now."

She nods and grabs my hand, pulling me inside her home. She directs me toward the couch as she goes to her little kitchen and grabs a steaming mug before settling down next to me.

"When your father left, I couldn't eat properly for weeks," she tells me, a wistful look in her eyes. "It's a horrible thing to be separated from your mate."

I rub the spot on my chest, the pain suddenly in sharp focus. Mother grabs my hand and squeezes tight.

"They'll both be home soon," her voice is barely above a whisper, and there's a hopeful spark in her eye. "And there's much to do to prepare. We'll keep ourselves busy until the moment they're returned to our hearts."

I lean into her and hug her tightly, realizing that she's spent years assuming her love was gone for good. I'm lucky to not know that pain, and I hope I never do. Just the last 24 hours without Kieran have been nearly unbearable.

We sit together on the couch for a while, chatting away about nothing in particular. There's a part of me that doesn't want her to know anything about my childhood. I'd like us both to focus on the idea that if I hadn't been taken, both of our lives would have been much happier and more fulfilled. She doesn't need to be privy to the abuse I endured at the hands of King Gavin and Queen Rowena, all while I thought I was their daughter.

Later, we head down to the plaza so mother can address her people after the events of yesterday. I look around at the people assembled, their features so much more closely matched to mine. A wave of gratitude hits me out of nowhere as I realize that I've found the place where I truly belong. Finally.

"Our scouts have told me that there have been no sightings of the troops from Dun's Crossing," mother is saying, and I realize sheepishly that I haven't been listening. "Still, we must remain cautious. I'd like to wait one more day before anyone else ventures outside."

There's grumbling from the same young men who wanted to fight yesterday, and I notice a young woman roll her eyes at them. She catches me watching her and blushes then shrugs at me. I smile back at her to assure her that I'm amused and not offended.

When mother dismisses the crowd, I approach her and introduce myself.

"Oh, I know all about you," she says excitedly. "You probably didn't see me, but I was at your wedding. I'm Melany."

I expect her to hold out a hand for me to shake, but instead, she embraces me tightly. This amount of kindness and affection still overwhelms me, but I hug her back with limp arms. She invites me to her home, and I look over to mother to see her smiling her approval. Not that I think anyone here would try to hurt me, but it still helps to know that my mother is happy with my choice of companion.

Her home is a bit larger than mine, with two bedrooms rather than my one.

"I still live with my mother," she explains to me, noticing me taking in the place. "I won't be old enough to be considered mature until next month, so I haven't had a chance to experience the Haze yet. Is it amazing?"

Melany is very chatty and easily excitable, though I can't blame her. She's spent her entire life underground, and I imagine I'm the first new person she's met in ages. I appreciate her kindness and candor, even if I'm still not entirely used to someone being so friendly to me.

"I can hardly explain it," I tell her truthfully, thinking back to the moment that changed my life forever. "It's as if the Moon Goddess herself is inside of you, pulling you toward your mate."

She sighs wistfully and collapses onto her sofa.

"I can't wait to find my mate, even if it is one of these idiots I've known my entire life," she giggles. "Maybe the Haze will mature them."

I think about how drastically Kieran has changed since then and tell her that was certainly my experience. She tells me all about her family. She lost her father during the war, as did many in Escuro. Her father was a nobleman, one of my father's closest confidants.

"If not for the war, I'd probably be one of your ladies in waiting," she giggles, her spirit light and carefree, despite the pain she's experienced in her life. "Can I be in your court when you become the queen?"

Her question rattles me, reminding me of when Kieran accused me of trying to take Dun's Crossing away from him. Yet here I am, with my own kingdom promised to me one day.

"Of course you can be part of my court," I tell her fondly. "And your future husband will be given a title too." My declaration reminds me of our earlier conversation about the Haze, and I suddenly feel dumb for not wondering this before. "How exactly does the Haze work here?"

"Oh, it's very contained," she tells me. "Your mother sends out scouts days beforehand to ensure it will be safe. Unfortunately, some people still go out year after year without finding a mate. Until our kingdom is restored, we can't exactly intermingle with others."

I nod sadly, remembering how badly I wanted my mate to be someone from a distant kingdom who could take me far away from all of my problems. Interestingly, I got exactly what I wanted, though it was in no way how I expected.

"Everything is different now that you're here," she tells me happily. "You're the key to our freedom! I bet the next time the Haze comes, everyone will find their mate because we'll be able to travel again. You've set us free."

A lump forms in my throat as I consider this. I was never important to anyone in Dun's Crossing. Most of the time, I got the impression that my disappearance would be a welcome change, even though I had nowhere to go.

"We're all free," I whisper, the tears spilling over to my cheeks.

39
OLD WOUNDS

Kieran

It's late in the evening when I finally reach my father's soldiers. The sun is low in the sky, threatening to set at any moment, and my body is weary after so many days of traveling. I'm grateful to see the men have already set up their camp for the evening. They've all shifted into their human forms, with one man still in his wolf form as the lookout.

He growls at me as I approach, but I tell him who I am and he bows low.

"Is that Prince Kieran?" a man asks, and I nod, disappearing behind a tree so I can shift and dress. When I reemerge, the men bow to me as well.

"At ease," I tell them, and they relax. "Until we're back at the castle, I'm just another one of you."

It's a small group, only half a dozen or so, and I can tell that at least two of the men are apprehensive of me. Is it something I've done? More likely, it's something they dislike about my father.

"I'll take the midnight watch, if no one's claimed it," I offer, hoping to win their favor. If they don't like my father, they are exactly who I need to get on my side.

"You wouldn't rather get your beauty sleep?" one man teases, causing several to laugh. I laugh along with them, showing them how good-natured I can be.

"I'm so good-looking, I don't need it," I shoot back. "But you look like you could use a few hours."

Now the other men are laughing with me rather than at me, and the man who teased me claps me on the shoulder in a gesture of acceptance.

"You're all right, kid," he says, and I can't help but beam. Winning their approval might be easier than I thought.

We work together to make a fire, and a couple men shift back into wolves to grab us something for dinner. My mind is drawn back to Raven, and I know she'd probably have a hard time eating freshly caught game. Of course, with her powers, she could probably convince a wild rabbit to hop onto an open flame. Not that she would, she's too kind.

I sigh loudly, missing my wife.

"Uh-oh," one of the soldiers says, coming to sit next to me. "I know a man in love when I see one. What's her name?"

I have to be careful here. Even as my neck burns and my heart is desperate to tell him everything about Raven, I know I can't. Even if these men have been away from the kingdom for a while, they'll soon know about Nessa and our engagement. I swallow down the bile rising in my throat and try to be as truthful as I can without betraying the actual truth.

"Nessa," I say, hiding my disdain.

"My wife's name is Pearl," he sighs. "It's been six months since I've seen her."

"So what, pretty boy?" another soldier grunts. "I haven't been back home in two years."

"Why is that?" I ask, curious. Surely, father doesn't need them out in the field so long when there are no active wars being fought.

Clearly, though, I'm mistaken because the two men eye me warily. Any camaraderie has been zapped out of the atmosphere.

"Tell you what," I say, turning up my charm as much as I know how. "I'll tell you one thing I hate about my father if you'll tell me one thing you hate about being a soldier."

"Bullshit," the gruffer soldier says. "You'll just listen to us run our mouths, then run to your daddy to get us fired."

I raise my left hand and place my right hand over my heart.

"I swear to the Moon Goddess herself that if I tell a single lie about my father, or repeat to him anything you say, I shall be separated from my mate forever."

A furtive glance passes between the two men. This is a solemn vow to make, even in jest. No one would ever make such a swear to the Goddess if they didn't mean it. Separation from one's mate is a horrible fate. The stinging in my chest is a sharp reminder of that.

The gruffer one still looks unsure, and he leans in close to me. "How do we even know you've mated?" he asks, pointing a dirty finger in my face.

I lower my collar and show him my mark, the only proof anyone needs.

"I'm mated," I tell him. "And I miss her terribly, so the sooner I can get home, the better. In fact, it's my father's fault that we're apart right now, and I'm pissed at him for that." There, none of that was a lie. I mentally high-five myself.

"Come on, Eric," the first soldier shrugs. "He'll be the king one day anyway. He might as well hear our concerns."

The gruff soldier, Eric, sizes me up again, but he must decide that I'm good for my word, because he finally opens his mouth to speak. "I haven't been home in two years because I can't afford to take the time off," he says slowly. "My wife and son need the money, and this is the best work you can get in Dun's Crossing."

"That's not true," the other soldier pipes in. "It's much better being a soldier in the palace, but you have to kiss a lot of ass to get that gig."

Eric spits on the ground, clearly disgusted by the palace soldiers.

That's interesting. I can't help but watch with rapt excitement. I wonder if the other soldiers feel this way too.

"Well, you don't have to kiss my ass," I tell them. "I could put in a good word for you."

"Wouldn't matter," Eric says sharply. "Your daddy only picks the youngest, strongest soldiers to protect the palace. I've aged out of consideration."

"At least you've seen real action," the other soldier says. "My dad used to tell me about the glory days of the army. About the wars we used to fight. I joined up because I thought I could be something. All we do now is patrol the border and make sure no rogues get in."

"We shootin' the shit?" another soldier asks, carrying the carcass of a wild boar.

Eric and the other soldier, whose name I've yet to learn, get up excitedly and help assemble a makeshift roasting spit.

"It's been a while since we've had a meal this good," the newcomer exclaims. "You must be lucky for us, Prince."

I shrug, and we relax by the fire while the boar cooks. My stomach aches with hunger, but I'll let these men eat first. They've had it much harder than I have, and I want to continue to appeal to their good nature.

I learn the other two men in my party are Aldritch and Ifan. Phinneas has taken the first night watch shift, and the men set aside a large portion of meat for him to enjoy. Graeme and Rege are also members of this band of soldiers, and they join us a little later with fresh water.

"Rege," Eric calls once the boar is ready to eat and we've tucked in. "Ifan was asking about the war earlier. His father told them those were the glory days."

Rege, an older man with a large scar across his face spits on the ground, much the way Eric had earlier.

"No offense to yer papa, son," Rege says to me. "But that was no war. It was a massacre. Those poor people didn't stand a chance. Well, you've seen Escuro, you know."

"He burned it to the ground," I say quietly.

"Easiest way to deal with all the bodies," Eric murmurs, a faraway look in his eyes. He's only with us physically, his mind is clearly back in Escuro, witnessing those horrors over again. "And to make sure no one ever rebuilt there."

"It was hell," Rege nods. "And I'd still go back to that than patrol the border for a threat that doesn't exist."

"What do you mean?" I ask him, curious.

"The Escurians are dead," Eric says loudly. "Your sister is dead too. Wasn't she trying to find Escuro? Maybe the very land is cursed."

I shudder as I remember the image of the dead wolf at the bottom of the cliff, and I try to swallow the lump in my throat. As far as they know, I hated her. I absentmindedly scratch at my aching mark and remember that she is safe and sound with her mother.

"Maybe it is," I agree quietly. "Or maybe it's full of ghosts."

The men laugh at this, and we turn the conversation to more pleasant matters. By the time we all settle down to sleep, I can barely keep my eyes open, but building these relationships is vital if I'm going to take a stand against my father. There will clearly be no love lost once he's gone. Then I can go back to my wife, to hold her in my arms again.

40

COMPLICATIONS

Raven

Melany and I spend the entire day together, and I even have the opportunity to meet her mother, Anya. She invites me to dinner, which I happily accept, not eager to go back to my empty home. When I do eventually leave very late that evening, I realize that the ache of being away from Kieran has been survivable today.

I think of my mother and how she's had to push through the pain of being separated from my father. She managed to survive these last 20 years without him, and I know it's because of this community. It's such a stark difference from the coldness and backbiting in Dun's Crossing. There's a genuine warmth and camaraderie among all of the people here. I'm sure it would exist even if the war hadn't forced them underground. There's a true kindness here that cannot be faked.

I manage to sleep, grateful to not have any dreams, or at least not to remember them. I have to spend so much of my conscious energy pushing away thoughts of Kieran running into trouble, I'm not sure if I could survive hours of nightmares. The morning brings a sense of refreshment, though, and I'm actually excited for the day.

Melany and I have already made plans to spend the day together, and I dress quickly, stopping by my mother's house to let her know. She's happy for me, telling me she's always liked Melany. She tells me we'll be returning the animals above ground today, so Melany and I can venture outside if we'd like.

It's hard not to feel a little sheepish that I've taken fresh air so much for granted in my life. These people have spent decades underground, some never allowed to venture outside. There are children in Escuro who've never felt the sun on their faces. I send a silent prayer to the Moon Goddess that Kieran and my father return quickly so we can begin to rebuild. My people deserve it.

Melany and I join a crew that helps lead the animals back to their above-ground stables. The poor things seem so depressed when we arrive, but by the time they're back settled into their normal environments, they seem much happier.

I press my forehead against a cow I've just penned and whisper, "Thank you for your cooperation."

When I open my eyes, I see Melany watching us, giggling.

"What?" I ask, suddenly feeling very self-conscious.

"I do that too," she says, her smile widening. "Whenever I have to use an animal's assistance, I thank it."

"Could you hear me?" I ask. I whispered my thanks, so she shouldn't have heard me, unless we were mind-linked. I surely would have realized it before now if that were the case.

She shakes her head. "I just know the look," she explains. "Those of us who have the gift to communicate, we all interact with the animals the same way. I'm used to getting weird looks when I'm especially affectionate with a squirrel."

I can't help but laugh at this. Anyone back in Dun's Crossing would call me a witch, but Melany understands me. Of course, she does. She has noble blood.

"My gift isn't as strong as yours, though," she tells me a little sadly. "I've practiced for years, but it takes me longer to make connections with the animals. I've only just mastered the art of getting a horse to follow me out of a stable without any external communication."

"I didn't even know I could do it," I tell her honestly. "I don't think I could before the Haze, but then it was like the animals were suddenly doing everything I wanted. The mice in my old castle were particularly helpful."

I tell her about my escape from my room as we walk through the fields, enjoying the warm sunshine on my skin. For a while, she doesn't say anything, and I look over to see that she's staring at me. I blush, feeling silly. I'm still not used to talking about this with anyone, and even someone who also has the gift is shocked by what I'm saying.

"I've heard stories about your father," she tells me. "His skills with animals are legendary. You probably got a lot from him."

"What about your father?" I ask too quickly, then internally cringe. "I mean, if you don't mind sharing. Sorry, I shouldn't have asked."

She smiles, though, not at all embarrassed.

"From what my mother has told me, he was fondest of bears. When he was in his wolf form, he loved to wrestle with them to get stronger. I can't even imagine being around a bear, let alone wrestling with one."

We both laugh at this, and she tells me the bears mostly stick to the mountains now, since King Gavin burned down so much of the forest.

"So many of the animals left," she says sadly as we walk through lush trees and overgrown grass. "And how could we blame them? Our water was poisoned, and the forests were burned down."

Anger swells in my chest as I think of the many injustices King Gavin inflicted on my people, and my hatred of him rages like the fire he set to this kingdom. My thoughts turn to Kieran, and I feel something akin to jealousy. If he really does manage to kill his father, he'll get the revenge my people desperately deserve. I can't help but think it would be more satisfying if we could witness his demise ourselves.

"Do you want to meet Bridgit?" Melany asks brightly, completely oblivious to my abrupt change of mood. "We keep her just over here."

I follow her down a path to an overgrown clump of trees. Melany steps between two large bushes, and on the other side I see a small enclosure that's been well concealed by the thicket of leaves.

Bridgit, I assume, is a large cow who's happily munching on grass, not remotely bothered by either of us. She looks up with boredom as Melany approaches, but I notice she tilts her head toward Melany as if she's expecting a scratch behind the ears.

"Bridgit is my favorite milk cow," Melany tells me fondly as she indeed scratches the animal behind her ears. "Well, technically, we've retired her. She prefers her solitude, so some of the men helped set up this enclosure so she can be alone as much as she wants."

Bridgit turns back to her grass and chews slowly, clearly unbothered by our presence in her space, and we leave her to it. We're near the hidden entrance to the tunnels when someone calls Melany's name.

We turn to see a girl chasing after us, but she stops abruptly when she sees me and her face turns sour.

"Everything okay, Sybil?" Melany asks kindly, but Sybil doesn't take her eyes off me.

"I was going to ask if you had plans today, but it's clear that you're too busy with the cows."

The way she looks me up and down, I assume she is lumping me into that group. I almost want to laugh in her face. Of all the insults and verbal abuses I've received in my life, this is probably the least offensive.

"We're all done," Melany responds, her kind voice unchanged, though it's clear she's trying to stick up for me. "Have you met Raven yet? We're just going down to wash up and get some lunch."

"My appetite has suddenly vanished," Sybil sneers, before brushing past us and running toward the tunnel entrance, disappearing inside in the blink of an eye.

"Don't pay her any mind," Melany tells me quietly, as we follow in her path, though much more slowly. "She's usually a very cool and level-headed person, but your presence has upended her life plan."

"How, exactly?" I ask, as we climb down the ladder back into the darkness of the tunnels.

"Her mother was your mother's head lady in waiting before the war. Her whole life, Sybil's just kind of lived with the assumption that she would be crowned queen one day because of how close she is to your mom. Your presence means she'll never see that dream come to life."

I can't help but laugh as I'm again reminded of how threatened Kieran used to be at the thought of my trying to steal his crown. I've given so little thought to ever ruling, yet I continue to threaten those who care about it so much.

"I'm sure she'll come around," Melany continues, her kind nature unable to fathom Sybil's jealousy.

"I'm sure," I agree, though I don't mean it.

Melany doesn't know what I've been through and the kind of cruelty I've experienced from my supposed family, from Queen Rowena, even from Nessa and her crew of sycophants. While Sybil may not be nearly mean as they are, I've seen how these kinds of things escalate.

I put it out of my mind for the rest of the afternoon, though, deciding it's a much better use of my time to enjoy Melany's company. When I'm finally on my own again, though, I can't help but remember Sybil's sneer. I really hope she's not going to cause me any problems.

41

MOURNING

The sun is high in the sky when we finally reach the castle. After days of travel, my home should be a welcome sight, but I can only think of the lives that were lost to build this place. This is not a home, I realize for the first time in my life. It's a monument to my father's ego. This castle exists because he's willing to kill innocent people to keep his power. My throat burns with anger at the thought.

All I want to do is go to my room for a hot shower and a long sleep in my bed. I'm so weary from the long journey, I could probably stay there for days without moving. Maybe I will, but first I have to see my parents. They'll want to know what happened. Surely, they'll have heard the news of Blanca's death by now.

In a way, she did kind of die. The girl they raised, the girl they abused, is long gone. She knows the truth now and her real name. She'd be their greatest threat if the Goddess hadn't made her my mate. Now, I'm their greatest threat because I'll never allow her to put herself in danger. It's my job to finish this.

When I enter my father's study, Mother looks at me distastefully.

"Darling, we're so happy you've arrived, but could you not have taken a moment to bathe?"

She wrinkles her nose, and it brings me a bit of joy. I'm happy to be ruining her perfect image of what her home should be. She deserves no less after how she's treated Raven all of these years.

"I apologize, Mother," I lie, bowing to her for added effect. "It's simply that I wanted you to hear the awful news from me before anyone else could relay it to you."

This is another lie, of course. I know the news of Blanca's death spread like wildfire once I told the closest pack of soldiers. I need to see the looks on my parents' faces when they hear it from me, though. It will add fuel to my growing hatred, making my task that much simpler. However, I do want to make my mother suffer through the indignity of my uncleanliness for a few moments longer. I settle in one of my father's chairs and begin relaying the story.

"Blanca was out of her mind when she left," I explain, laying it on thick. "She was saying all kinds of nonsense about our family, about you, Father,"

He nods and rolls his eyes. Mother's attention is focused on the pristine chair I'm dirtying.

"I chased her as far north as I could, and I was hot on her tail for most of the journey. I would have had her in my clutches in a moment, but I was attacked by a flock of birds. Have you ever heard of such a thing?"

I notice father pale a bit, but his expression remains unwavering. My mother is likely not listening at all, probably deciding if she can burn this chair once I've vacated it.

"Well, the attack lasted for hours! It seemed that once I'd managed to get my way out of the flock, more birds would arrive. It's truly unnatural behavior, is it not, Father?"

He's fuming under the surface, I can tell. His breathing is slightly labored, and I see the tell-tale signs of a flush creeping up his neck. He's imagining Raven sent the birds, I know it. But he obviously isn't going to admit that to me. After all, he thinks I still think of her as my sister. If he suggested that she was controlling the fictional birds, he'd have to admit the truth about her parentage. He won't crack that easily.

"Finally, I managed to escape the deranged beasts, and I'd lost all sight of her. It took me two entire days to track her down, and she clearly got herself lost. She'd strayed too far east and somehow ended up in the mountains."

"Yes, well she always was a stupid girl," Mother mutters under her breath.

"Rowena," Father hisses lowly, and I'm sure I wasn't supposed to hear it.

Have they always been like this, I wonder. Were they always so cruel and hateful toward her, and I was just too blind to see it? Even worse, I participated in it. My stomach is sick at the thought.

"All of this to say," I continue, "when I finally caught up to her, it was too late. She must have lost her footing on the rocks and slipped to her death. She's gone."

They barely respond at all. Mother looks at her nails in boredom, and my father's face doesn't change at all. He's still just looking at me with a stoic expression.

"Yes, well," he says, clearing his throat. "That is, of course, terrible news."

"Terrible," my mother echoes in a monotone. "Terrible news that we did receive prior to your arrival. So, perhaps now might be a good time for you to freshen up?"

"Mother, you've just lost a child," I tell her, my voice thick with false concern. "Perhaps you're in shock. Should I call for the royal healer?"

"I am quite well," she tells me, her posture stiffening even more, if that's possible. "She was a nuisance to me in life; she won't be a nuisance to me in death as well."

"What your mother means," Father interjects, "is that, while it is a great sadness to us, there was always something off about Blanca. After all, she met her fate while trying to find a kingdom that is long gone. She was mentally unwell. Thank the Goddess she can now be at peace, and so can we."

"Yes," Mother nods enthusiastically. "We can be at peace and not speak of this nasty incident again."

She looks at me expectantly, waiting for me to get up and acquiesce to her demand that I bathe. Perhaps it's petty of me, but I settle into the chair further, pretending to be contemplative.

"Well, of course, we all know what a nuisance she could be," I answer slowly. "Goddess knows she's been a thorn in my side since the day we were born. But the people of the kingdom aren't aware of her shortcomings in life. Would they not find it odd if we don't mourn our dead princess?"

Mother sighs heavily and rolls her eyes, and my father shoots her a weary look.

"You are right, of course," he says to me, though he's still looking at her. "She was our daughter, after all. We do need to acknowledge her death so that the people may mourn her for an appropriate amount of time and move on."

"How much did the people really like her, anyway?" Mother snaps. "It's not like she was some beloved princess like Candace or Ingrid. There will hardly be wailing in the streets over her."

"No one is suggesting a public gathering, my love," Father tells her through clenched teeth. "But we must at least announce to the people about her passing."

"And say what, exactly?" she gripes, her hand going to her head in frustration. "Our useless daughter died a useless death? I'd rather we just never speak her name again."

"Then let us speak just of her one more time, and then the matter is settled," my father says in an authoritative voice that she cannot refuse.

I nod and finally get out of the chair slowly, telling them that I'll let them hammer out the details while I wash off my travels. Mother so visibly relaxes it's almost comical, though everything about the scene makes my blood boil.

If Raven truly were dead, a thought I can barely stomach, I would be devastated. They can't even pretend to be a bit sad that their supposed daughter is gone. Would I have even noticed their reaction if this had happened before the Haze? Probably not, which sickens me further. I was awful to Raven our whole lives and treated her only fractionally better than they did. I'll spend the rest of my life trying to make it up to her.

The steam of the shower helps dull the ache in my chest, and I wash off the days of grime and the disgust my parents have left me with. I could stay in the shower forever if I weren't so damn tired.

I'm just about to crawl into my bed when there's a knock at my door. A moment later, a paper is slipped underneath, and I pick it up, reading it quickly. It's a royal proclamation sent to the entire kingdom.

"It is with great sadness that we announce the death of Princess Blanca. She left home to find her mate and died on the journey. Our brave son, Prince Kieran, followed behind and tried to save her from herself, but was ultimately unsuccessful. At this time, we appreciate you giving us our privacy as we mourn as a family."

I roll my eyes and crumple the paper, tossing it in the wastebasket where it belongs.

42
POWER INSIDE

THERE'S A LOUD KNOCK ON MY FRONT DOOR, AND I'M SO EXHAUSTED I have to actually take a moment to remember where I am. Thankfully, my eyes have gotten very used to the dark, and I manage to make it to the door without turning on any of the lights. Mother is on the other side with a steaming mug of tea and a smile on her face.

"Morning, sunshine," she says cheerfully as she pushes the mug into my hands. "I hope you've enjoyed the last two days of reprieve because that's the last you'll have for a while."

I stare at her blankly, but she's still watching me cheerfully. When I make no motion to move, she claps her hands loudly, causing me to jump.

"Let's not waste the daylight. We've got to work on your training!"

She hurries me to get dressed, and I quickly down the tea she's provided and make some toast to eat. She tells me I'll need my strength, which is a bit worrisome. I'm not exactly sure what my "training" will entail.

A few moments later, she leads me through the winding tunnels until we're ascending to an open field.

"We're in the middle of the old kingdom," she tells me. "We don't often see any travelers come through these parts because it's so far into the kingdom. Plus, we're quite a distance from the forest. It'll be a good test to see how far your powers extend."

"What am I supposed to do, exactly?" I ask hesitantly.

I was never allowed to participate in any of the tactical training my siblings went through. Fake siblings, I remind myself. Though it's been easy to accept that Kieran isn't my brother and King Gavin and Queen Rowena aren't my parents, it's been harder to reconcile that the other three aren't my siblings. Especially Candace, who was finally showing me kindness right before I left.

"We'll start off easy," Mother encourages me. "All you have to do is call some birds to us."

The words have hardly left her mouth when I look up to see a murder of crows approaching us from the forest. She turns and sees them too, nodding and smiling her approval. They arrive and circle over head, before she tells me to send them back home. Immediately, they are taking off again in the direction they came.

"Very impressive," she compliments me, and I can't help but blush a bit. It's been a rarity to receive praise from anyone. "Now, I want you to call squirrels here. When they arrive, I want you to direct them to go back to the forest and collect acorns for you. Let's see how well you can handle multiple tasks."

Again, the words have barely left her mouth when I look toward the forest and see an animal approaching. It's scurrying toward us, so tiny in the distance. A few more join it, and a dozen or so squirrels all hurry toward us until they've all assembled in front of us, waiting for instructions. They're so cute, I can't help but bend down and scratch their little heads. They crawl toward me, each desperate for my affection.

Mother clears her throat, and I'm reminded of my task. I think of what I need, envisioning them going back into the forest to collect acorns to bring me. The squirrels incline their heads toward me as if they're listening, and then take off back toward the forest.

With the travel time, it does take them several minutes, but soon there is a small pile of acorns assembled at my feet, and the squirrels are all looking up at me. I'd almost swear they're smiling, so pleased with themselves for a job well done. I look over to my mother, who rolls her eyes and nods.

"You may pet them now," she laughs, as she bends down to give a squirrel one of the acorns it's just brought us. "It's important to show them your gratitude," she tells me. "This ability is a rare gift, and we do not take it for granted. When the animals help us, we want them to know that they are appreciated."

When all the squirrels have received an acorn and an ear scratch, I direct them back to their homes. Slowly, they all leave, and I smile contentedly. What I thought once was a fluke is actually a very important skill that I can control. I've never felt so accomplished in my life.

We spend nearly an hour in the sun, calling different animals to the field and seeing how well I can control them. I get a herd of deer to run around us in a tight circle, defending us from anyone who might be watching. I call two large black bears down from the mountains, and we watch as they gently feed seeds to a flock of ducks who've come from a nearby pond.

It's all a bit overwhelming, knowing that I've done this, yet the pride swells in my chest nonetheless. When the animals have all dispersed, Mother smiles brightly at me and pulls me into a long embrace.

"You've done so well, my love," she whispers into my ear. She pulls back slightly and I see a misty look in her eye. "You are every bit the natural your father was . . . *is*," she quickly corrects, wiping at her eyes. "Goodness, it's still strange getting used to the fact that he's alive."

"And he'll be back soon," I assure her, squeezing her arms.

"Luna Queen Delaney," someone calls from behind us.

We turn to see a young woman approaching. She leaves me to speak to the woman, then walks back to me with an apologetic look.

"I'll be right back, darling," she promises, patting me softly on my cheek. "The job of a queen is never done!"

"Is everything okay?" I ask, concerned.

"Nothing for you to worry about," she says wearily. "Just a silly horse who doesn't like to stay locked up. I'll be right back."

As she leaves, I sit on the warm ground and lean back on my elbows, turning my face to the sun. I've nearly dozed off when I hear footsteps approach and I open my eyes expecting to see my mother, but instead Sybil is standing there, her arms folded.

"You must be feeling so proud of yourself," she jabs, her snarky tone such a sharp contrast to her words. "I've been able to control animals since I was five. You aren't special."

"Good for you," I mutter, closing my eyes and trying to ignore her.

"It's such a shame you couldn't go back to your kingdom with your mate," she practically growls. "Nobody wants you here."

"Tell that to my mother who's been waiting twenty-one years for me to return," I shoot back, not even bothering to look at her. She wants to get a rise out of me, but I can't let her.

"And what a disappointment that you came without our king," she goes on. "You're too useless to even get that much right."

She's clearly not taking the hint, so I open my eyes and sit up to face her. Clouds have started to gather, and the sun is barely visible now through the darkness.

"Is there a point to all this?" I ask, my voice coming out colder than I intend. "You can dislike me all you want, but it's not going to change the fact that I am back, and I am the rightful heiress to the throne."

"You'll be a horrible leader," she spits just inches from where I'm sitting. I quickly move to avoid it, and stand to face her as she continues. "What do you even know about us? What do you know about leading the people of Escuro? We'd be better off if King Gavin came back and killed us all."

Thunder rolls somewhere in the distance, and the wind starts to pick up. Her hair whips around her face as she leers at me, her disgust evident in her eyes.

"Now who doesn't know what they're talking about?" I can't help the anger that's rising in me. "You have no idea how cruel that man is. If you did, you wouldn't wish him on your worst enemy, and you certainly would never wish that on these beautiful people."

In my mind, I'm not even speaking to Sybil. Instead, I'm directing all my anger at Queen Rowena, at my siblings, at Nessa, at King Gavin himself. She's a combination of every person who's ever hurt me, her words a cocktail of every insult and abuse ever thrown at me.

The wind is really blowing now, and fat drops of rain start to fall from the heavens. Sybil shields her eyes to look up at the sky as the droplets start coming faster. A bolt of lightning flashes in the distance, and the ground shakes ominously.

"Girls, get back inside," I hear and look to see my mother running toward us, ushering us toward the tunnel entrance. We rush in, and she slams the hatch behind us as another peel of thunder shakes the earth.

43
UNEXPECTED ALLIES

THE WALK TO THE DUNGEON IS COLDER AND DARKER THAN I REMEMBER. It's always been dingy, sure. Truthfully, I've only ever come down to chastise Raven for being here when she shouldn't or yell at her father. *How did she stand it*, I wonder. The stench alone is enough to send people running in the opposite direction.

The guards stand at attention when I round the corner, but I motion for them to stand at ease. They look understandably surprised to see me. I wasn't the "twin" who spent all my free time here.

"The king would like me to deliver a special message to that bastard, Blake," I growl out.

They nod with amused understanding. He's likely their favorite to beat. It makes my blood boil. No king deserves to be locked up in the dungeon of another. If these men knew who it truly was they were torturing, they'd probably beg for mercy. They will beg for mercy when the time comes, unless they wake up and choose the right side.

"Discretion is of the utmost importance," I tell them quietly. "You understand. There are certain things my father prefers to not be overheard."

The men smile again and nod before one whistles to call another guard over. He conveys the message that I need privacy with Blake, and the newly arrived guard has the same smirk on his face. He simply nods, and they clear out, leaving me alone in the dank space.

One guard lingers behind. "He's back in his cell now, Sir."

I nod, and he shuffles away.

I know my way to his cell very well now. He's standing under the same high window, the way he always does, and I'm struck immediately by how similar he is to Raven. How could I not have noticed? Of course, I couldn't have comprehended the truth before, even if I had made the connection. Yet, it's evident in his long dark hair, even in the way he holds himself. There's a raven perched on his windowsill, and he seems to be in deep conversation with it.

Weeks ago, I would have considered that a ludicrous idea, but now it's just another puzzle piece fallen into place. My heart lurches at the thought that this is probably his only way to stay sane. It's all so fucked up. I look down at his feet and notice the silver shackles clinging to his ankles. I will make this right as soon as I can.

"Mr. Blake," I say lowly, pretty certain he already knows I'm there. He has that funny way about him.

He turns to look at me, the cuts and bruises on his face still evident, though they've healed a lot since the last time I visited him on a hospital bed. The bruises, especially, are in various shades creating a kaleidoscope effect.

"I wondered when you would come down to see me," he says calmly, his lips twitching as if he's about to smile. "It was such a shame to hear about the death of your sister."

Now he's smiling fully, and I know he knows the truth. The guards probably delighted in telling him about Raven's death, knowing she was the only one who would ever show him kindness. He's much too wise to have fallen for it, though. Maybe he senses her still, all these miles from where she is. If that's the case, I envy him that.

"Yes, it's a shame Blanca is dead," I say loudly, without any emotion. "And I'd like to discuss your role in it."

This is mostly for the guards' benefit, just in case they're listening. I wink at him, and he nods. He shuffles over to the bars, pained by the small movements. I can't disguise my own wince, and the fury continues to build. He didn't deserve this. It's just one more injustice to level against my father.

"I left Raven safely with your wife," I tell him more quietly, and his eyes light up brightly. "It was a beautiful reunion."

He clings to the bars when he reaches them, though I can't tell if it's from physical exertion or his excitement to hear about his beloved wife.

"How is she?" he asks, his eyes quickly filling with unshed tears.

"She's very well," I confirm, wishing I could show him how well she's adjusted to life, even without him. Though, I don't know if that would hurt him or help him. "She misses you terribly, but she was ecstatic when she heard you're still alive. And I intend to ensure you stay that way."

He rests his forehead against the bars and sighs, his body seeming to relax.

"And tell me, should I be calling you son, now?" he asks in barely more than a whisper. I nod curtly.

"We were wed before I left. Perhaps we'll celebrate again when you can join us," I can't help the smile that spreads across my face as I remember my wedding. I can't wait to get this over with so I can return to her. That's all that really matters anymore.

"That's a bold promise," he answers solemnly.

"It's one I intend to keep," I assure him. "I promised your wife and mine. Your kingdom needs you, and so does your family. This is no place for a king."

He chuckles quietly to himself, and I realize that this is likely the first time in 20 years that anyone has ever referred to him as what he really is.

"Well, I'm certainly glad you've taken the blinders off your eyes, finally, to see the truth," he breathes out. "It's been frustrating to see you two circling each other without understanding."

"Did you know?" I wonder aloud, the thought just occurring. "Before the Haze, I mean. Did you know that she and I would be mates?"

"I'm not psychic, Kieran," he chuckles again. "However, I do know your father went to great lengths to make sure that very thing could never happen. Having his kingdom allied to mine was his greatest fear. He never could accept that we are stronger as allies than as enemies."

"That's why we have to get rid of him," my voice breaks, though my will is still resolute.

His eyes meet mine briefly, and they flash with something I don't entirely understand. Revenge? Anger? Fear?

"How exactly do you plan to do that, son?" he asks, his tone almost condescending.

"I'm still ironing out the exact details," I answer honestly. "But he has to be overthrown. And he has to be killed."

The look in his eye is clearer to me now. It's doubt.

"You could never do that, son," he says gently. "Despite his flaws, he is still your father. You could never do that to him."

He pities me, I realize. For what I have to do, and the belief that I don't have the strength to do what it takes. Somehow that crystalizes my need to do it even more.

"With all due respect, Your Majesty," I bite out sarcastically, mentally chastising myself for being rude to my father-in-law, "you have no idea what I'm capable of. And you haven't been home in twenty years. You have no idea how hard it is there, how your own people have to live because of what my father did to them. He can't be allowed to live."

He bristles at this, clearly angry at the mention of his home. Truthfully, I don't know exactly how much of the damage he bore witness to before he was forced to make a deal with the devil to save his daughter. What I do know, though, is that he underestimates how much I care.

"While I appreciate that, Kieran, it takes an awful lot more than concern for others to have the stomach to take a man's life," he says in a quiet, yet urgent whisper. "Especially the man who raised you."

"The man who abused my wife for twenty-one years." I growl as quietly as I can so as not to alert anyone else. "The man who enslaved her father and left her mother thinking she was a childless widow. The man who burned an entire kingdom to the ground out of fear. I can and will kill that man because I have to. The future of my family depends on it."

I don't realize until he takes a step back how close I've gotten to him through the bars. I'm practically spitting in his face, and I mirror his movement, taking a step away and shaking my head to right myself.

"I believe you will do what you set out to do," he says with a resolute nod. "What can I do to help?"

I slide down to the ground, my body half turned toward the cell so we can still talk privately, but this will be a much longer conversation. He settles down across from me, on the other side of the prison bars, and we discuss my plan. I wait with some anxiety for him to tell me I'm just being a stupid kid, that it will never work, but he doesn't. He listens patiently and asks questions when he doesn't understand. It hits me suddenly that he respects me, and that's the greatest gift he could possibly give me.

44
A STORM IS BREWING

RAVEN

THE SKY IS BRIGHT AND CLOUDLESS WHEN WE EMERGE THE NEXT morning. The storm from yesterday left the ground soaked through, and mud squishes under my shoes as we make our way back to the center of the field.

Mother's been strangely quiet all morning as if she's lost in thought. I can't seem to shake her out of it no matter how much I try. I asked her many times if anything was wrong, but she only looked at me with amusement in her eyes that I couldn't decipher. Though I have no reason to be afraid of her, I can't help but be reminded of Queen Rowena's cruelty.

We finally stop walking at roughly the same spot we were in yesterday. The forest to the north of us, the mountains to the east. She picks up right where we left off, instructing me to call animals to the center of the field.

The air is much hotter today, especially with the sun beating down on us mercilessly. It's soaking up all the water from the ground and creating a humidity that is nearly unbearable. Even the animals seem to be affected by it, coming to us more slowly and seemingly grumpier. If they could speak, they'd probably chastise us for making them leave their cool, shady homes.

Still, they're compliant, obeying my every silent command. It's still strange that I can just think something into reality. It makes me wish I could bend the weather to my will. A stray cloud would be a mercy from the unseasonable warmth. Even a light breeze would make a huge difference.

No sooner have I thought it than I feel a small breeze kick up around my arms and face. It's gentle, barely a whisper of wind, but it cools my sweating brow. I close my eyes enjoying the sensation, and when I open them back up, I notice a wispy cloud is now covering the sun.

I look at my mother, who is staring back at me in wonder. I don't understand why, though. We haven't done anything more extraordinary with the animals than yesterday. When she catches me looking at her, she nods her head, as if she's answered a question that I didn't ask.

"Remind me when you first started noticing your powers, Raven." Her tone is demanding, rather than questioning.

"It wasn't too long after my birthday," I answer, picturing the moment I had a cat attack Ness and Kieran. "This woman at the castle was bothering me, and there was a cat nearby watching us. I wanted it to help me, to get her away from me, and suddenly it was scratching her, and when Kieran came to help, it scratched him, too." I do remember the raven from the prison that happened that day, too, but I don't think that was me.

Mother nods, her eyes darkening.

"Did they all bother you?" she asks sadly. "Your adopted family, I mean. Did they show you any kindness at all?"

I think on this for a moment, grateful that the steadily increasing wind is bringing tears to my eyes so I can explain them away when they start to fall.

"No," I answer honestly. "Not a bit. I had a small room with a tiny bed while my siblings had luxurious bedrooms and private living rooms to host their friends. Not that I had any friends to host."

"Why do you think that was?" she poses, a pitying look on her face. "Why do you think you didn't have friends?"

I know she doesn't mean for it to, but her question stings. Why didn't I have friends? I think of Nessa with her mean girl minions. She didn't like me from the moment she arrived in Dun's Crossing, and she made it abundantly clear that no one who was kind to me could be friends with her. Even the girls who'd just ignored me most of my life started to bully me.

"A diplomat came to live with us, and he brought his daughter," I explain. "She didn't like me from day one, and she made sure no one else did either."

"Did you do something to her?" mother asks, tipping her head to the side. I'm again reminded of Queen Rowena, and I try to even out my breath. This is my true mother, she isn't trying to hurt me. She just wants to understand. I shake my head.

"I never did anything to her. I tried to befriend her, but she wasn't interested. From the moment she arrived, all she cared about was making my life a living hell."

"And your parents allowed it?" Her face is like a mask to me now. It must be as hard for her to ask me these questions as it is for me to answer.

"The king never really paid me much mind unless I was in serious trouble," I explain, no longer needing to refer to King Gavin as my father. "The queen doled out punishment pretty regularly. The mean girls were nothing compared to her. She probably encouraged it."

Mother nods, looking down at the ground, her face impossible to read. I look up to the sky as the tears start flowing freely from my eyes. More clouds have gathered now, blocking out the sun completely. It looks like another storm is coming up.

"Some parents believe physical punishment is the best way to discipline misbehaving children," mother says, bringing my attention back. "It's hurtful, of course, but they're just doing what they think will best get their children in line."

Her words twist like a knife in my heart. She has to know that I never misbehaved. I never did anything to deserve what they put me through. I've been able to see that clearly now. For so many years I wondered why I had to be so bad, why everything I did was so unbearable for my family. The moment I left, I realized that I'd done nothing wrong. They hated me because I wasn't theirs. And I hate them because they stole me from those who would have loved me.

"They were not punishing me for bad behavior," I shoot back, my voice thick with emotion. The wind is picking up more now, but I ignore it. I step closer to my mother, trying to get her to understand. "I never acted out, never stepped a foot out of line, but they treated me like I was willful and unlovable."

Tears fall rapidly from my eyes now, rolling down my cheek and falling to the ground. A moment later, rain begins trickling from the sky, as if the sky itself is weeping for me.

"I was not a bad child," I say louder, trying to be heard over the whistling wind. "I was not disrespectful or disobedient. All I ever wanted was to be loved and accepted, and they punished me for even that."

The mask on mother's face seems to break, and I realize there are tears falling from her eyes too. She closes the distance between us, wrapping me in her arms and holding my head against her shoulder.

"Of course you weren't a bad child," she whispers gently into my hair. "I'm sure you were a perfect child. I'm so sorry I wasn't there to protect you."

"You couldn't have known," I sob against her. "I know you would've been so much kinder to me."

She releases me and takes a step back, grasping both of my hands in hers. She turns her face to the rain falling from the sky, and I do the same, letting the droplets wash the tears from my face.

"But look what you can do, my love," she slightly yells over the sound of the storm, a tinkle of laughter in her voice.

I look back at her confused, and the rain abruptly stops. Does she mean? She couldn't possibly.

"You did that, Raven," she confirms, looking me in the eye, then back to the sky, where the clouds are starting to disperse.

I drop her hands and step away, looking back up at the sky in amazement.

"I did that?" I whisper back to her, no longer having to compete with the wind. She simply nods.

"You are amazing, my darling," she says back, her voice cracking with emotion. "When it stormed yesterday, I had my suspicions, but you've just confirmed it. You have a very rare gift, indeed."

A shudder runs through me as if I'm afraid of my own capabilities. Maybe I am a little, but I also feel powerful in a way that I never have.

"You'll need to learn to control it, of course." Mother nods her head, again as if answering a question no one asked. "We'll start small. Try to send a bolt of lightning down to that tree," she instructs, pointing in the distance.

I envision it in my head, and a moment later, a flash of lightning engulfs the tree, sending its inhabitants scurrying and flying away.

"Sorry," I scream to the animals and birds. Mother just laughs, pulling me against her and squeezing tightly.

45
WHO CAN YOU TRUST?

An hour later, I'm walking back toward my room when I see the absolute last person I can stomach at the moment. Nessa. The moment she locks eyes with me, she's running toward me, latching herself around my neck. Her little minions titter in excitement behind her. Were they not there, I'd maneuver to the side and let her run into the wall.

Instead, I reluctantly wrap my arms around her and pull her against my chest. Even before I knew the truth about Raven this was torture. Now, my mark burns so much I nearly cry out in pain. Even that can't compare to the nausea I feel churning in my stomach.

"My love, you're home," she screeches, planting sloppy kisses on my face. It takes a concerted effort not to wipe them away. "I've been so worried about you!"

I push her away gently and smile at her awkwardly.

"No need to worry, darling, I'm home now," I say in my smoothest, most charming voice. "I can't wait until we can put all this nastiness behind us and finally wed."

261

My mark burns sharply, and I have to reach up to grab it, smiling at her sheepishly. There's a blazing look in her eyes that nearly screams at me, "Make this look convincing or I'll make your life hell."

My life is already hell without Raven, but I'm never going to admit that to her. If all goes well, a day will soon come when I never have to see her again. It can't come soon enough, in fact. I don't need any extra complications, though, so I gently grab her hand, raising it to my lips for a tender kiss. I could be on the stage for the performance I'm putting on.

"I'm so sorry that I must again depart from you, my love, but I'm meeting with my friends to discuss their roles in the wedding," I explain.

Her eyes light up in excitement, and I hear her friends giggling again. Having a mate is exciting on its own, but being mated to the future king is more than they can imagine. Some of them eye me as if they wish they owned the hand I just kissed. I'm very much looking forward to never having to see them again either.

"Until we meet again," she giggles, and lets me go. Not a moment too soon.

I nearly stumble down the hallway, trying to put as much space between us as possible. When I'm finally out of her sight, I wipe my face on my sleeve, rushing back to my room so I can properly wash my hands and face. My lips tingle unpleasantly from kissing just her hand. There's no way I could have ever gone through with marrying her. I'm beyond grateful I no longer have to.

When I feel satisfied that there's no trace of her scent left on my skin, I decide I probably should hang out with my friends. We aren't actually going to talk about the wedding, of course. There's nothing I want to talk about less with them. But I'm able to mind-link with them and let them know that I want a guy's night.

We decide to raid the kitchens, and that's where I meet with them. Each gives me a half hug or a clap around the shoulder, and I feel grateful for the true bond we all have. Taner loads up his arms with desserts while our friends Whyte and Lucias gather up whatever savory dishes they can find.

The kitchen staff glare at us, as we're clearly in their way and stealing food that was likely intended for something else. I could not possibly care less, though. Stealing food that is likely meant for my parents somehow doesn't bother me at all. It's just another one of the small rebellions I'm becoming increasingly comfortable with.

I grab as many bottles of the good liquor I can carry, and we head off to my private drawing room. All of my siblings have one. Not Blanca, of course, not that she was my sibling. I try desperately not to think about her or I'm bound to spill a secret to my friends that I'm not ready to share. Instead, we eat, drink, and catch up on everything I missed while I was away on my travels.

Taner is sickly in love with his mate, to no one's surprise. She's all he can talk about, and the longer he goes on about her, the more we all groan. Poor Lucias didn't even find his mate, so he understands the draw the least of any of us. Part of me wonders if his mate isn't up in Escuro herself. Whyte adds a bit about his mate as well.

My chest aches thinking about Raven there without me. I wish I could just tell my friends about her, but I'm not sure how much I can trust them just yet. We've been friends since we were children, but what if I slip the wrong thing to them and my plan unravels? It's too important to see this through. Until Taner says,

"Goddess, we're all assholes. We haven't even told you how sorry we are about Blanca's death."

I look up at him in surprise, a little uncomfortable with his sincerity. Partly because I know she isn't dead, but mostly because I'm still not sure how to react to the news. Everyone knows we weren't the closest siblings, that at most times we basically hated each other. Still, the pain from my mark throbs just imagining her death. I must be contemplating my response for too long because he keeps talking.

"I know you two weren't exactly bosom buddies, but she was still your sister. Your twin, at that. That can't be easy."

His words split open something inside me, and I know that I can't keep lying to him, to any of them. If I'm going to have to put on a mask for everyone else in the kingdom, it's the least I can do to be real with the people who care about me the most.

"Do you remember what your father told you about Escuro?" I ask him, testing the waters to see how far I can take the truth.

Taner blinks at me in surprise, but he leans forward in curiosity. He nods at me silently. Our friends look between us, wanting to be in on the secret, so I fill them in on what Taner told me several days previously. It feels like years ago. Whyte and Lucias listen to the tale in open-mouthed horror.

"Can I trust you three?" I ask them when I conclude my story.

They nod solemnly.

"You know you can trust us with your life," Taner confirms, and it's all I need.

"Blanca wasn't my sister," I breathe out in a rush. "She's the princess of Escuro."

They stare at me for a beat before they burst out in laughter. It's not until they notice the deathly serious look on my face that they realize I'm not joking with them.

"She's also my mate," I growl when they've finally stop laughing.

The tension in the room is palpable as they digest the truth I've just told them. Finally, Lucias breaks the silence.

"Your mate died?" he whispers in horror. Maybe he understands better than I give him credit for.

"No," I shake my head quickly. "She's not dead; that was just a ruse. But I need my parents to think she is."

They're still clearly confused, so I tell them everything. I tell them about the Haze and how, understandably, disgusted I was at first. Taner smirks at this, but he says nothing as I continue to speak. I tell them about Nessa's blackmail and Raven running away. I leave out the graphic bits, the parts where Raven and I literally couldn't stay away from each other, but I give them the gist of our journey. How I misled my father's soldiers so we could make it safely.

"Why did you do all that for her if you didn't think she was really your mate?" Lucias asks, but it's Whyte who responds.

"When it comes to your mate, your body does things your mind can't comprehend," he answers solemnly. Lucias just shrugs and relaxes back against the sofa, pouting a bit that he's still without a mate.

I continue my story, telling them about the wreck that I found Escuro in. In my mind, I still see the scorched trees and the devastated forest. I imagine the slightly sunken look on the faces of the Escuro residents. What was done to them was inhumane, and it's my father's fault. I tell them all this, praying to the Goddess that they understand. Because I can't do the rest without their help.

They're still intently listening when I go over my plan to stop my father. Whyte wiggles in his chair uncomfortably, and Lucias is still relaxing against the sofa, though Taner is on the edge of his seat. All three stare at me in wide-eyed wonder.

Finally, I ask them the question that is burning in my chest.

"Will you help me?"

4 6

ELECTRIC CHARGE

The next day, Mother guides me through a few more exercises to help me master my powers. It's not much harder than controlling animals, but the feeling ripples through me like an electric charge. I still just think something and watch it happen, but the elements seem to shift around me and inside of me. It's like nature and I am one being, communicating with each other. It's profound and a little shocking.

When she's satisfied with what I can do, she heads back down to the tunnels for some lunch. She invites me to join her, but I'm not ready to go back into the darkness just yet. It's like the sun is calling to me, telling me to take every opportunity to hone my skills. She promises to bring me something in an hour if she doesn't see me and starts walking back to the hidden entrance.

I stand in the field and will a cloud to start pouring rain next to me. A solitary black cloud gathers and big, fat raindrops fall rapidly in a small, contained circle. I walk around it, marveling at how well contained it is. I stick my hand into the downpour, the icy cold water feeling like a treat in the heat of the day.

I splash some of the water on my face and will the cloud to stop raining and cover the sun. The cloud moves, growing slightly bigger to accommodate to block all the beams, and the earth around me becomes darker and cooler. I imagine a gentle breeze again, remembering how nice it felt earlier, and the wind starts to blow.

None of this makes any sense to me, but I don't question it. There's no doubt that I'm the one controlling this. Mother told me earlier that only a handful of people from Escuro could control the weather since the beginning of our history. It was a gift that would skip generations and generations with no rhyme or reason.

"But it chose you," she'd told me, her eyes shining with unshed tears. "My brave, darling girl, you are special."

My heart swells now as I think of her words. Queen Rowena would have called me a "freak" or a "witch." She probably would have arranged to burn me at the stake if she thought she could get away with it without the villagers asking questions. But then, King Gavin wanted me for my potential powers, so he probably wouldn't have let her.

My mind drifts to Kieran, and I feel guilty that I've barely spared him a thought all day. The electricity inside of me has been the only thing I could focus on for hours.

I miss him terribly now, though, and I notice the wind picks up a biting edge.

"Stop," I say out loud, almost involuntarily.

The wind stops altogether, the air deathly still around me.

I'll have to get used to this, I know. Mother told me that a lot of this power is attached to my emotions, and I'll have to find a way to control them so that I don't accidentally cause a natural disaster. Still, I can't help but wonder how far these powers extend. Could I create a blizzard all the way down in Dun's Crossing? Could I cause a tornado to wipe the kingdom away the way King Gavin tried to wipe all of my people away?

No, I'm nothing like him. I'll never be like him, and I realize with delight that I'm much stronger than he is. His fear will be his down-fall, and that's enough to lift my spirits. I send the cloud away so that the sun can shine on the field again, but I keep a calm breeze blowing to cool off the day.

I'm not sure how much time has passed when I hear a voice. I turn around, thinking my mother has come to bring me lunch, but it's Sybil, much to my annoyance. Melany is a few paces behind her, shouting something to Sybil that I can't hear.

"Leave it alone, Syb," I finally hear Melany call.

Sybil stops and turns around, whispering something in her face. Then, she turns on her heel and starts marching toward me, a scowl on her face.

"It isn't fair!" she screams, stopping just a few paces in front of me. I see her chest rise and fall with quick, angry breaths.

Melany comes to stand next to me, pulling on my arm to get me out of Sybil's clutches, but I'm not afraid of her.

"What isn't fair?" I ask, raising an eyebrow in challenge.

"You don't get to steal my crown and my gift!" she whines. "My mother told me those powers run in our bloodline. They should have come to me!"

"You know that's not how the Goddess works," Melany tells her in a soothing manner. "She bestows gifts how She sees fit."

"Then she's blind," Sybil screeches. "You are nothing but a spoiled princess from a kingdom that tried to destroy us. You're the last person in the world who should have received those powers!"

The laughter escapes me before I can stop it. She thinks I'm spoiled? She has no idea what I've escaped from. She wouldn't last a day with Queen Rowena.

"That's enough," Melany shouts back to her. "You're out of order, Sybil. Raven hasn't done anything wrong, and if you tried to get to know her instead of letting your jealousy cloud your judgment, you might actually like her."

"I could never like you," Sybil spits as if I'm the one who suggested it. "You were raised by filth, and you deserve to rot in that kingdom like the filth that you are."

Anger boils up inside me with such a blinding flash, I don't realize at first that there actually is a blinding flash of lightning happening in front of my face until I hear Sybil scream in horror.

"You bitch!" she screams, putting distance between us. "You could have killed me! You're a psychopathic bitch!" Her dress is burned, and her hair stands on end. Thankfully, I didn't hit her directly enough to kill her. I would feel bad about that.

She turns to run, but I'm still blinking at the spot on the ground where the lightning struck—mere inches away from where she'd been standing. My anger is replaced by guilt. I had no intention of doing that. I bury my face in my hands and groan before I feel arms wrap around me.

"That was the funniest thing I've ever seen," Melany whispers conspiratorially in my ear. "Don't tell her I said so, but her face went as white as a sheet!"

"Melany," I squeak. "That was horrible! I could have really hurt her!"

I uncover my face and look her in the eye, trying to convey that I'm truly sorry for what I just did.

"You could've," she agrees. "But you didn't!"

"I wasn't even in control," I confess, taking a step back from her in case I accidentally strike her too. "She just made me so angry and I . . ."

"Nearly electrocuted her?" She laughs.

I shoot her an admonishing look.

"I'm sorry, but that was incredible!" She giggles, grabbing my hand and squeezing tightly. "I've heard legends about people with the gift, but we've never seen it in person! It's been nearly a hundred years since the last weather bender died."

I shake my head as I digest this information. King Gavin must have never heard this legend, or he would have killed me as a baby just to be safe. He was scared enough of our ability to communicate with animals.

"Raven?" Melany calls, and I realize I've not been listening. My heart beats so loudly it's all I can hear. "Raven, it's really okay! Her pride is hurt more than anything. She's going to be fine."

I turn toward my new friend and pull her into a hug, feeling overwhelmed and a little afraid of myself. She rubs my back as my breathing starts to slow, and my heart rate returns to normal. She stays quiet for a long time, but she must sense I'm feeling better because she pulls away from me and starts speaking.

"You are amazing, Raven," she tells me firmly. "You have a power that other people in Escuro only dream about. It's why Sybil is so angry. But you were chosen by the Goddess, and She chose you for a reason."

"What do you think that reason is?" I whisper, feeling completely unworthy of it.

She smiles brightly at me, pride etched in her features. "Because the Goddess believes in restoration," she answers reverently. "She's seen us suffering all these years and heard our prayers. Now you're here, and you're the strongest of all of us. I've said it before, and I'll say it again. You have the power to free us. Literally."

The electricity surges within me, mixed with a feeling of hope.

"And I bet there are some other people you could use that skill against," she says with a gleam in her eye.

I picture King Gavin in my head, and I know she's right. Kieran's gone home to finish the job, but if he somehow fails, I'll be able to step up and end this once and for all.

47
THE ESCAPE PLAN

KIERAN

I STARE BACK INTO THE BLANK EXPRESSIONS OF MY THREE BEST FRIENDS, my heart pounding in my chest so loud I'm sure they can hear it. This might have been a bad idea. A really bad idea. Even though these are the three men I would trust with my life, I've asked them to stomach a lot in the last hour.

Plus, I've told them I plan to kill my father. Their king. That's treason of the highest order, even if I am the prince. If we were to fail, their lives would be on the line. It's a big ask. What was I thinking? Part of me wants to tell them I'm kidding, that this whole thing has just been an elaborate joke. I open my mouth to speak, but I'm cut off.

"Of course we'll help you," Taner finally says, breaking me out of my spiraling thoughts and breaking the palpable tension in the room.

My head snaps up, and I look him in the eye, seeing nothing but sincerity looking back at me. He's all in. I turn to look at Whyte and Lucias, who both nod solemnly.

"It's messed up," Lucias says. "I've heard rumors about your father, of course, but I never thought he could be capable of that."

My eyes widen in surprise, and it occurs to me how sheltered I've been. My entire life has been shielded by this false belief in my father, the pride of his legacy and what it would mean for me as the future king. Naturally, my friends would never share with me what they've heard or what they truly think about him.

"We deserve a king who cares about everyone," Whyte breathes, his body deflating as if he's been waiting years to express the thought. "Things in Dun's Crossing are far worse than he'd have people believe. We need a strong leader."

He nods curtly, and I hear the words he didn't say. They need me to be that leader. This is as good of a place to start as any. The four of us huddle closer together as I go over the plan King Cole and I discussed earlier that day, mentioning there are other soldiers who will help us. Lucias goes a little pale listening to the finer points, but I have faith in what we've come up with. It's going to work. It has to work.

"So all of this relies on us breaking that old kook out of prison?" Whyte asks, earning a stern glare. He quickly realizes his mistake. "I mean, King Cole, erm, your father-in-law, that is."

Taner whistles lowly. "It's not going to be easy," he grumbles. "Those guards are not friendly."

"You wouldn't be either if you had to be surrounded by that stench all day," Lucias shoots back with a shudder.

"And poor Albatross," Whyte whispers with some pain in his expression. "Could you imagine having your . . . you know . . . chewed off by–"

"All the more reason we have to be careful, and we cannot divert from the plan, okay?" I cut in firmly, trying to rein their attention back in. I love my friends, but they can be idiots when they get off-track.

They nod sheepishly, and we bide our time for the next few hours as we wait for nightfall. The time finally comes, and my stomach is in knots. This is the beginning of everything. If this doesn't go right, the entire plan falls apart. Most importantly, though, it has to work so that I can keep my promise to Raven and Queen Delaney. It's time for Cole to return to his family after all these years.

We leave my private sitting room, strolling slowly through the castle as if we're just screwing around on a regular night. No one even notices us, or they pretend not to care because it's easier that way. We've been known in the past to stir up a little trouble. I'm grateful for it now, as most of the servants just rush past us without a glance.

Once we reach the dungeon entrance, the three of them post up against the wall, pretending to be deep in conversation. I leave them there as lookout while I descend into the deep darkness.

"Come back for more?" a guard smirks at me. "The old fool has been silent since the moment you left. You must have done a number on him earlier."

I put on my best wicked smirk and simply nod as I slip past them. As I walk by, I pretend to trip on a loose stone, and when one of the guards reaches out to steady me, I swipe his keys off him. He doesn't even notice, too focused on the well-being of his future king. This is almost too easy, but I don't delude myself. The hard part is coming.

I start walking down the long, dark corridor toward King Cole's cell. A few of the other prisoners look at me in interest, some even throw out verbal insults, but I ignore them as I focus on my destination. He's sitting on his bed when I arrive, waiting for me. I quickly look around to make sure no other guards are around before I slip the key into the lock and slowly turn until I feel the gears give way.

I pull the padlock off of the door, placing it on the bed as soon as I enter the cell. I kneel in front of King Cole, searching for the right key to undo his shackles. When I look up at him, there are tears in his eyes. The gravity of the moment sinks down onto both of us. This will be the first time in over 20 years that he will go outside. In a few days, he'll see Raven again and be reunited with his wife after all this time.

He swipes at his eyes, and I swallow hard, trying to bury my own emotions. We stand together and he puts his hand on my shoulder, nodding to me that it's okay. He's okay. There's a rustling noise, and I look over to see Albatross standing in the doorway, a murderous expression on his face.

"Well, well, well," he spits out, "I knew that sister of yours was a freak, but I never expected to see you showing kindness to a prisoner, Prince Kieran."

He says my name like it's a curse, and my heart sinks. We can't have failed that quickly. I try to say something, to come up with a convincing lie off the cuff, but I'm saved by the scurrying sound of rats. He hears it too, and his eyes widen in horror. No wonder; it did not end well for him last time.

He rushes past us, pushing himself against the wall, pleading with King Cole to call them off. I use his distraction to punch him squarely and knock him out. My hand stings from the collision, but as his head hits the floor, I know he won't be a problem for us. I nod at King Cole, and he tilts his head to the side.

I watch in fascination as the rats, who were just about to enter the cell, turn around and scamper in different directions. Though I've borne witness to Raven's powers, it's not something I think I will ever fully get used to.

We leave the cell together, quickly making our way back to the entrance.

"Can you send your rats to distract the guards at the top of the stairs?" I whisper to him. "Maybe leave them with their balls intact, though?"

He chuckles at this.

"That was all my daughter's doing, I'm afraid. She didn't know how to control them well enough." He sighs happily, not sounding remotely sorry for Raven's actions.

My heart swells as laughter rips through my chest. Of course it was. I look down to see the rats are organized again, running up the stairs to hopefully clear a path for us. We hear the sound of disgusted screams as the rats reach the guards, and I smile to myself. We're almost home free.

When we get to the landing, though, I realize that our luck has run dry. The two guards have indeed fled, but there is a battalion of soldiers waiting there for us. I realize that Albatross must have sent them a mind-link before I knocked him out.

The soldiers standing in front of us seem to have a stronger consistency than the usual prison guards. They don't seem to notice the rats scampering over their heavy boots. Instead, their eyes are focused on us, weapons raised. I look at King Cole, who has his eyes trained steadily on the soldiers. His face is an unreadable mask, but there's fire in his eyes. He looks at me and nods once, firmly. We haven't gotten this far to just get this far. We're going to have to fight our way out.

48
LIGHTNING STRIKES

EVERY TIME I CLOSE MY EYES, I SEE LIGHTNING STRIKE DOWN JUST inches from where Sybil stands. Guilt gnaws in my stomach no matter how much I toss and turn in my large bed. If Kieran were here, he'd hold me, tell me that it's all okay. He'd probably laugh about it. I can almost hear his laughter in my mind, and it sends a pang through my heart.

I miss him so much it's eating me alive. Each day I hope that the pain of his absence will somehow lessen, but it's only grown with each passing hour he's gone. How has Mother endured this for all these years? It's only been a few days, yet my heart feels like it doesn't fit inside my body anymore. It exists somewhere out there with him, wherever he is, whatever he's doing now.

I sit up in bed and throw off my covers, giving up on any pretense that I'll get to sleep tonight. If I'm not feeling guilty about what I did to Sybil, I'm missing my husband so much I can't breathe. The walls feel like they're closing in around me. I quickly dress and head out the door before I consider the wisdom of my plan. It's the middle of the night, but I really need my mother right now.

It's a blessing to actually have a mother worth needing, I don't take that for granted. Never once did I wake up in the middle of the night wanting Queen Rowena. She was the subject of many of my nightmares, in fact. My true mother will make this all feel better; I'm sure of it.

When I reach her house, there's a light shining through the window. Thank goodness. I would feel even guiltier if I woke her up. I tap lightly on the door, but she throws it open immediately, as if she's been waiting for me. She opens her arms, and I fall into them, unable to stop the tears that fall.

She guides me to her sofa where we sit for a while. She holds me and strokes my hair while I sob. Everything about her is comforting, from her touch to her scent. She exudes warmth and love, which I'm still getting used to. I didn't know true love until recently, and it fills all the cracks in my heart that my "family" created in Dun's Crossing.

When I've finally stilled, my mother gently prods.

"What has you so upset, little one?"

I sit up and wipe my face, not wanting to look at her as I admit what I did to Sybil earlier.

"I lost control earlier today," I admit tersely. "Sybil confronted me in the field, and I couldn't stand it. I sent a bolt of lightning down just inches from her."

To my utter surprise, Mother laughs. It's a light, tinkling sound that somehow makes the whole room feel brighter.

"Her mother did tell me there was some sort of incident," she says with a delighted sigh. "Truthfully, love, she's deserved a wakeup call for years. The way she prances around this place thinking she's going to be the next queen."

I snap my head up in surprise. "Did you not choose her to be your successor?" I ask curiously. She laughs again. "Darling, I don't plan on dying any time soon!"

She pulls me into her side and begins stroking my hair again. I sense a sadness coming over her as she continues speaking. "What you have to understand is that we are survivors here. We've done the best we can with what we've been given, but it doesn't leave much time to plan for the future. Any notion that Sybil had of being queen one day was entirely her own."

I snuggle closer to Mother until I can hear her heart beating in her chest. Our hearts beat in the same relaxed rhythm, and I sigh happily against her. This is love. This is what I've been waiting for my entire life.

"What's going on in your head, my darling?" she asks me after a while.

"It isn't worth sharing," I tell her honestly. It's still hard for me to talk about my abuse to her. There's nothing either of us can do to change it, and it would only make her upset. I never want to make her sad if I can help it.

She grabs my chin firmly and makes me look her in the eye, though, and I know that she's going to pull it out of me if she has to.

"There's nothing you can't share with me, love," she tells me earnestly. "We've already lost so much time together, I never want you to feel that you have to keep things from me."

Tears fill my eyes again, and I nod. "I can't help but think about my old family," I admit reluctantly. "They ignored me in the best of times and were unbelievably cruel in the worst. Queen Rowena was only happy when she was making my life miserable. I had no one."

I finally meet her eyes to see that they're glassy from her own unshed tears. She strokes my face gently then grabs me and pulls me against her again, holding me while we both cry.

"There's nothing but evil in their hearts," she says bitterly. "If I had known you were alive and under their care, I would have traveled to Dun's Crossing myself to get you back. I could kill them for how they treated you."

"And how they treated Father," I say glumly.

"How they killed half of our kingdom," she remarks, and I see another bolt of lightning behind my eyes. Only this time, it isn't a guilt-ridden memory. I have an idea.

I pull away from her once more and look her seriously in the eye.

"We can kill them," I breathe out, excitedly. I can tell by her confused expression that she needs more. I stand and start pacing the room as I think through my plan.

"If Kieran succeeds in killing King Gavin, they're going to come after him," I say breathlessly. "He'll lead them right to us, and we'll trap them at the river. I can send down lightning and electrocute them all. It'll be over. We'll finally be free!"

I stop pacing to garner her reaction. Her face is pale, but there's an unmistakable light in her eyes.

"I don't know, darling," she says warily, wringing her hands. "It's a risky plan. There's so much that could go wrong."

"Yes, but there's so much that could go right," I say, kneeling in front of her and grabbing her hands. "Mother, they killed off half our population without blinking. They kidnapped me and treated me like I was filth my entire life. They imprisoned Father and beat him mercilessly. They deserve this."

Tears stream down her face as she considers my words, but her posture is stiff and resolute.

"Our warriors aren't ready for a fight," she argues. "They have as much passion and desire as you, my love, but they don't know how merciless the soldiers from Dun's Crossing can be."

"But I do," I say, moving to sit beside her. "And Kieran does. We'll lead the charge right alongside them. Besides, there won't be many left to fight if this works."

"It's a big if, darling," she says, cupping my face. I look down in disappointment, my excitement waning. "I'm not saying no, I just need time to consider it."

I nod, but I can't help but feel the sharp sting of rejection. She forces me to look into her eyes, a kind expression meeting me.

"It's a good plan, Raven," she says gently. "Please don't think that I have any doubts about your abilities. But as queen, I have to make sure that my people are safe, no matter what."

She hugs me tightly, and I sigh against her, realizing that she really doesn't want to hurt me. But I do want to hurt King Gavin. I want them all to suffer for taking me away from this wonderful woman, for destroying our family, for destroying our kingdom.

"Do you want to stay here tonight?" Mother asks when she sees me yawn. "It is quite late."

I shake my head, though, because I need the walk back to my house to think. We say goodnight, and I slowly make my way through the tunnels of my new home, my anger toward King Gavin growing with every step. With equal measure, I will for Kieran to come home to me safely so we can finally end this war and begin our life together.

When I make it home, I crawl into bed, my spirit lighter as I think about the look on King Gavin's face when he realizes he's failed. I imagine my father returning with Kieran and our kingdoms united at last. Finally, I imagine the swift end I will put to the soldiers from Dun's Crossing, and I can't help but smile. It's my last thought as I crawl into bed and finally succumb to sleep.

49

FINALLY FREE

King Cole and I lock eyes, and for a moment, I see his fire. Despite his physical weakness from the harsh beatings he's recently received, he's ready to fight.

'*A little help here,*' I mind-link with my friends. The dungeon doors swing open, and Taner, Whyte, and Lucian storm into the space behind the soldiers, already in their wolf forms.

The air fills with the sound of terrified screams as soldiers at the back of the formation are unexpectedly attacked by my friends. This distracts the soldiers at the front enough for me to knock one out and steal his sword for Cole. I pull my own sword and get into a tussle with another soldier on the frontline.

It's pandemonium around us as my friends tear into the soldiers on one end, and Cole and I engage in hand-to-hand combat on the other. A flock of birds swoop in through the windows and start pecking at the eyes of the soldiers we can't handle. All I can hear is the sound of flesh being torn and mangled, the scent of blood so heavy in the air it turns my stomach.

I don't stop fighting, though. I can't stop. If I show these soldiers one moment of weakness, I'm a dead man, and so is Cole. As my sword clangs with that of yet another guard, I see him stab a soldier out of the corner of my eye. The man goes down swiftly, tripping one of the soldiers fighting behind him.

The crowd is finally thinning out with just a few stragglers left to get through before we can safely get out of the dungeon. King Cole's gift is certainly helping as the rats attack from below and the birds from above. We wouldn't have had much of a chance of success without them. I manage to catch my breath for a moment while I watch Whyte take down the last remaining guards. I collapse briefly against the stone wall, exhausted from the battle.

"We have to go." Cole grabs me by the shoulder and pulls me upright, whispering encouragement in my ear as he pushes me forward over the pile of bloody bodies.

"Whyte and Lucias will get you through the gates," I say loud enough for all of our party to hear. "You'll need to shift the moment you're off the property, and do not stop running for a moment."

Cole releases me, and we stop briefly so my friends can shift back and dress quickly. When we're reassembled, we go over the plan one more time. The dead guards in the dungeon are already a big snag in the plan, but Cole is free from his prison, at least. We just need to get him off the grounds, and he'll be safe. He and I both know he'll be much better protected in nature

When we're satisfied with the next steps, I say a heartfelt goodbye to Cole. I know I'll see him again soon, and this will all be over, but I can't help but worry about his safety. He's my father-in-law, after all.

He takes my face between his large hands and squeezes gently.

"I could not have asked for a better mate for my dear Raven," he tells me, his eyes shining with pride. "These next moments will be difficult for you, Kieran, but you have the strength within you. Don't forget that you don't fight alone."

He embraces me tightly then takes off with Lucian and Whyte, as Taner and I head back to my private chambers. If this plan is to work, I can't be seen with him in the castle. Thankfully, we don't encounter anyone else on our way to the throne room. That's all the better because we're both covered in blood.

I don't breathe fully until Whyte mind-links with me to let me know they've cleared the gate with no issue. Surely, most of the grounds guards were called as backup and are now dead in the dungeon. There would've been little chance of any guards stopping Cole when he could've called on any number of creatures to help him outside of the castle. I tell Whyte and Lucian to head back to the castle and get changed. For their own safety, they can't be connected to the escape in any way.

Barely two minutes later, I get the message I've been waiting for.

'Where the hell are you, son?' my father asks through a mind-link. *'Find me. Now.'*

I look over to Taner and nod.

"Showtime," I tell him, and he grins wickedly.

We enter the throne room, the evidence of our fight displayed proudly on our clothing. I take pleasure in the disgusted look on my father's face as I track my blood-stained shoes through the throne room. He's probably thinking he'll have the flooring completely replaced after I leave. Any inconvenience I can cause him feels like a victory.

"What's the meaning of this?" he snarls, indicating our clothing.

"It was awful, King Gavin," Taner interjects, his tone bordering on weepy. Of the two of us, he's the better actor, so I agreed to let him take the lead. "I was reading a book in the library when I heard the soldiers heading down to the dungeon. I mind-linked with one of the guards, and he told me that someone was trying to stage a prison break."

"And where were you during all of this?" my father asks, tuning his ire on me. His expression is equal parts fury and curiosity.

"Well, as soon as Taner knew what was going on, he mind-linked with me and called me in for backup," I tell him with a definitive nod. "As you know, my room is quite far from the dungeon, so it took me quite some time to find him."

"And by the time he did, half the guards were already dead," Taner cries pathetically. "It all happened so fast."

"What exactly happened?" Father seethes, his frustration palpable. "How is it that two dozen of my best guards are now lying dead in the dungeon?"

"It was Albatross," I tell him confidently. I would've left him out of this, but he just had to complicate our plan by showing up. He's dead anyway; there's no harm in sullying his name further. "I can't say for sure what got into him, but somehow, Blake convinced him to set him free."

"He what?" Father barks, his face nearly purple with rage. He stands up and begins pacing the small platform his throne is set upon. "Where is Albatross now?"

"I'm sorry, Father, I killed him," I say, feigning shame. Technically, it's not a lie. "I managed to corner him when I arrived, but it was like he was possessed. I threw him against a wall thinking maybe he would snap out of it, but he fell and hit his head. There was so much blood."

"It's no matter now," Father snaps, putting his hand up. "Saves me the trouble of executing him for treason. But what of Blake?"

"It was such a bloody mess," Taner cries. "There was so much fighting, it was hard to see anything. But he managed to create confusion among the guards and slip away."

"He's gone," I confirm. "I checked through the bodies myself. He wasn't among them."

Father begins pacing again, muttering to himself as he goes. When I'm sure he's paying us no mind, I conspicuously give Taner a thumbs up. He played his part to perfection.

"Perhaps all is not lost, Father," I suggest, as if I've just had the most ingenious idea.

He stops pacing and gestures for me to continue.

"After my brief . . . adventure," I look pointedly at Taner to communicate to my father that I'm keeping up the ruse about Blanca, "I know the path to Escuro well. That must be where he's headed, right? Let me pursue him and bring him back here."

"No," my father shouts gruffly. "He's had enough chances. When you find him, you must kill him."

"Fine," I agree, nodding sharply. "I will find him, and I will kill him."

"You won't go alone," he tells me, not a suggestion but a command. "I trust you to lead the charge, but you will take an army with you. The man is more dangerous than you can possibly understand."

"Do you not believe in my ability to fight him?" I challenge. Maybe it's risky to be so bold in this moment, but Father is so distracted by his fury he doesn't notice the attitude I'm giving him.

"I believe in you, Kieran," he tells me firmly. "But look what he's done. He took out two dozen guards on his own. It's a miracle you and Taner are not counted among the dead."

He steps down from his platform and loosely embraces me, leaving some distance between us so that my bloodied clothes don't come in contact with him. He nods to Taner, an indication of his approval.

"Lead the troops, and bring the bastard to justice," he commands. "Show me that you have the makings of the king I know you'll be."

"You can trust in me, Father," I tell him, my anger burning brightly in my chest. "You will see exactly the king I'm going to be."

5 0
ASSEMBLE THE TROOPS

I watch Mother as she paces back and forth among the line of troops. No one would call this an army. It's more like a rag-tag team of poorly trained teenagers. They aren't all so young, but they are scrawny, pale, and a little gaunt. It's evident that many of them have not seen the sun in ages. Even outside in the bright light of the sun, most of them squint, unused to the bright glare of natural light.

"Raven, a little help please?" my mother calls to me.

I imagine a small cloud covering the sun, and the next moment it's there, shading the worst of the early afternoon brightness.

Mother still isn't fully certain that my plan will work. I can't blame her. We have to take into account a lot of variables. Her main concern is that, if I fail, there's no backup. Her "troops" can take on a small band of old, overweight soldiers if the need arises–thankfully, it hasn't yet. My plan involves a much scarier possibility. We might be met face to face with the full force of Dun's Crossing's warriors. They're battle ready at all times. While the people of Escuro have been hiding underground for the last two decades, the warriors of Dun's Crossing have stayed fit and sharp.

Then there's the sheer number of them. Every man in Escuro has the option to join the army when he turns 18. Some of them even lie about their age so they can join earlier. It's considered the highest honor in the land to be chosen. The army is never lacking in numbers, and those numbers include the strongest, healthiest, most loyal members of the kingdom.

There are maybe 100 soldiers from Escuro, and none of them have proper battle training. They don't have a general; they have my mother. That isn't to say mother isn't excellent at what she does, but she's never fought in a war either. She's experienced great loss from war, sure, but she's never had to fight. She's never had to kill.

Still, she and my Aunt Nola have done their very best, and what Escuro's soldiers lack in size, they make up for in speed and cunning. Then there is the small contingent like Sybil and Melany who can control the animals. They are exactly who King Gavin fears the most, and Sybil is definitely the angriest person I've ever met. She'll rip his head off herself if Kieran doesn't do the job.

I watch from one side of the field where Mother taught me to use my gifts. Mother guides them through sparring drills, hand to hand combat and weaponry. She makes the group with gifts fight extra hard, warning them that, in the heat of the moment, they may not necessarily be able to rely on their gift to help them. She shoots me a meaningful look as she says this. She still isn't sure about this, I know.

"With all due respect, Luna," a young guy shouts to Mother, his chest heaving with exertion from his sparring practice. "We're ready to fight. We're thirsty for it."

"Be that as it may, Braden," she responds with a withering look that could shoot daggers through the young man. "You've never seen the warriors from Dun's Crossing. I have. You haven't experienced their savage cruelty. I have. While it's all well and good to feel passion, to feel a hunger for the fight, even, that isn't enough to win a war."

"We aren't just hungry for it," Sybil spits. "We're bloodthirsty. It's time that Dun's Crossing pays for what they did to us."

A loud chorus of cheers rings through the air as a palpable energy rips through the crowd.

"And what if they kill you all?" mother asks gravely. "What if your bloodthirst isn't enough to beat them?"

"The animals will help," Melany says sweetly. "They've helped before and they will again. And King Gavin won't be able to poison half our people this time."

'Mother,' I call through our mind-link. *'We've got this. I know you're afraid, but we're ready for the fight. We can't keep hiding underground. Our people deserve to live in the sun.'*

She turns to look at me over her shoulder, shielding her eyes from the brightness that's still shining through the wispy clouds.

'You know these soldiers better than any of us,' she answers reluctantly. *'Do we have a shot at defeating them?'*

'Only if you trust me,' I tell her firmly.

Mother nods to me and claps loudly, bringing everyone's attention back to her.

"All right then," she tells them decidedly. "We don't want to waste all of our energy on sparring when there's an actual war to fight. Raven is going to walk us all through our plan of attack."

I stand, surprised at this, and walk over the group, ignoring Sybil's characteristic snarl. There's nothing she can do or say to get to me now. When Escuro is free, and the soldiers from Dun's Crossing are defeated for good, she won't have any choice but to respect me.

"We're going to need the strongest of you near the river bank," I tell them. "If any of the soldiers manage to survive the crossing, we'll need our best line of defense ready to take them out."

We spend the next several hours organizing our soldiers and going over the plan over and over again. By the end of the day, I'm sure I can recite it in my sleep. I can't help but feel a swell of pride at how well most of the soldiers listen to me. They trust me, and they know that I will fight as hard as I can to lead them to victory.

When Mother is finally satisfied that everyone has a good handle on the strategy, she finally dismisses everyone, reminding them to rest up and be on their toes. We don't know exactly when the warriors will come, but I know they will, especially if Kieran succeeds in his plan of killing King Gavin.

Mother and I walk toward the river to assess the best hiding spots. The bank is full of overgrown brush that will easily conceal our fighters. Back just a few feet is a lush part of forest that wasn't burned down by Dun's Crossing. Wildlife abound inside, our backup should we need them. I'm more confident than ever in our success. I just wish Mother felt the same.

"I know what you're thinking," she says from behind me as we pick our way through the thicket. "You think I don't believe in you."

I stop walking and turn to face her.

"That isn't it, exactly," I say hesitantly. "You've shown me more faith in the last several days than I've received from anyone in my entire life. But you seem resigned to think we have no hope in winning."

She grabs my chin gently to look up at her.

"You have no idea how hard it was to lose you," she whispers. "How hard it was to lose your father. I went from being a queen of a vibrant kingdom, a wife, and a mother, to having absolutely nothing at all. Those people took away my kingdom and my family in one fell swoop. I'm not sure that I can take losing what little I have left."

I cover the hand she has on my face with my own then grab her other hand with my free one and squeeze gently.

"When this is all over, you're going to get it all back," I promise her. "You have me back, Kieran is going to bring Father back, you have Kieran as a son now, and when we defeat the soldiers, you'll have your kingdom back. They'll be stronger than ever, and you'll get to be the queen who ushers in a new era of prosperity for Escuro."

She laughs and swipes at tears that are racing down her rosy cheeks.

"My darling," she chuckles, "you have seen more cruelty in this world than most, but you've kept a brave and kind spirit. I'm so proud to be your mother."

"I'm proud to be your daughter," I say earnestly, pulling her into a tight embrace. "You have no idea how relieved I am that you're my mother and not that witch."

"You and I both," she laughs again, running her fingers gently over my face. She seems so much lighter and happier than I've seen her since I arrived, and I know she's starting to truly have hope. Her expression abruptly changes, though, and she looks across the river, searching for something I can't see.

"What is it?" I ask, worried. Surely the troops from Dun's Crossing aren't here already.

She gasps and nearly collapses, but I steady her, holding her tightly as she continues to stare in the distance.

"I can feel him," she says in a daze. "Your father. I can feel him! I never thought I would sense his presence again, but he's on his way home."

I continue holding her to me as we both stare across the river. I hope she's right, because if he's nearby, that means Kieran is too.

51

THE BATTLE CRY

There's little time to prepare for the journey. Father wants us to leave the castle as soon as possible so we don't delay in hunting down King Cole. He makes me bring Anwen along because, in his words, "Anwen needs some toughening up."

More like, Anwen is getting under foot, and Father wants him out of the castle. He'll be under my feet now, though. I mind-link with Taner, Whyte, and Lucian to signal my displeasure at this turn of events. It's one thing to get the troops to turn against Father. Half of them seem to have one foot out the door anyway. My friends are hanging back with them now, sowing as much discord as possible.

Anwen will be another story, though. He's completely loyal to Father and to Dun's Crossing. He might be another complication.

"You're being quiet," he tells me now, as we enter the forest, the beginning of the long journey toward Escuro. We're preparing to shift.

"I'm not," I lie. "I'm just focused on the mission."

"Are you?" he challenges, a superior tone in his voice. "Because I heard-" I cut him off, pushing him squarely in the chest.

"I don't care a bit about the idle gossip you've picked up lurking around corners, Anwen." I snap at him. He doesn't even have enough grace to look humbled. He just smirks at me, and I know that whatever he's heard is probably important. I won't give in, though. I need to get the troops far enough away from the castle to tell them the truth.

We take a much more direct path to Escuro this time, Anwen and I leading the troops from the front of the pack. I direct them to spread out to cover more ground because I know it's what my father would do. For now, everything has to appear above board until I can get them out of mind-link distance from the castle.

I'm going to tell them the truth the moment we are far enough away that they can't communicate with anyone at the castle. They deserve to know that the king they've been serving for all this time doesn't care about them. He only cares about gaining power and keeping it. I'll remind them of the horrible conditions they've endured for the last two decades and tell them my plan to change those conditions.

They need to know that they aren't fighting for a noble cause so that they will be inspired to join my fight. If I must, I'll fight anyone who dissents, even kill them if I have to. Then, we'll head back to Dun's Crossing to lead the coup. That will give King Cole plenty of time to reach Escuro and assess the situation there.

Once my father is dead, I'll head back to Escuro myself and get Raven. We can decide together what happens next. For all I know, she'll never want to come back to Dun's Crossing, and I'll honor that decision if that's her wish.

That's a problem for the future, though. For now, Anwen and I run in silence, ripping through the countryside on our way to Escuro. King Cole has at least two hours on us, by my estimation. I just don't know how strong he is. If we get too close, though, I know he'll send animals to slow us down. Either way, we'll make sure he arrives in Escuro before we do.

It was already late into the evening when we left, so we didn't manage to get very far before we needed to stop to make camp. I've also stopped us a little earlier than strictly necessary to give Cole as much of an advantage as I can. The troops don't complain when they arrive at our stopping place and shift, some of my new friends even thanking me for not pushing them too far.

"Since when are you friends with soldiers?" Anwen asks suspiciously. "This is exactly what I was talking about."

"I don't–" I start, but this time my brother cuts me off, pulling me out of earshot of the troops.

"I know you say you don't want to hear what I know," he says between clenched teeth. "But trust me, brother, if what I heard is true, you're on a suicide mission."

My heart drops into my stomach and my curiosity gets the better of me. I shake him off me and face him down, ready to fight him if need be.

"Fine," I spit. "Tell me this incredible gossip I simply must hear."

"You helped King Cole escape," he says simply with a smarmy grin.

My heart races in my chest, but I maintain my facade. "That's ridiculous," I say as nonchalantly as I can. "Where would you even have heard such a malicious rumor?"

"It's not a rumor," he answers evenly, sure of himself. "One of the guards sent a mind-link before you killed him. And if I heard it, brother, you can rest assured that Father heard it too."

Shit.

I have even less time than I thought. I push past Anwen and walk back toward the assembled troops. They all stand at attention, waiting for my directions. There's a large contingent with us. Father sent them because he said he wanted me to be safe, but now I realize that his deception ran as deeply as mine. I had to get it from somewhere, after all. My only saving grace is that these men don't know the truth about my father, and when they do, they'll turn on him. I'm sure of it.

"Gather round," I command, my voice as steady as I can make it, despite what I've just learned. "I have something important to share with you all."

The men surround me, curious expressions on their faces. There's something else, I notice too. They all look weary and underfed. Despite promises that joining the army is an honor, my father has neglected the well-being of these men for far too long.

"You are the best of the best in our kingdom," I tell them, appealing to their egos first. "You've been selected because you are brave and hard-working. You were promised to be well taken care of if you took up arms and fought for your king. But that was a lie, wasn't it?"

Some of the men begin grumbling among themselves, but mostly there are confused faces staring back at me. Only the older soldiers with less to lose are willing to be honest about their dissatisfaction. I have to push them further.

"My father does not care about you," I go on. "He's underpaid you for years, he's worked you to the bone, and he's sent you to slaughter innocent people all in the name of a foe that doesn't exist. You have been deceived for years, and it's time for you to know the truth."

"Brother, what are you doing?" Anwen whispers urgently, coming to my side.

"The kingdom of Escuro was never a threat to us," I bellow, loud enough that they can probably hear me at home. Father wouldn't like that, but he's too far away to do anything about it now. "My father, your king, wiped out half of their population with poison before a single troop could arrive on their soil."

There's more grumbling this time, and a few shocked gasps. I've got them on the hook now, I know it.

"He kidnapped their princess and imprisoned their king," I admit. "He raised the girl as if she were his own daughter, as if she were my twin sister. He thought that her people were a threat to us, and that's what he's told us all for two decades. But it's a farce. The man we're pursuing is not an enemy of Dun's Crossing. He's the rightful king of Escuro, and he is my father-in-law."

"What?" Anwen hisses, grabbing my shoulder and turning me to face him. "What are you saying right now?"

"My true mate is Raven, Princess of Escuro," I say, loud enough for the troops to hear. "I've been with her to Escuro, and I've seen the devastation my father has brought them. He attacked them, unprovoked. They were left with nothing, and he still wants more. What happens when there are no more kingdoms to conquer? What happens when he decides that his enemies are in Dun's Crossing?"

"It's true," Taner adds from somewhere in the crowd. "My father was part of that attack. He told me everything."

"We stand with Prince Kieran," shouts Lucian, leading more than half the men in the chant. "We stand with Prince Kieran!"

I raise my hands to silence them.

"This is our chance to write a new story for Dun's crossing," I shout over the cheers. "Anyone who joins me now will be on the right side of the coming war."

There's more cheering, but it starts to die down slowly. I can't begin to understand why until the crowd begins to part and there's one single man clapping. When he reached the front of the crowd, my blood freezes in my veins.

It's my father. It's safe to say he knows my plan now.

52

THE RIGHTFUL KING

Mother wakes me early, her excitement and anxiety evident in her face and posture.

"He'll be here tonight," she breathes out, standing over my bed. "We must prepare. The soldiers will be close behind him."

I sit up quickly, trying to process her words. "Were you able to mind-link with him?" I ask breathlessly. "Did he say anything about Kieran?"

"I'm afraid I haven't been able to speak with him," she tells me, her bravado faltering just a bit. Her hand goes to her heart, and she presses against her skin. "But I feel him, Raven. My mark hasn't felt like this in years. We have much to do to prepare!"

We spend the morning in her home, preparing for Father's arrival. It's so endearing watching her flit back and forth across the space, worrying over if he'll like it. I don't tell her that anything is an upgrade from his dungeon cell. She doesn't need that image in her mind.

After a quick lunch, she packs some things–food for the journey and clothes for Father when he arrives. She leaves nothing to chance, ready to cater to his every need. There's also a shyness in her movements, a nervousness that I can only speculate about. I suppose if I was about to see Kieran for the first time in 21 years, I would feel a little shy too. What I do feel is relief. It won't be long until everything and everyone is back in their rightful place.

We begin spreading word through the mind-link for the soldiers to assemble in the plaza. She wants to address them all before we begin the journey to the river. As we make our way to the meeting place, I feel the buzz of energy throughout the space. Even those who are too young or too weak to fight are humming with it. They'll stay below, hidden and safely out of sight until they receive word that it's safe. Then, they'll begin rebuilding our kingdom from the ground up. From under the ground, really.

"Thank you for assembling so quickly." Mother addresses everyone a few moments later when the plaza is brimming with soldiers. "The time has finally arrived for us to take back our kingdom. I can't promise your safety. I can't promise what the future will hold after we make our stand. The only thing I can promise you with absolute certainty is that we will fight together until the bitter end."

Cheers go up, the rowdiest coming from the young men in the crowd. Many have waited their whole lives for this day. Escuro will either be free or they will die trying to make it so. The threat of death doesn't seem to remotely dampen anyone's spirit. Everyone is chomping at the bit to get above ground and get in our fighting position.

"May I say a few words?" I ask my mother quietly. She looks at me with such affection and admiration, I feel the tears burn in the back of my eyes. Wordlessly, she steps aside and motions that the floor is mine.

"I know that I haven't been here long," I say by way of greeting the crowd. "You've all embraced me with such kindness and warmth, and you'll never know what that means to me." I purposely ignore Sybil's face as she is the exception. "The people of this kingdom deserve to live in the sun. You deserve to breathe fresh air and find your mates.

You deserve the same basic human rights as the citizens of every other kingdom."

A few people in the crowd clap while others just look at me in awe.

I continue. "Like my mother, I can't guarantee that this will go in our favor. But I can guarantee you this: I will fight until my last breath for you. You are my heart; you are the blood in my veins. Finding my true kingdom was one of the best things that has ever happened to me, and I will not fail you."

Another cheer goes up, nearly deafening in the confined space. Mother squeezes my shoulder and nods her approval. We lead the troops out of the tunnels and begin the long journey to the river. The closer we get, the braver I feel. We're going to win this, I just know it.

It's late when we finally arrive and begin settling into our positions. There's no way of knowing how long we'll be here waiting. It could be a day or two before they arrive, though Mother is sure that Father is going to arrive at any moment.

There's something so poetic about making our stand here, at the very river that King Gavin poisoned all those years ago. There are soldiers here now who were orphaned by his cruel act. Everyone here has lost someone because of him. It fuels our hatred toward the foreign king, and our hatred makes us braver, stronger. We're done hiding out of fear and mere survival.

Night falls around us, and we settle in, ready to pounce at the earliest sign of trouble. It's past midnight when one of our scouts signals to Mother that they see something coming across the river. Mother runs out of her hiding space and stands at the river's edge, straining her eyes against the dark to see. I follow her, ready to defend her if need be.

As the object gets closer, we realize it's a lone wolf. Mother shouts with unbridled joy, wading into the river to meet him. It's my father! I run back to our hiding spot to grab the bag of supplies she packed earlier. Murmurs sweep through the soldiers as they try to understand what's happening.

"King Cole has returned!" I shout, running back to the bank as I watch my father shift and embrace my mother with wild abandon.

I'm several feet away, but I watch as she tackles him, sending them both into the water, the sound of their laughter carried over the night wind. He rights them, lifting her in his arms and spinning her around. I've known this man my entire life, always seeing him behind prison bars.

The man in front of me is unrecognizable, though. His face is transformed by an overwhelming happiness and relief. In all the time I've known Mr. Blake, I've never seen him smile so brightly. Then he looks up at me standing there and beckons me to come over, and my feet move of their own volition. I wade into the river myself, not minding the sharp sting of the cold as I run into my parents' embrace.

After our joyous reunion, I hand Father the clothes Mother packed for him and return to the shore to allow him his privacy to change. The entire army is assembled there, all coming out of their hiding spots to see the miraculous return of the king they'd assumed was long dead.

When he finally reaches the bank, everyone drops into low bows, and I can't fight the sobs that rip through me. I notice the tears in his eyes as well. He's back in his rightful place, no longer a prisoner, but the rightful King of Escuro.

I stand back with Mother, gripping her hand as we allow him to be properly greeted by the soldiers. The eldest warriors rush forward to embrace him, weeping as they do. Mother cries beside me as she watches, and I realize this is a day she'd long given up hope of every seeing.

When Father has been properly greeted by everyone, he raises his hands to quiet them, though there's little he can do to quell the excitement of the moment. Everyone waits with rapt attention to hear what he's going to say, Mother and myself included.

"You have no idea how good it is to be home," he chokes out, his voice thick with emotion. "And while I'm not exactly sure what you're all doing here, it is beyond comparison to receive such a warm welcome. I'm afraid I don't bring happy news. Dun's Crossing follows close behind with a large army. We must retreat! I do not want to lose you all so soon after finding you again."

"Father," I say, grabbing Mother's hand and pulling her toward him. "We are here because we expect them. We're going to fight them, and we're going to win."

He looks between us in shock.

"I admire your bravery, my little Raven, but you can't possibly take on an entire army."

"Actually," Mother interjects. "She can."

She tells him of my abilities and the plan to lure the soldiers to the river. His eyes are wide as he listens, often finding mine and staring in awe and pride.

"I never imagined," he whispers. "But, of course, my darling, you are exceptional. That's no surprise at all!"

He pulls me into a tight hug and holds me for several long minutes. We both begin crying while mother stands beside us, one hand on each of our shoulders.

"You have to know that I stayed in that awful prison for you, my love," he whispers against my hair. "I had to make sure that Gavin kept you alive. I had to make sure you were safe. Seeing you was the only thing that kept me going for all of those years."

I cry against his chest, overwhelmed by the love I feel for him. I've always loved him on some level, always somehow knew deep down in my subconscious that he was my father. Now, he's here, and my family is almost whole.

53

DIVIDE AND CONQUER

KIERAN

"THAT WAS QUITE A SPEECH," FATHER SAYS COLDLY, COMING TO STAND within inches of my face. "You've certainly spun quite a tale."

He's saying this for the benefit of those around us, I know. The fury blazing in my eyes is a sharp reminder of the truth of my words. When he deems someone a threat, there is no stopping his atrocities, and I've just made myself public enemy number one.

"I should have known this would all be too much for Prince Kieran," he shouts louder, for the troops to hear. "He's been off ever since The Haze. I suppose being mated to your own flesh and blood can cause any man to lose his mind."

"She's not my sister!" I spit. "You kidnapped her!"

Anwen pulls me back before I can swing on my father. Family or not, there are men in this crowd who would still see a punch in the face as an act of treason. I can only pray to the goddess that I've convinced enough of the men to join me.

"As you can see," he chuckles sadly, waving in my direction, "my boy has lost his way. Nothing he's said can be taken as truth. The Haze muddled his brain."

"You're lying," I spit at him.

"And you're a traitor," he says lowly, just loud enough that only I can hear. His tone is dangerous, murderous, and I know that he wouldn't be above stabbing me here and leaving me to die. He won't, though. There would be too many witnesses. He'll wait to deal with me at home.

"Prince Kieran is clearly unfit to lead this kingdom," he turns back to the crowd. "My son Anwen is now the crown prince. You will take your orders from him. Anwen," he calls to my brother, "since you've already got Kieran restrained, take him into custody."

My brother's grip tightens around me, and I see my plan fall apart in an instant. Anwen is smart when he wants to be, even kind on occasion. But he is also fiercely loyal to my father. He's always resented my position, and this is finally his chance to usurp me. My father would have known this. It's why he sent Anwen on this mission here in the first place. I can only hope King Cole will reach Escuro and warn the others.

"No," Anwen says quietly, surprising both me and my father. He lets go of me completely and faces me. "I believe Kieran."

The silence is deafening; the only sound is the wind blowing through the trees. The men clearly don't know what to do, who to believe. Anwen taking a stand against Father might just be the support I need to turn the tide.

"I stand with Prince Kieran!" he shouts, raising his fist in defiance.

There's shouting again, and many fists raise in one accord. My father reaches for his sword, but I grab Anwen's hand and start running, mind-linking with him to tell him to shift—and fast.

"Run!" I call back to the men who've protested with me. The moment they see me shift, they do too, and we are a blur of fur, taking off as fast as we possibly can.

There's no way for me to know how many men are with me. I run as hard and as fast as my legs can take me, and soon I'm flanked by my closest friends. I'm relieved that they've made it safely away from anyone who is still on my father's side, and I turn to see my brother just a hair behind me, keeping pace.

I'm the one who knows the way, and the group behind me understands that there is no slowing down between here and Escuro. I have no idea what will happen when we arrive. I don't know how far ahead King Cole is, but I know that behind us is certain death. The king retains control of enough troops to kill us. Just when the fear threatens to swallow me whole, I hear the flapping of wings.

It's too dark in the night sky to see what's coming, but the creatures are flying in a tight formation so close together that they block out the light of the moon. There are hundreds, maybe even thousands of the creatures, and they fly overhead, completely ignoring us.

It isn't long before we hear the howls of pain, but we keep running.

"Bats," Anwen cheers in his head. *"I'm still linked with Father. He's warning his men not to get bitten."*

"A gift from King Cole," I tell him, and I would laugh if I could. Wherever he is, he knew we would need backup. We keep running, but Anwen tells me that the bats have slowed Father's group of soldiers down. They've given us a chance.

King Cole must not be too far away, which is a relief. The moment we cross into Escuro, he can help us regroup. Even if most of the army followed my lead, my father will not stop until every last one of us is dead. I can only hope that the soldiers in Escuro have prepared in some way. There weren't many from what I could see while I was there, but they were passionate. They were just as bloodthirsty for my father's men as he was to destroy their kingdom.

It won't be much, but it's the only advantage we have. My father doesn't know that anyone is left in Escuro. He doesn't know that Raven has powers, and at least with her and King Cole on our side, we'll have some help.

Even with the help of the bats, I know we must push on. We'll likely have to run all night to stay out of my father's clutches.

'What do we do now?' Lucian asks from somewhere behind me. *'Do you have a plan?*

'*We have to take out the king,*' I tell him, wondering if I've accidentally mind-linked with anyone else in my tired state, but it's nothing these men won't have already guessed. We're in a position to kill or be killed.

'*They're still fighting the bats,*' Anwen confirms, giving me some peace of mind. '*How much further is it to Escuro? It won't be safe to stop until we're there.*'

'*We'll run as long as it takes,*' I hear an unfamiliar voice, a soldier behind me, I'm sure. '*We're with you, Prince Kieran.*'

'*We stand with Prince Kieran!*' I hear a chorus of voices shout.

It's going to be a long night, that's the only certainty. There's nowhere for our large group to hide, and I don't know if we have the numbers to fight on our own. If we're powerful enough to win.

So I run faster, pushing my body harder than it's ever been pushed. I am pure adrenaline, imagining Raven, and how happy I will be when I finally have her in my arms again. She started all of this. As much as I wanted to be the one to kill my father, maybe it's right for us to be together when it happens.

'*So,*' Anwen starts, linking with me again. '*Blanca isn't our sister?*'

'*Her name is Raven,*' I correct. '*And no, she isn't our sister. And you better start being nicer to her now. She's my wife, and I'm not going to put up with any shit from you.*'

'*I promise, I promise.*' He laughs. '*Goddess, what a weird day. I had no idea when I woke up that I'd be running myself ragged for my former sister turned sister-in-law.*'

'*It just sounds weird when you say it like that,*' I complain, annoyed with my brother but grateful for the distraction.

In a few more hours, we'll be in close enough range that I'll finally be able to mind-link with Raven again. I wasn't expecting to be back so soon, and definitely not under such precarious circumstances, but the realization makes me feel like I'm flying.

This time away from her has been hell for so many reasons, but soon, she'll be back in my arms. Hopefully not long after, my father will be dead, and all the danger will pass. It doesn't seem like I'm asking for too much with that request.

'I'm sorry, by the way,' Anwen continues, pulling me from my thoughts. *'I'm sorry for how I treated her. How I've been treating you. There's probably more of Father in me than I would care to admit.'*

My heart hurts for my little brother. It's been a whirlwind of a day, throwing everything he thought to be true into chaos. Still, he's by my side, choosing me over our father. It's more than I could have hoped for. When this is all over, I could probably stand to be a little kinder to him too.

'You'll have to apologize to Raven,' I tell him. *'As far as I'm concerned, I owe you my life.'*

'Then we better make sure that you live a long time because I plan to cash in on that for several years,' he jokes.

I can't help but laugh at this, the joke lifting my spirits. We'll be at the border soon, and then we'll have backup. I'll have Raven. No matter what happens after, we'll be much stronger when we're together.

54

JUST GET ACROSS THE RIVER

THE NIGHT DRAGS ON, HEAVY WITH ANTICIPATION AS WE WAIT FOR THE soldiers to arrive. Mother and Father don't let go of each other for much more than a moment. When they aren't holding each other, they're simply gazing at each other. Mother looks at Father like he's the most precious thing in the world, which is probably true after all these years apart. Father looks like a starving man who's been offered a buffet. For their sake, I wish I could just tell them to go back home and let us take care of the threat. They will never leave, though. As travel-weary as Father must be, he stays up all night, watching and waiting with us.

The first light of dawn creeps over the horizon, bathing the river-bank in a soft glow. The night felt like an eternity, but the sun brings little relief. Father told us a bit of Kieran's plan, and we know the army will be coming soon. We just don't know when. And I don't know where Kieran is in all of it. Is he safe? Is he even alive? If his father has gotten even a whiff of his plan, he'll be running for his life, just as Father was.

The morning dew settles, and everyone is back in position, watching the horizon for any sign of a disturbance. The pale sun begins to rise, but a dense fog settles over the river, so thick that we can barely see over the water. I command it away, giving us a clear line of vision. My heart beats at a steady, eager pace until I hear the voice I've so dearly missed.

'Raven? Can you hear me?'

Kieran. I cover my mouth to keep from shouting with joy, not wanting to alert anyone of the recent development. Selfishly, I just want a single moment to enjoy the sound of my husband's voice. Though it's only been a few days since I saw him last, his words are a balm for my soul. Relief and joy surge through me in powerful waves.

I think of Mother wading into the river, so overcome with emotion at seeing Father that she couldn't stay still for a moment. Yet, I must stay in position, ready for whatever comes. As overjoyed as I am to hear his voice, I know that if he's this close, the entire army of Dun's Crossing is likely close behind. There won't be time for a sweet reunion until the army is taken care of.

'I'm here,' I tell him, my heart pounding so loud that it's the only sound I can hear. *"I've missed you so much!'*

'I've missed you, too,' he assures me. *'I've been dying to be back in your arms since the moment I left. But there's something you need to know.'*

I brace myself against the cold ground, unsure if I'm ready for whatever it is he has to tell me. Based on his tone, it isn't going to be good news. I focus on slowing my breathing as I anticipate what he's going to tell me.

'I'm sure by now your father has filled you in on my plan. Unfortunately, there was trouble last night. We'd gotten far enough from the kingdom that I thought I could safely tell the troops the truth about us and the real reason we're going to Escuro.'

My heart stutters in my chest from fear. I've never met a soldier from Dun's Crossing I felt I could trust. The men I've met have been cruel and crass, but most importantly, they've been loyal to the king. It's not that I don't trust Kieran's judgment, but I can't imagine that going well.

'Father was among the group,' he continues, and I feel as if I might collapse. My stomach turns so violently I'm glad I'm already in position on the ground. Kieran was King Gavin's hope for the future, but he's ruthless enough to kill him on sight for that kind of perceived betrayal.

'I had no idea he was with us,' he continues. *'But it all went to shit, and the army split. Many are with me, but I have no idea how many are with him. It all happened so fast, I just told them to run. We're on our way to you, but Father's group is close behind. I'm so sorry I've brought this shitstorm to your doorstep.'*

Even with the anxiety coursing through me thinking about Kieran's confrontation with his father, I can't help but smile that he is so concerned about my safety. It's been unbearable being without him, but I know what I'm capable of, and I'm not afraid of King Gavin anymore. I'm much stronger than he will ever be. He's the one who needs to be afraid of me.

'It's okay, Kieran,' I comfort him. *'We're ready for them. While you've been gone, we've been working on a plan. I just need you to get yourself and your followers across the river. Once you do, I'll take care of the rest.'*

My heart swells with pride at the thought. There's something so satisfying about knowing that I'm going to be the one to bring the kingdom down. King Gavin won't see it coming from a mile away.

'What are you going to do?' Kieran asks, interrupting my vengeful thoughts. There's a hint of curiosity and fear in his tone. I can't wait to show him just how powerful I've become.

'Just get across the river, and you'll see for yourself,' I tell him. *'This is all going to be over soon.'*

'Are you sure?' he asks, not from doubt, but concern for my well-being.

'I am,' I reply firmly. The only thing I've ever been more sure about in my life is my love for him. What I once thought of as a horrible mistake, a cruel prank by the Goddess, has been the single best gift I've ever received. A very close second is my ability to control the elements. And I can use the second gift to save the first.

'I love you,' he says, his thoughts sounding terribly forlorn. *'Whatever you're going to do, please be safe.'*

'You're the one running for your life,' I reply wryly. *'You are my heart. I need you to return to me in one piece. I love you more than you could imagine.'*

I break the connection, knowing he needs to concentrate on his journey. If he's truly going to return to me safely, he'll need all of his mental and physical strength to carry him through the rest of the journey. Still, it hurts my heart to let him go. I ache for him the moment I can no longer hear his voice, but soon he'll be back in my arms.

I look over to Mother and Father again, who are still staring at each other like they still can't quite believe they're back in each other's presence. It pains me to break up their moment, but I have to tell them what Kieran's shared with me.

I make my way through the tall weeds, making as much noise as I can to alert them of my presence, just in case they're whispering sweet nothings to each other. As full as it makes my heart to see them together, I absolutely don't want to witness any physical displays of affection.

Mother sees me first, and her happy demeanor quickly morphs into worry. She drops Father's hand and rushes to me, searching my face.

"What is it, darling?" she asks with such motherly concern. "What's happened?"

Father comes to stand behind her, and I tell them everything Kieran's shared with me. King Gavin knows everything, and he's on his way to destroy us for good.

"Nothing's changed," I assure them, but my words do nothing to soothe my mother's worry lines. "The plan is still on, exactly as it was before."

I lock eyes with my father, who has a hint of a smile in his eyes. We have an instant moment of connection, and I can hear his thoughts though he's not mind-linking with me. He trusts Kieran completely. He already loves him like a son. This is all so evident in his gaze. More than that, though, he trusts me and has every faith in my ability.

"Well then," he says, saluting me. Mother turns to face him and swats the salute away, but he just winks at me. "We are ready and waiting for your command, little Raven."

The three of us embrace tightly, 21 years of love conveyed in that single moment. Mother holds us both tightly, the worry still evident in her posture and expression. The last time the soldiers from Dun's Crossing darkened her doorstep, they took everything from her. Today, I'm going to ensure she gets it all back.

We let go of each other, and my parents finally, reluctantly, let go of one another so they can get into their battle positions. I leave them to hide in my own spot, watching the shore for any sign of my love returning to me.

5 5

IT ENDS TODAY

KIERAN

WITH RAVEN'S LAST WORDS—*I LOVE YOU MORE THAN YOU CAN IMAGINE*—ringing in my ears, I pound across the open plain toward the river that is apparently our only hope of survival. We left the forest half an hour ago, and since then, my father's forces have been gathering behind us. More men stayed with him than I hoped. Fewer than I feared. I still don't know that we could take them in a fair fight.

Luckily, we have Raven on our side.

We reach the river. At the last possible second, I call across the mind-link, *'Jump!'*

My brother's gray body flies through the air to my left, Taner's white wolf on my right. We land in a cloud of dust on a seemingly empty riverbank.

'My love?' I ask.

'Here.' Her voice washes over me like cool water. *Just waiting.*

'I'll join you.' Blake—King Cole–steps out from behind some brush with his wife at his side. They hold hands like they'll never let go again.

After only a short time away from Raven, I understand.

My father's forces stop on the other side of the river, and he strides forward in human form, already laughing.

"Pitiful." He shakes his head. "You betray our family for *this*? There really are witches in Escuro."

"No witches," King Cole replies. "Just love."

That makes Father laugh even harder. "And how did love save you last we met, Cole?"

"It kept me alive." He lifts his chin, every inch the Alpha I want to be. Once my father's blood paints these shores.

'Come here, love,' I say to Raven. *'Please. I'll keep you safe.'*

She steps tentatively out of her hiding spot, also in human form, and joins me on the riverbank.

Father eyes her. "So you are alive. Pity."

Raven clenches her fist in my fur. My beautiful wife, who I've seen face so many dangers, shrinks in the face of my father. He's spent too long making her feel small. Not anymore.

'Raven Blake, Crown Princess of Escuro, is my mate!' I roar over the mind-link. *'And the only one to pity is you, Father, because she is the reason you're going to fail.'*

He snorts. "That pup has only ever failed herself. Advance!"

'Thank you.' Raven releases my fur. *'That's exactly what I needed.'*

My father's men splash into the river in a frenzy of fur and water. She looks up at the cloudy sky, and suddenly, the clouds darken to pitch back. I have to squint to see. My love, my mate, raises her hands.

A bolt of lightning cracks through the sky, shattering the darkness, and strikes the surface of the river. The water lights with a thousand smaller arcs, and pained howls fill the air.

She's brilliant.

'Now!' King Cole barks over the mind-link. *'Catch the stragglers.'*

A couple of dozen Escurian warriors leap from more hiding places and form up on the bank, drooling and readying their claws. I command my men to join them, and the real fight starts.

It's almost not fair. Soaked, singed wolves stagger out of the river in groups of two or three, and we tear into them. I sink my teeth into a haunch and yank until something cracks. Taner tackles one to the ground and digs into him like his chest is soft earth. Lucias and Whyte tag-team, pushing wolves back into the still-crackling river with a couple of Escurian fighters. Amidst us, King Cole shifts into a pure black wolf and joins the fray as though he was just another soldier. Blood turns the sand a slick red.

Suddenly, the clouds clear. I look back, panicked that my father somehow snuck through and found Raven, but she's standing whole and resolute, staring out over the river.

She's looking at my father–who didn't even bother to shift, much less enter the river with his men. Raven cleared the storm so I might cross the river safely.

This kill is mine.

I plunge into the water. The remainder of the lightning sparkles over my skin, but it doesn't hurt me. Raven never would. I shoulder the corpses of Father's men out of the way, choking on the stink of charred skin. And then I emerge.

Father looks at me. "You honestly believe—"

The time for words is over. As I've learned, Father has preferred words to fighting for far too long. I throw myself at him, my jaw wide.

Not all of the rumors of his fighting skills were exaggerated. He flips backward, exploding into a shift and landing on four paws. Before I can even gauge his weakness, he's charging me. I dodge, curl around, try to catch his leg, and miss. He's faster than a wolf of his age has any right to be, and his silver pelt warns that he's just as strong as I am. I can't just overpower my way through this one.

Still, I dive at his side, hoping to knock him off his feet. He rolls, but I get the sense he's letting me do this. Sure enough, we come to a stop with him on top. Command rolls off him in thick waves as he snaps at my throat. I tuck my chin and fight for purchase.

'This is the man I was proud to call my father,' I yell. *'Not the one who poisons and lies.'*

'*You're naïve if you think you can have one without the other,*' he replies.

I snap my chin up and smash into the underside of his jaw, jarring both our skulls and giving me a split second to roll us over. I land on top, and he snarls at me.

'*You barely deserve the honor of a clean death.*' I shove his face into the wet earth with one paw and open my mouth to tear out his throat.

'*Kieran!*' Raven screams. '*Behind you!*'

I throw myself to the side before even checking, then twist. My father's Beta stands behind where I lay mere seconds ago, a sword plunged into the dirt next to my father. He was going to stab me in the back.

Father chuckles over the mind-link. '*All this, and you still expect me to fight fair?*'

'*No,*' I reply. '*But I have someone watching my back now.*'

He narrows his eyes, and I see my opportunity. His Beta's sword is stuck. He can't get up.

My paw flashes through the air, silver hair and silver claws blurring into a single streak. I claim the throats of my father, and his Beta in a single stroke, leaving them to bleed out just the same way they left the men they couldn't be fucked to fight with.

'*The king of Dun's Crossing is dead,*' Anwen calls somberly across the mind-link. '*Long live the king.*'

The cheer goes up from all the wolves on the far side of the river. '*Long live the king!*'

5 6

CLEANING HOUSE

Raven

Escurians and people from Dun's Crossing celebrate all around me, but I only have eyes for a bloodstained, silver wolf on the other side of the river. I shove through the crowd, desperate to touch him and know that he's safe. That we all are.

King Gavin is dead!

Kieran seems to have the same idea. He charges back into the corpse-choked river, and when we meet in the middle, he shifts. He crushes me in an embrace, and his lips collide with mine, both of us hungry with relief. The water swallows us up to my neck, his chest, and it's not like anyone would be looking in the middle of this chaos, but I love knowing that his body is all mine. The moon-shaped mating bite on his pale skin declares to the world that the Goddess Herself blessed our love, and no one will tear us apart.

Finally, when I think I'm going to pass out if I don't take a breath, I pull back. Kieran stares down at me, his blue eyes glowing.

"I love you," he says, "my queen."

That startles a laugh out of me. With King Gavin dead, Kieran is Alpha, and we're married, so….

"I'm Luna of Dun's Crossing!" I laugh again.

"And the most beautiful woman I've ever seen." Kieran dips me into another kiss.

"Wait." I push his chest until he releases me. "You just killed your father. Are you really happy to just celebrate?"

His triumphant expression crumples for a split second, a shift no one who didn't grow up with him would notice. "I… don't know. I can't imagine a world without him in it." He shakes his head. "But I have to because I know that's the only world where we get any peace."

I cup his cheek. "You don't have to know everything right now. We've got time."

His smile brightens again. "Time. What a wonderful word."

"This is all very cute," Anwen says to us through the mind-link, *"but you don't think Father left the whole palace unguarded, do you? You have to finish what you started."*

Kieran squeezes me. "He's got a terrible habit of being right. We'll party for days when the palace is ours."

I kiss his cheek. "And get started on that big family."

He laughs.

* * *

My footfalls blend with the massive pack of wolves I'm running with, and for the first time in my whole life, so does my coat. Dun's Crossing still outnumbers us, but I'm far from the only black pelt in the crowd. I howl for the sheer joy of hearing my own voice as we approach the palace.

Other wolves take up the call. Escurians, those of Dun's Crossing who support Kieran, Mother. Father, Kieran himself, who shoulders me teasingly. We were never planning on a stealth approach anyway.

As we get within range, crossbow bolts begin flying through the trees. As expected.

'Split!' Kieran calls.

Just like we planned, most of the army keeps charging forward, bobbing and weaving so the archers can't land a shot, and those of us who know the castle peel off–all the Solbergs, and Kieran's friends, me. Father, and because she refused to be separated from him, Mother. Low and fast, we dart for a secret tunnel that will let us right into the palace proper.

After a few moments of running, the sounds of crossbows still humming in the air, Kieran skids to a stop and shifts. Mother and Father politely avert their eyes. He depresses one light-colored brick at the base of the castle, and a doorway's worth of them start to fade out.

Then fade back in. Then out again.

"Fucking Wordsworth," Kieran mutters.

I huff a wolfish laugh. The court magician is yet another thing to get rid of once this palace is ours.

Finally, the bricks settle into a half-dissolved position, leaving a narrow gap for us to shimmy through. Kieran rolls his eyes and shifts back into a wolf. I nudge Mother and Father, and we head inside one after the other.

I was never allowed in these tunnels before, but I'd like to see Queen Rowena stop me now!

We pound up a set of stairs built between wolf and human strides and explode into the throne room. Queen Rowena, sitting on her throne, screams. A few other nobles in the room scatter back.

"King Gavin is dead!" Kieran roars. *"I killed him. By right of blood and right of combat, the throne of Dun's Crossing is mine!"*

"Th-that can't be." Rowena looks from Kieran to me, frantic. "She's a witch! She ensorcelled you into doing this, believing this."

'She is our daughter,' Father declares. *'Crown princess of Escuro, Raven Blake.'* His Alpha blood allows her to hear him.

'And my mate,' Kieran says. *'My wife.'*

"No!" Rowena wails. I brace for pain.

But she only crumples to her knees, weeping. Lucias and Whyte shift then start dragging her toward the dungeon.

Suddenly, everything clicks into place. She tortured me for years, made me feel less than dirt. But she didn't do that to her husband, her children, anyone else in her life. Because I was the only one she had enough power over. I couldn't even begin to challenge her. She was a weak, scared woman who took out her anger about that on a weaker, more scared child.

I snap at her heels. I may never be the person I would've been without her in my life, but she doesn't frighten me anymore.

"They're lying!" Nessa steps out of the crowd with her hands on her hips. "Tell them, Kieran-Wieran. *We're* mates."

Without Rowena here, I have nothing to lose, no one to fear. I shift and stare Nessa down.

"Say that to my face." I raise my hands, and dozens of mice scamper out of the walls to swarm around my ankles.

She pales. "Um—"

"Exactly." I look at the crowd of people who didn't blink at my years of torture. "Now, I'm going to give you two options. You can shut the fuck up about me, my family, and my mate, or"—I look at Kieran. Even without a mind-link, he's ready to open the door for me. I nod—"you can get the fuck out!"

I conjure a roaring wind, targeted in a single column and blast Nessa. She tumbles ass-over-teakettle through the door Kieran just pulled open and lands far enough away that I can't hear her complaints, but I can see she decided to skip underwear today.

Nervous laughter fills the throne room, but I feel incredible. Nothing can stop me today. I'll never have to hide in this castle—

My stomach twists, and I vomit on the stones at my feet.

5 7
LONG LIVE THE KING

KIERAN

I RUN MY THUMB NERVOUSLY OVER THE BACK OF RAVEN'S HAND AS Fleming, the royal healer, looks her over in his study. The wizened old man mumbles to himself as he works but never anything I can understand. My heart pounds. I will not have gone through all of this to lose my wife at the end. I will fight the Goddess herself, if that is what it takes.

She squeezes my hand, just as strong as usual. She doesn't seem much weakened, other than the sudden burst of vomiting.

"Mm-hmm!" Fleming sits back with a sharp nod. "Just like I thought."

"What is it?" I spend all my willpower not biting the little man's head off.

He grins. "Your lady wife is pregnant."

I can't imagine five more perfect words.

* * *

Three days later, I stand at the foot of the throne dais, staring up at the towering, moonstone chairs that have symbolized power all my life. One for the Alpha King, one for his Luna Queen. And by the end of today, they will be in good hands for the first time since the kingdom was created. I take a deep breath and glance at Raven next to me. She shines in her coronation dress, but she looks a little unsteady, like she often has since her first bout of morning sickness. It seems her pregnancy won't be an easy one, but I know my wife is strong. I'm not worried.

A holy woman from Escuro, Aylin, raises her hands. "Today, we gather to crown the Alpha King and Luna Queen of Dun's Crossing. This is not my land, but the moon shines the same on all lands, and so does the Goddess." She smiles. "Or they will from this day forth."

Slightly nervous chuckles fill the room. Behind us, people of both packs mingle, trying to overcome years of fighting.

"Kieran Solberg, first of his name." She looks to me. "You have claimed this throne by right of blood and combat. Which do you believe gives it to you truly?"

I blink. The Escurian ceremony is different from ours, from the words I've spent my whole life practicing. But Raven squeezes my hand, and I know the answer.

"Combat." My voice rings through the hall, proud and true. "This land, these people, were led by a king who was not honoring them. I may be his son, but I've earned the right to lead them by saving them from that fate."

Aylin smiles softly. "And how will you lead?"

This is the answer I know, and I realize Aylin is giving a blended ceremony, as much Escuro as Dun's Crossing. Exactly what we need.

"Bravely as my wolf. Proudly as my ancestors. Steadily as the moon in the sky."

She looks at Anwen, on her left. Were my father stepping down, he would do this part. Instead, it feels right for the brother I've worried about my whole life to drape my silvery royal robe around my shoulders.

'Maybe not as proudly as all our ancestors,' he says through the mind-link.

I smirk. The heavy fabric settles over me, a reminder of the duty I've sworn to uphold. Anwen steps back, and Aylin turns to Raven.

"You have claimed this throne by right of mating, but you were raised as blood. What do you believe gives it to you truly?"

Raven swallows. "I think… I wasn't raised as blood. I was raised as nothing. So I know firsthand the cruelty that people outside of Dun's Crossing have known for years." She nods. "That's what gives me the right. That, and my desire to change it."

Aylin inclines her head. "And how will you lead?"

Raven answers with the words I taught her just this morning. "Bravely as my wolf. Proudly as my ancestors. Steadily as the moon in the sky."

Candace steps forward with Raven's royal robe, which we had to have made special for the occasion. The robes match the pelts of our king and queen, and centuries of silver, white, and gray had no space for my wife. Instead, she glows in jet black, embroidered all over with jagged lightning strikes in the same silver and blue as the flecks of her eyes. A new robe for a new day in Dun's Crossing. Aylin gestures us to the thrones, and we sit. The power of the moonstone courses through me.

"May the Moon Goddess bless and keep you," Aylin says. "And may we all raise our voices in honor of Alpha King Kieran Solberg and Luna Queen Raven Blake of Dun's Crossing!"

Howls split the air just as easily as a grin splits my face. I kiss my wife.

With the ceremony over, we leave the throne room for the ballroom next door, already decorated in a striking blend of Dun's Crossing silvers and Escurian blacks. Raven and I proceed to the middle of the floor and lead the first dance. She fits so neatly in my arms, and I can't help but wonder if this is why Mother and Father forced us to have separate dance lessons so long ago. Other couples flood the floor, and an air of celebration fills the room. We're done being somber. There's no more fighting to do, no more enemies to conquer. Nessa chose to remain in the palace after Raven's threat, but she sulks along the wall, not saying a word. Mother remains in the—at Raven's request—much better tended dungeons, where I imagine she'll be for the rest of her days. There is peace in the kingdom.

I dip Raven and see King Cole and Queen Delaney spinning over to us.

"Mind if I cut in?" King Cole asks. "I'll offer you my partner in exchange."

"How could I refuse?" I pass Raven into her father's arms and accept her mother into mine.

Queen Delaney is a brilliant dancer, despite how long her people spent underground, I quickly learn. She puts me through my paces and chuckles kindly every time I stumble.

"Is this how things are going to be?" I grumble. "You and King Cole laughing every time Raven and I stumble in our leadership?"

"Never." She smiles. "This partnership is only until my husband and I decide we tire of leading. Then, all of Dun's Crossing and Escuro are yours. We'll teach you, not laugh at you."

"Then start by teaching me that complicated little weaving thing you're doing with your feet," I challenge.

Queen Delaney rises to it, like I knew she would, and the party blurs into a series of feasting, dance partners, and laughter. As the night starts to grow old, I finally find myself dancing with Raven again. She looks tired, but she's still smiling like everything is right in the world, and I struggle to disagree.

"Well?" I ask.

"Well what?" She raises an eyebrow at me.

"Are you ready to lead, my queen?"

She laughs. "I have no idea. But I know I can do better than your mother, and you can do better than your father."

"That, I won't deny." I kiss her. She arcs up into me, hungry, and my body responds. "Do you think they'd notice if we left?"

She giggles against my mouth. "As far as I'm aware, the Escurian ceremony is over. What about Dun's Crossing?"

I grimace and pull back. "I owe them a final speech."

Raven runs a finger over my lower lip. "Well? Who are you going to disappoint?"

Her touch burns through me. "You've taught me the value of compromise, my love."

I hook an arm under her knees and lift her into my arms, then bellow, "I am your king, and I will do right by you, but now, I need to do right by my wife!"

Laughter chases us out of the ballroom as I carry my impossible mate up to our room.

5 8

A BRIGHT FUTURE

I PRESS KISSES ALONG KIERAN'S NECK AS HE CARRIES ME THROUGH THE palace I felt so alone in for so long. Now, not only am I its queen, but there's no shame in my husband dragging me out of a party after announcing he needs to fuck me. I feel beautiful and wanted for the very first time within these walls.

His skin burns under my mouth, rich with his scent. I want him, need him, even with the baby already growing in my stomach. It's lucky we want a big family because I don't know how I could ever stop feeling like this.

Kieran kicks open the door to our room, and I expect him to toss me on the bed. His scent is growing headier, proof of how much he wants me. But he lays me down like I'm glass, nothing like the brother I thought I grew up with.

"I love you," he says.

"I love you too." I grab the collar of his royal robe. "Now come here."

He obliges with a smile and crushes his mouth to mine. When he joins me on the bed, flattens his body against me, I can feel his cock already responding. I grind up into him, resenting the layers of robes and my dress. He's so close and so far away.

I break the kiss in frustration. "Do you think they dress us like this in the hopes we'll have a small family? Something lesser nobles dreamed up so they could steal the throne more easily?"

Kieran chuckles. "Antsy, my love?"

I meet his gaze, trying to press all my love, trust, and hope for the future into him. The man I've come to know as my mate won't deny me. "Tired of waiting for our happy ending."

His amusement softens, and I see my love reflected back in his face. "Then stop waiting."

He reaches down then slides his hand up the inside of my leg. There are a thousand layers of fabric between us, but beneath my dress, there's only a little cotton. He presses kisses to the tops of my breasts, light and teasing. When he cups my wet heat, already soaked through the thin barrier, I groan and start unlacing the front of his pants.

But Kieran knows how to drive me even wilder. He stills my hands, presses them against his bulge, and rocks into me. I repeat the rhythm against his hand. He slips beneath the final layer and circles the bud at the apex of my legs. I moan his name.

"Louder," he murmurs. "Let everyone know you're mine, and I'm yours."

"Kieran!"

His thumb settles against the sensitive bud as he fucks two fingers into me without hesitation. Pleasure builds in my gut, but I need more. I pull one of my breasts, the one marked with his sun-shaped mating bite, out of the top of my dress and press his head toward it. He doesn't disappoint. Kieran scrapes his teeth over the mating bite, sending bolts of euphoria down my spine, then takes my hardened nipple between his lips and twirls it. I groan and squeeze his cock harder.

"Please," I gasp. "I need you."

"Louder." His voice is sing-song, teasing against my skin.

"I need you!" I shout. "Please, Kieran, fuck me!"

"Beautiful." He ducks his head back to my breast, sucking into my mating bite, and pulls out of me to yank down his pants.

I squirm at the loss, shameless. This is my castle, my home, my mate. Our child in my womb, my promise of a brighter future. Kieran shoves my underwear aside, pushes up my skirts, and slides home in a single, smooth motion. I nearly scream. Happy tears bead at the corners of my eyes. I'm so full, so surrounded by his scent. I could spend forever here, pinned beneath my powerful mate.

And then he starts moving. I realize his teasing was a flimsy façade as he sets a punishing pace. He's just as hungry as I am. He needs me as badly as I need him. I claw at his shoulders, writhe, moan at the top of my lungs. He grunts in rhythm, muttering half-nonsense praises. I'm beautiful, perfect, exactly what he never knew he was looking for.

Pleasure explodes through my body, and my vision nearly goes white. Kieran follows me a second after with a stuttered groan of my name. Then, he collapses onto his side, still half-hilted within me. I suck in deep breaths of cool air, those happy tears sliding down my cheeks.

"My love?" he says with a note of worry. "Is something wrong?"

I shake my head. "I'm just so happy."

He laughs. "Well, that's okay."

"No." I twist onto my side so I can face him, trying not to dislodge his cock. I don't want to be any further away from him than I am right now. "I'm so happy. Happier than I ever thought I could be."

He cups my cheek, his eyes shining. "So am I."

"We're going to fix this place." Visions of a kinder Dun's Crossing, one where no one ever goes through what I did, dance through my head. "Us—and our child, our heir."

He puts a hand on my stomach. "And we're going to raise our children better than my mother and father raised us."

"That won't be hard." My smile fades as the years of pain here try to force themselves into my focus.

"Don't think of them now," he says.

"What should I think of instead?" I ask.

He smirks. "Our future."

"I know you, Kieran Solberg." I trace his lips with one finger. "You're not thinking of the kingdom anymore."

His smirk deepens. "Well, when a man's future also happens to involve stripping his very sexy wife out of her clothes and making love to her all night long, can you blame him?"

"Not when my future involves the same." I grin and reach for the clasp on his royal robes. We'll lead tomorrow. Tonight, we just get to enjoy each other.

5 9

ON THE HORIZON

I sit at my desk in my study, poring over a new trade agreement the representative from Snowcrest Canyon, Floyd, delivered yesterday. So far, being king has included far less heroic resolution of my father's sins and far more approving announcements of his fall that include apologies and offers of future friendship, followed by the very official refusals from various kingdoms. It's headache inducing, but I just keep reminding myself that I need to prove I'm completely different from him, and this is the first step.

Going to bed with Raven every night is certainly making bearing that burden easier. At this rate, I'm starting to worry she's going to have twins conceived on two different nights. Not that that's possible.

I look out the window at where the Haze has started gathering. Anwen's birthday was last night, and it's moving in quickly. Is it possible the Haze considers him old enough now to participate? I'll have to see if the palace staff needs any help with preparations for the Haze, but I doubt they will, with the last one having happened so recently. Back to the agreement, then.

Someone knocks on my door.

"Come in," I call.

Taner, now officially my Beta, steps inside and closes the door behind him. "I've got news."

I lean back from my desk, happy to abandon the trade agreement. "Good or bad?"

"Not sure." He frowns. "The scouts spotted a boat on the horizon."

"A boat? Here?" I sit bolt upright. The only water that we can access from the palace is the Lonely Sea, and the only kingdom who might reach us across it is Sundrop Gem–whom we haven't heard from in a century and were feuding with even before that.

Taner nods. "They've dropped a rowboat into the water, and it's on the way here now. Clearly, they want permission to dock."

I run a hand through my hair. "The Escurians haven't all left yet, but their king and queen have. We're still figuring out which soldiers are actually loyal, and don't get me started on the nobility." I shake my head. "No. Things are just too volatile."

"They're flying a white flag." Taner shrugs. "And you were the one saying the letters were all well and good, but you didn't think they meant anything until we actually got other packs to visit."

"I didn't think it would be this soon." I sigh. "And I didn't think it would be Sundrop Gem." But turning them down will look much worse. "Give the rowboat the go-ahead. I'll start gathering people for a formal welcome."

* * *

A couple of hours later, I stand next to Raven in our royal robes once more, watching a four-masted sailing ship of strange design dock in our harbor.

"Are you sure this is a good idea?" she asks. *"We don't even know why the feud started."*

"I'm sure we can't send them away," I reply.

She takes a deep breath and squares her shoulders. The ship

judders to a stop. A wooden gangplank slides out and *thuds* onto the dock. Showtime.

Four people in beautiful clothing parade down it in twos. All of them have warm, sand-colored skin, and rich brown hair. The man and woman in the front are middle-aged, perhaps as old as my parents. The man and woman behind them are younger, perhaps our age or a bit younger than that. They smell like nothing I've ever encountered before.

The older pair reach us first and bow deeply.

"King Kieran. Queen Raven. Apologies for the abruptness of our arrival," the man says in a rumbling voice. Up close, his gray eyes are striking, closer to a Dun's Crossing blue than anything else in his complexion. "We received your letter on an auspicious day, and our holy woman said our trip would have the best luck if we left immediately."

I bow as well, and Raven follows, after a split second of hesitation. These people talk and dress like royals, and I'd rather not insult the first outsiders to believe something could change in Dun's Crossing.

"No apologies needed," I say, "but I'll admit you have the advantage of us. What is your name, if I may ask?"

He laughs an equally rumbling laugh. "Apologies again. We don't travel often, and it seems I've become used to being recognized. I am Alpha King Isai Sollabella, of Sundrop Gem, and this is Luna Queen Suniva. Behind us are our children, the crown princess Estrella"—the young woman curtsies—"and her younger brother, Castor." He bows as well.

"Wonderful to meet you all." I bow again. "Sundrop Gem has a certain reputation for... isolation." I carefully leave our centuries-old feud unstated. "What brings you here now?"

Luna Suniva clears her throat. "If I may be frank, my husband and I have begun to think that isolation no longer serves us. We were discussing opening lines of communication with various kingdoms when we heard from you and thought there was no better way of re-entering the world than to patch relations with our oldest enemies."

"We wish to form an alliance," Alpha Isai finishes. "Or discuss it, at least."

'I like that they're honest,' Raven says. *'And they're right for both of us. Repairing old wounds would show everyone we really are a new Dun's Crossing.'*

'I was starting to think the same thing.' I eye the royal family. They seem comfortable around each other, moving in easy orbit now that the introductions are done. None of them shy away from each other like my siblings and I used to from each other and our parents.

"I would be honored," I declare with a smile. "Come, stay in our palace. You ought to know, though, that our current crown prince had a birthday last night. A silver Haze is imminent."

"How auspicious." Alpha Isai smiles. "Our Estrella became of age a few months back, and the Haze has yet to visit our land."

Auspicious, indeed. I don't know how I feel about this royal family's seeming attachment to predictions and omens, a branch of Moon Goddess worship I've always found suspect, but a mate bond between someone in Dun's Crossing and their princess would certainly ease relations.

"Follow us." I turn and lead them into the palace. "We're so happy to have you in Dun's Crossing." I hope this is the beginning of a great friendship.

60

EVERYTHING GOES HAZY

Anwen

I stand in the open gate as the milky white Haze silvers with the rising moon. Not everyone finds their mate during their first Haze. I keep reminding myself of that.

This is my first time in public since Father's death, other than mandatory political appearances. I can't believe my siblings are acting so normal. We lost our parents. And, fine, I accept that Father was a crueler man than I thought, but that doesn't make his loss mean nothing.

The moon hits its apex, and a wild drumbeat seizes my blood. For the first time in days, the strange ache of Father's death fades out of my mind. I am all instinct and need.

I leap forward into a shift. My bones slide smoothly, and pure white fur explodes from my skin. My wolf has always felt more natural than my human form, but tonight, I can barely remember the human I'm leaving behind. I howl, and answering howls split the air.

A mouthwatering scent catches my nose, like something sweet baking in the oven and a flower I can't name. I tear off after it. Speed has always been my wolf's greatest grace, and tonight, I bend every scrap of it toward finding this scent. The smell of my mate. Animal need fuels my bunching muscles as I weave through tents and trees. Human sounds—moans and yells—threaten to puncture my single-minded focus, but I shove them aside. Nothing has ever been more tempting than this smell.

I skid to a stop, and the Haze shifts out of my way. There, close enough to a tent that I can see the shape of it behind her, stands a wolf. I can't pick out the color through the dampening mists, but it's dark, and her stance is tall and proud.

Something in my twangs like the plucked string of an instrument. My mate. *Mine.*

We howl in unison.

I sprint to her, rub my body along the length of hers—her scent is intoxicating up close, so thick I can taste it—and continue to the tent behind her. She twists like she can already read my thoughts and races me to the door.

A competitive urge lights in my blood. She wants to prove herself to me? Let her try.

She started closer, so she's nearly on my heels as I tumble through the flap, shifting immediately. Not bad. But she can do better. I know it.

When she shifts behind me, I whip around to catch her instantly and crush my lips to hers. That same drumbeat still hums in my veins, heating my blood. I grab fistfuls of her long, soft curls, stirring more of her scent into the air. She molds herself against me. We collapse onto the soft floor. I press my tongue to her lips, begging access, but she doesn't open.

Mine, that animal voice in my head snarls.

I flip her over so I'm on top, grab her jaw, and pull her mouth open. As soon as she notices what I'm doing, she parts with a moan, but I don't release her face. Holding her here, pinned, is almost sweeter than her scent on the night air.

Almost.

I palm one of her breasts roughly, find it to be the perfect handful topped by an already pebbled nipple. A snarl of pleasure tears from my lips. She's perfect for me. Made to fit me. And the rougher I handle her, the louder her moans grow. A perfect symphony of primal pleasure. I need her. My cock twitches, and I move to line it up.

Distantly, my human mind reminds me that few shifters experiment like I have before the Haze. This perfect creature might not be ready for me.

The snarl this time is one of displeasure, but a protective instinct surges up to meet it. I don't want to hurt her.

No. I will never hurt her. She's mine.

I devour her mouth and release her face to cup her core. She moans and bucks into the pressure. She is already slick and wanting. But I will not hurt her. I swipe my thumb over her clit, listen to the beautiful waterfall of noises she makes, then slide one finger inside her.

Her moans reach a fever pitch. She is hot, wet, and so tight I can barely move. Her smell fills the tent.

I have to taste her.

I abandon her mouth and dive between her legs. The pooling slick there tastes like the nectar of the Goddess, the sweetest dessert I've ever had. I lap, lick, savor. She rocks against me, coating my whole face in her. I fit a second finger inside her, then a third. She is crying out, every twitch of my hand or my mouth setting off a new cascade of reactions that I want to watch forever. My cock aches and burns.

When I slide the fourth finger in with only the barest resistance, I know she's ready. I pull out, position my cock against her pussy, and plunge forward. Her whole body arcs off the ground as if electrocuted. I catch her in my arms, quickly reposition so we're both sitting up, and she rides me in desperate thrusts. Our harsh breath echoes off the walls of the tent. I groan and drop my mouth to her shoulder as my own pleasure races toward its crest. She kisses along my neck, my back, anywhere she can reach with our chests pressed so closely together. We move in perfect unison, two pieces of the same machine.

As pleasure overtakes me, my teeth sharpen, and I sink them into the flesh of her shoulder. Sweet pain sears through my upper back, surrounded by the relief of her lips.

* * *

THE FOLLOWING MORNING, I BLINK AWAKE WITH HAZY MEMORIES OF the night before. A few pieces click into place immediately. The tan canvas of a tent surrounds me, and a warm weight covers my chest.

I found my mate.

Something hot and sharp tears through me. This wasn't supposed to happen now. Not yet.

Still, I glance down to see who's asleep on my bare chest. Dark brown hair covers my pale skin, and I can just make out the edge of a sand-colored hand which could only belong to one person.

The newly arrived princess of Sundrop Gem.

Fuck.

Mated to Four Alphas

Threats Against the Breeder

At War for the Breeder

The Stolen Breeder

Four Alphas, Four Babies

Becoming the Luna Queen

Descendants of the Breeder

Desired by the Devil series

Whispers of the Devil

Banter of the Devil

Murmurs of the Devil

The Mafia Kings series

Indebted to the Mafia King

<u>Loved by the Mafia King</u>

Claimed by the Mafia King

Secrets of the Mafia King

Burned by the Mafia King

Kidnapped by the Mafia King (coming soon!)

Dark Stalker Romance series

Tempted by Sin

Fated to Sin

Secret Billionaires series

Finding the Secret Billionaire by Olivia Bhelle Kildare

Falling for My Secret Billionaire by Bella Moondragon

Driven by the Secret Billionaire by ID Johnson

Wolf Shifter Alpha Kings series

Ravens and Ruins

Sundrops and Shadows

Snowflakes and Sabotage

The Vampire King's Feeder series

Claiming the Alpha's Daughter

Loving the Alpha's Daughter

Finding the Alpha's Daughter

Writing as B. Moon

The Boy Who Died

Sign up for Bella's newsletter here.

Or get a free novella from The Alpha King's Breeder series when you sign up here:
The Beta and the Maid

Follow Bella on Facebook here.

Follow Bella on Bookbub here.